Also by Graeme Connell

Tide Cracks and Sastrugi: An Antarctic Summer of 1968–69
(2011)

Finding Dermot
(2014)

Uncharted

An Inspirational Novel

For Norma a Grant
Endless possibilities
Hope, patience, faith.
Rom 12:12
Graeme
Oct 2016

GRAEME CONNELL

WESTBOW
PRESS®
A DIVISION OF THOMAS NELSON
& ZONDERVAN

Cover art: Broken Fences, watercolour, by Lois F. Connell

Editor: Nancy Mackenzie, Bronze Horse Communications, Edmonton, Alberta

Scripture quotations taken from the New American Standard Bible®, Copyright © 1960, 1962, 1963, 1968, 1971, 1972, 1973, 1975, 1977, 1995 by The Lockman Foundation. Used by permission. (www.Lockman.org)

This is a work of fiction. All of the characters, names, incidents, organizations, and dialogue in this novel are either the products of the author's imagination or are used fictitiously.

WestBow Press books may be ordered through booksellers or by contacting:

WestBow Press
A Division of Thomas Nelson & Zondervan
1663 Liberty Drive
Bloomington, IN 47403
www.westbowpress.com
1 (866) 928-1240

ISBN: 978-1-5127-5143-7 (sc)
ISBN: 978-1-5127-5144-4 (hc)
ISBN: 978-1-5127-5142-0 (e)

Library of Congress Control Number: 2016912323

Print information available on the last page.

WestBow Press rev. date: 08/05/2016

—

For Lois,

who brings colour to my world every day.

Chapter One

A hand brushes aside his scarf, and Brewster McWhirtle feels the softness of two warm fingers nudging their way toward his windpipe for the rhythmic beat of life. He stirs and slowly liberates the young lodgepole pine that has anchored him through the night. His arm is locked, maybe frozen; it hurts to uncurl his hand. His free arm, folded above his head, is stiff, the muscles beyond feeling.

His cramped fingers rest on the smooth, flat rock he'd poked a few hours earlier under the low branches between the trunk and earth. *Melanie*, the laser etching says on the underside, *Blue Aster.*

A slight nudge to his left foot. *What's that? A nosy coyote?* Brewster lies still, half-frozen, half-asleep, facedown in dirty, slushy snow. *How do I get out of this life?* Again, a tentative tap-tap.

Let me die.

His leg twitches from the stiffness of the hours he's been lying there. *Cold, so cold.* He turns his head a degree or two, licks and spits the muck from his lips.

I should be unconscious by now. With no more pain. With no more daylight. Let there be peace.

"Hey, fella, you okay?"

Not a coyote, just the toe of someone's boot.

"Hello-o. Can you hear me?"

Brewster inches out from the tree. His groan from the pain in his arms is nothing compared to the howling he did during the snowstorm

1

in the early morning hours. The blood starts to run as he stirs—a severe case of pins and needles. Slowly he twists onto his side, lifting his dirt-smeared face toward the leaden sky.

"I'm fine, just fine. Just wanna lie here, meld with the earth." He gives a croaky laugh.

Fresh, wet snowflakes decorate his dirt-smeared cheeks. He blinks. Through half-closed frozen lids, he squints at the shadow leaning over him.

Just what I need—Ranger Rick to the rescue. Why can't I just disappear?

"Man, you okay? Looks like you're in pretty bad shape," the voice says. "Wassup? Name's José. I'm with the parks service. Let me help you outta this wet snow and get you warmed up. Maybe go see if we can find a coffee."

"S'okay. I'm fine. Just wanna lie here."

"Nope. Can't do that, buddy. You been drinking or something?"

"No, no. I'm okay. Just got caught in this spring snowstorm. Then I figured, what the heck. Maybe it was meant to bury me here."

José interrupts, reaching for Brewster's arm. "Now, that's taking winter just a bit too personally, my friend."

Brewster, now half-sitting and resting on one very cramped arm, twists and gently shakes the snow off the pine branches. "This tree here ..." He bats another branch, and snow falls on him. "See? It's for my wife; we claimed it for her. She was killed. Year ago today." Brewster mumbles to himself, "Just wanna ..."

"Here, lemme help you up." José picks up Brewster's numb, ungloved hand and pulls him to his feet, away from the partial covering of the little tree. "Think you can stand? How're the legs? Pretty stiff, I bet. Easy does it. Steady, steady. Man, you're a mess!"

"I thought I was in the very best place when I started to feel drowsy. Lying here stretched out in a snowy blanket of silence. I don't want to go on. I just don't. She's not here. This symbolic tree. Why am I here?" Fresh tears ripple down his muddy face. He stumbles as if blind as José leads him down the snow-covered hill.

"My truck's over here. I was looking out for who might belong to the SUV in the parking lot. No tracks around; looked like it's been there all night. Just as well I spotted you. I actually cruised past and then thought, well, I haven't seen that mound before. Might've been your black boot that caught my eye. Supposed to snow even more today, and if you'd stayed there much longer, you'd've been a goner, I reckon." José keeps up his patter to encourage his stumbling, mumbling invalid. "Think I should maybe get you to emergency. Bit worried about hypothermia. You been there all night?"

"'M okay. I'm fine, fine."

"The field office is not far. Let's get you inside and see what you look like."

José's truck is idling, the heater running. A shivering, shaking Brewster sighs deeply as he slumps into the enveloping warmth. José helps him with his seat belt, steadies him and closes the door.

"Don't wanna be a bother," Brewster mumbles. "Car's down there somewhere. I'll just head ..."

"I like my idea better," José says. "We'll brush you off, clean you up a bit, and go for coffee. I've got all the time in the world." His chatter keeps Brewster from nodding off during the short two-kilometre ride to the field office. "Yeah, I hear you, about your wife," he continues. "My wife, she died from cancer five years ago now. I miss her. I still look for her, thinking she'll just turn up. We had the advantage of talking about my life without her before she went. Still a huge shock, though. Bit of a vacuum now. Kids have grown and gone on with their lives. Now it's just me and the cat. Got too much baggage for anyone to be interested in me now."

In the cosiness of the portable field office, warm water takes the dried tears and mud from Brewster's stubbly face. The mottled backing of the aging mirror admits a still-presentable face—no frostbite. He hears José on the phone. "Found a fella in the snow. Yeah, he needs some company for a bit, so we'll go find a coffee. No, not much happening down my way. No cars and no people. Yep, been right round the park at this end, and all is as it should be."

The comforting buzz in the crowded coffee shop blankets the two men as they sit and relate their shared experiences. Brewster's not saying much, but he warms to the questioning and idle chitchat of the park warden as he tucks into a bowl of chilli. José talks about the long years of treatment until his wife finally succumbed. "At first they only gave her a few months. We got three plus years, so that was something. Really tough for me to handle, though," he says. "I quit work just to look after her. What made you plant a tree in the park?"

"Melanie and I were working on a project for ourselves," Brewster says. "We enjoyed the natural wilderness of this park looking for the wildflowers, especially the natives. It was something we did together. All wasted now. I've not been near my material in the year she's been gone. Not worth it." His eyes moisten. "Sorry," he says, wiping his cheeks with the back of his hand. "Can't seem to hold back."

"You were going to tell me about the tree," José says.

"Oh, yes. The tree. It seemed like a good idea, and then we found out we couldn't identify the tree as a memorial with her name because it's in the park. So we just looked around until we found that lodgepole. Nicely growing, and we decided that was hers. It kinda told us it needed an owner, so the kids and I sat there and quietly claimed it. It's in a place where we'll always be able to find it. It's nice that it's the Alberta provincial tree too, and will be there a long time, maybe even a hundred years."

"The kids and I thought about that too," José says. "But we wanted a tree with Mizzy's name to it and found another memorial garden in the city. So that's where I go."

Calmly and quietly, the park warden gets Brewster to open up about himself—his interest in wildflowers and why they mean so much.

"Melanie loved flowers, their colour and their beauty and what they mean to so many people," Brewster says. "We used to come here to walk, and then she started to point the wildflowers out to me. She had a bit of a gift, I reckon; could see a flower where to me there was just grass or scrubby undergrowth. I got the idea to photograph them— macros—and use the pictures to decorate her flower shop. We own The Blue Aster up the street from the reservoir."

"I know that place," José says. "You guys did the flowers for my wife's funeral. Small world, isn't it?"

"I don't know how she did it, and every time I asked, she'd just say to look for a change in the colour of the undergrowth," Brewster says, his eyes closed while recalling so many wildflower expeditions and adventures. He sighs. "We became absorbed with the fascinating world of the colour and courage of wildflowers, masked and protected in the clutter on the forest floor." So many and yet too few outings with his bride.

For almost an hour, he talks about their visits, his photographs, and Melanie's ability to see what most people miss. "There's the obvious stuff like goldenrod and the berries, but it's something else to uncover delicate wintergreens, coralroot and other orchids. She did that for me."

"You should consider keeping it going," José says. "For her. I'm sure your wife would want that. Now that you've told me all about it, I'd like to chat with my colleagues about it. Sounds like something we could use in our educational programs."

"I've dozens and dozens of images in the computer. All wasted now. I really don't know the names of the plants; that was her. I just like taking the pictures. Without names, the pictures are useless."

\#

A week later, Brewster looks out his kitchen window. He watches his neighbours, a husband and wife, head off to work. Warm water fills the sink as he loads in his breakfast dishes: one mug, one dish, one bowl, one knife, one spoon. He sighs. The surprise spring snowfall that had almost trapped him was a one-day wonder. There are signs of renewal, the miracle of the season. There's even a slight green tinge to the grass, as well as transformation in the trees as leaf buds swell in the sunshine. A robin skips across the lawn, his red breast a delightful contrast. The rumpty look of the gardens, strewn with the leaves of last autumn, reflect his own barren, lonely soul.

The phone rings, and he lets it go. Telemarketer probably, or a pollster. No message.

Half an hour later, it rings again. Brewster stirs from his seat in the front window of his silent house. He listens as the voicemail clicks on.

"Hey, Brewster, it's José—the guy in the park. How's it going? I have a meeting with park management tomorrow. They're quite excited about what you've got. Call me."

He swivels his chair around and stares at the framed wildflower pictures hanging on the wall and self-standing on the bookcase. *A house of flowers, and the best one has gone.* Brewster throws his newspaper aside and thumbs through the contacts on his iPhone. He taps José's number.

"José? Brewster."

"Well, about time, my friend. Missed you. What have you been up to these days? I hope you're not just sitting around and feeling sorry for yourself."

Surprised at José's bluntness, Brewster stands and paces the room. As he listens, he pauses to close in and focus intently on each wildflower picture on display. He has the distinct feeling Melanie is listening in on the call.

Chapter Two

Brewster dodges direct answers to José's cheerful questions by mumbling something about being out of town for a business meeting. He's not sure why he reacts like the old Brewster, the devious alcoholic of more than 20 years ago.

José pauses. "That's right. We never did talk about your work. Funny thing: I thought you must have taken one of those early retirements."

"By trade I'm actually a sheet metal and plumbing journeyman, but it's been a long time since I practiced," Brewster says. "I built up a big business during the city boom years, sold out and bought an office and retail tower. Now my main business is leasing office and retail space."

"I can see that would keep you busy," José says. "Now, what I called about is that my team got pretty excited when I told them about your wildflower photos and your wife's information. They'd love to meet you. Major interest because the park does have a need. Do you have something to show the education group?"

"Well, um, I haven't done much since Melanie died," Brewster says. Distracted, he looks out to the street and waves to an elderly couple on their morning walk. *An activity Melanie and I will not get to do.* "I hadn't really thought about the education bit. Um, I do have a couple of printed—oh, shoot, I just spilled my coffee. Ah, sorry for that José. I may still have a slideshow in my laptop."

"Why don't you come to the park offices and show us what you've done, and what your plans could be for this flower season?"

"Not sure I can do that. Y'see, it was really ... well it was her work, her interest. I loved taking the photographs, but they were for her, just something we could do to be together."

"I understand, Brewster. It's just that we're currently fleshing out plans for this summer's education program, and we have the idea your work could really kick-start that. From what you've told me, you have a good grasp on what can be found underfoot, so to speak, in this park."

"Yeah, I appreciate what you're trying to do here, José. Um, I'll call you back in 30. Is that okay? Just want to check my computer."

"How about I put you on the agenda for next Tuesday's meeting? Say, a 30-minute show and tell. Okay?" José says, doing his best not to sound anxious and pushy. "They'll want to know about costs and that sort of thing. Call me back as soon as you can."

Brewster pours his third coffee for the morning. He watches the kids heading off to school. A yellow bus rounds the corner with a loud clatter and diesels off up the street. Since Melanie died, he hasn't been near the photograph file in his computer. It feels like an intrusion into the world he had with Melanie. Now he wishes he'd never said anything. It was theirs. It was hers and not for a park officer to parade around. Maybe he'll just say his hard drive crashed and all their work has been lost. But that would be a whopper that could leap up one day and bite him.

Throw something, smash something. He's frustrated. The living room phone rings as he searches around for something to lash out. He stares at the phone. What now?

"Dad, you there? Pick up, pick up, pick up."

Brewster dives. "Hello, Hannah, hello." He feels the heat of emotion behind his eyes. "How's student life in colourful Nova Scotia?"

"Things are pretty good out here, but I was worried about you because I didn't call you on, on ..." Hannah says. "I meant to, but the day actually got the better of me—you know, the remembering, and Mom not being around anymore."

Father and daughter share the silence. No need for conversation. Enjoy the tele-nearness.

"I thought I was doing well and was heading to my class when I had a meltdown, realizing it's been a whole year." Silence. "You still there, Dad?"

"I am, sweetheart. Just listening and thinking," Brewster says. "Lovely to hear you talk. You sound just like your mother."

Hannah tells how she was overwhelmed with grief and sat down under a tree on campus. Her tears had rolled. "I must have been there about five minutes or so, and this guy … well, he's the chaplain. He walks by, sees me and sits right down.

"'Rough day?' he asks. He just sat there, Dad. Didn't say a word while I sobbed my heart out. He opened his briefcase, pulled out a couple of tissues and handed them to me. I cried till I ran out of tears. My mascara was a mess. He didn't even comment, just suggested we go for a walk around campus."

As she talks, Brewster walks downstairs to his office and wakes up his computer. It's been asleep for a long time.

"It's really beautiful here. Just like a park. The trees, the spring blossoms and all this sunshine. I miss you, Dad."

Brewster clears his throat and pauses. "I miss you too. So you walked around the campus with the chaplain?"

"Yes," she says. "We got up and just walked. That's when I started to tell him about how we lost Mom. He still didn't say much and just listened. It was so nice to be able to talk, whether or not I made sense. Then we walked in the quiet, enjoying the morning. Finally I say to him, 'Thanks for listening, but don't you have something important you should be doing?'

"'Yes,' he says. 'I'm doing it. Walking beside you.'

"We talked a bit more, and he told me about grief and stuff. Very helpful. Then he simply gave me his card and said I could see him anytime I wanted to talk. We were in the atrium by then, and he continued on his way. I sat down by the window, thinking things through."

Brewster coughs. What could he say? How to reach out and hug his daughter? She was so many miles away and beginning the second year of her earth and environmental sciences degree at Acadia University.

The phrase "walking beside you"—he's heard that before. Melanie, perhaps? He offered, "Sounds like your chaplain was in the right place at the right time for you."

"It was lovely. He seemed to know exactly how I felt," Hannah says. "Dad, I wanted to tell you I won't be home for Christmas break," Hannah says. "Several of us have a chance to head to Europe on an exchange. We're not sure if it will be France, Spain or Germany. We still have to firm things up with our professor. Do you mind?"

"Sounds brilliant," Brewster says. Surprisingly, he gets upbeat and starts talking about the park's interest in her mom's wildflowers. "That stuff your mother and I spent so much time on," he says. "I have to give a show and tell for them next week. If anything comes of it, I'll be kept busy this summer."

"Terrific, Dad. Heard from Harris at all?"

"Your brother's doing really well. I got an email from him a couple of days ago to say he has his skipper certification now, so big, ocean-going sailboats are under his command in the Whitsunday Islands. I think he's looking for a berth in some major yacht race down there. Never thought our sailing excursions on the reservoir would take him as far as Australia."

He enjoys chatting with his energetic daughter—Happy Hannah, they'd called her. She was always bursting with enthusiasm. He'll have to become more proficient with fingertip technology like FaceTime or Skype to keep up to date with his worldly children. Life has taken them a long way from home, yet they remain very close, and he knows they will all laugh around the barbecue again one day.

"Let me know what funds you'll need for Europe," he says. "We'll see what we can do."

"Okay, Dad, I will. Not sure just yet," Hannah says. "I may have enough, or there may be a scholarship or grant or something."

With that, they end their call, hesitation in each of their voices. They give cheerful and quick goodbyes.

Brewster reheats his coffee, returns to the window and looks out to the street. This has been quite a week: his rescue, interest in the wildflowers, Harris's news, Hannah's call.

With a lung-filling sigh, he rouses himself and finds his photo files. Hundreds of wildflowers. *Man, they look beautiful,* he thinks. He decides to put together 20–25 of Melanie's favourites for the presentation.

The last time he looked through the pictures, disaster had struck. That's exactly what he was doing when the doorbell rang. Melanie had wanted to check through her list to see what they could uncover as summer returned. At first he thought Melanie had forgotten her key. He'd driven her to the hair salon. She'd phoned and said she had to get some groceries and wanted to walk home in the sunshine.

Two cops stood in the doorway.

"Mr. McWhirtle?"

"What's happened?" *It's Melanie.* He knew right away. How did he know?

"We're sorry to have to tell you there's been an accident, and your wife died at the scene. She's been taken to the hospital. Would you come with us to identify her?"

It's as if the words have appeared on the computer screen, overwritten on his picture of a striped coralroot. Whimpering like a child, he tips forward and slowly smashes his head again and again on the edge of his desk.

Chapter Three

Brewster is scared of each day. The moment of waking up always frightens him. He has to bother about how to occupy himself through the long hours. Somehow, he can't shake away the loneliness, can't shake away her silent presence, can't shake away the fact that he is alone in the silence of their home. Nothing is going to bring her back. She has gone.

He lies in their bed. She is not beside him. He looks up. The ceiling looks the same today as it did yesterday. Does that mean today will be the same as yesterday? Nothing; just stippled whiteness. A couple of dust hangers over by the window. A new day? Ha. The same old drift. A wander through nothingness. What is there to get up for?

Brewster pokes a leg out from the covers and rolls to his side. His feet find the floor as he shakes off the duvet. For starters, he has to pee and drain the night away under a warm shower. Her towel is still where she left it on the bathroom rack. Her name was embroidered: Melanie, red on blue. Her robe hangs on the back of the door. Maybe it's time he cleaned house. How, though? Does he just pick up her stuff and send it away? She's everywhere—every shelf, wall, closet and cupboard. Her room, her table, her chair. When does it end? He buries his head in the foaming shampoo, and with his eyes closed tight, he lets the hot water soothe over him. He steps from the shower, hauls his towel off the rack and tosses it to the floor. Musty smelling. He's glad Hannah convinced him to get a cleaning and maid service as he picks a clean folded towel from the shelf. He dries himself and wonders aloud if there's a service he can get that will come in and magically deal with Melanie's belongings. But how? How can he just let all her stuff, her very presence, disappear from every nook and cranny in a house they'd lived in together for 27 years?

The house is a home, an accumulation of their 34 years of marriage.

With his morning latte, he heads to the dining room table and flips open his newspaper. War in the Middle East, Ebola in western Africa, women missing, police brutality. *Where's some good news? Show me something.*

Where will this day go? He stands with his coffee at the front window and waves to a woman walking her dog. He doesn't know who she is, but she passes his house most mornings about this time.

Perhaps I should get a dog. Make me get out and walk or do something. A dog. Worth a thought. Someone in the house beside me. Hannah is the dog person, though. Maybe I should send her an email later. But what sort of a dog? Doesn't matter. They all mess up the yard and have to be taken for walks, and then you gotta pick up their poop and walk around with a plastic bag. No, a dog is not really my thing.

He finds a spot amongst a week's worth of dishes in the smelly dishwasher, adds the detergent pouch and turns on the machine. He rubs his chin and decides it's time to get rid of his three-day growth, brush his teeth and stop being a wuss—a person his Melanie would not like to have around the house. He'd have breakfast at McDonald's, do a bit of grocery shopping and see what he could do for the rest of the day.

He imagines a combine in a wheat field as the razor buzzes and pulls his greying whiskers into the foils. He mows slowly around his face and under his chin, mesmerized by the sound of stubble meeting cutters. His skin smooths and freshens. He lifts the foils, blows the whiskery dust from the comb, replaces the foil and drops the razor head first into the cleaner. He flosses and brushes his teeth, runs the water hot and relishes the steaming cloth on his face. He rubs an aloe cream into his cheeks, under his chin, around his neck, up around his eyes and across his forehead. *Hmm. New man. Another new day.*

After putting on jeans and a fresh shirt and sweater, he looks at the bed, a twisted and tangled mess of sheets and duvet. It troubles him that he's just pulled everything together each day for a couple of weeks. Maybe it's a laundry day, a chore he always shared with Melanie. But not now. He shrugs and leaves the messy room. *Laundry can wait. Breakfast first.*

#

As he eats his egg and bacon breakfast, Brewster finds a certain comfort in the noise and warmth of the fast food outlet. He sits back and watches people of all ages come and go, some for a breakfast sandwich, some for a muffin, and others for a coffee to go. What about those old guys over in the corner table? Are they like him, living alone?

"Well, look who's here, slumming it with the rest of us."

"Hello, John," Brewster says. "Yep, good place to come every now and then. Gonna join me here, or …?"

"I'm just in for a pickup," John says. "Myra's gone off somewhere—early shopping with the kids. I bailed for a bit to grab a quick coffee."

Brewster waits for the inevitable question—the one about his freewheeling bachelor life. He gets it every time he comes in contact with old friends. Today, will they chit-chat about nothing: the weather first, how the kids are doing, recent holidays. Then the question, always the question. "I'm on my way to the supermarket, and then I'm taking the car down for a lube and spring check," he says.

"I do have time to catch up with an old buddy," John says, plonking himself down. "How you been? Haven't seen you in a while. Myra was saying just the other day we should have you over for a meal. Been away?"

"Nah, just moseying around and getting a few things organized, y'know." Brewster imagines himself back on the scaffolding as a young apprentice plumber, holding a pipe in place with one hand and staring at the parts he needs still on the ground. "Wonder what our politicians are up to?"

"Yeah, it's hard to see," John says. "The oil price diving, the economy, unemployment."

Brewster is folding up his newspaper as John's youngest arrives and tugs at his father's sleeve. "Looks like I've gotta go," John says as he gets up. "Well, good to at least say hello. I'll tell Myra and give you a call. Take care."

Brewster reopens his paper to read the editorial to see what might be relevant in the strange world of politics, Alberta-style. Eventually he picks up his breakfast junk, dumps it in the bin and heads out the door.

He'll avoid the local supermarket and avoid any chance of banging into someone else he knows. Seeing John has rattled him; he realizes just how much he's dropped out of circulation. Curmudgeon, Mel had said. If he didn't watch out, he'd turn into a curmudgeon, an old man who'd yell at an out-of-place snowflake.

I need milk, and I need eggs and bread. He drives to a supermarket across town. *Not likely to bang into anybody I know here. Not ready yet to talk with people. Maybe I should leave town.*

He collects his groceries and drives to the lube shop. It's nice and quiet today; he has the waiting room to himself. He scans through the pages of a pop magazine. Scandals, divorce, beauty, better boobs, more sex, more lies, diet, and riches. He tosses it back on the pile, stands and looks through the workshop window. There's his Jeep, up on the hoist. The technicians scurry round it. He's been coming here for years and likes how his vehicles have always been well cared for. The staff knows him. It's a comfort stop.

"Mr. McWhirtle?" a voice says. Brewster turns. "Hi. I'm Gord, your technician today. We've finished everything, and all looks good. I will say though that perhaps you should get a new cabin air filter next time. This one's okay for now. And you might consider new wiper blades next time round. Otherwise, you're good to go. They're just taking it off the hoist." Then he's gone.

There's nothing to pay as he checks out. Gotta love this service. Free lube and check-up with a new vehicle as long as he owns it. "Thanks, Bill," he says to the guy behind the counter as he picks up his key and heads out. "You guys do good work."

Back home, there's a call from his lawyer and another from his accountant. *It'll be about the business,* he supposes as he puts his groceries away. All this stuff that has to be done. These are things he did with Melanie. They'd always worked together, and he enjoyed their partnership. Now it's just him. The joy of doing anything is gone.

He thinks about their occasional discussions around co-dependence. A decade ago, it had been a sort of topic du jour and a regular discussion among their friends, especially those in their church group. There was no reason why, but perhaps church was a place where people spoke a little more freely and were not so guarded. He thought of close friends who'd suggested he and Melanie were joined at the hip. In reality, they were quite independent. They simply enjoyed being together, and being together had little to do with thinking freely or making their own decisions.

Now, though, he's adrift. Lawyers, accountants, business managers. He had to handle the fallout from her sudden and tragic death. It came down to having to take her name off the papers. Take away the name, and she's not there. Throw away her toothbrush; she'll not be back to use it. But he did not want to blot her from the house she'd put so much into over the years.

The house phone rings as he puts a couple of cans of baked beans into the cupboard. He lets it roll to voicemail. "Hello, Brewster. It's Jo at the shop. Please call me when you can. We have an issue with a supplier who's playing hardball. I'm not sure why. Thanks."

Jo's managing The Blue Aster, Melanie's shop, and he hasn't been near the place in the year she's been gone. He leans against the kitchen counter. Melanie's life had always been about the flowers at work, at home and at play. Now the best bloom was gone, ripped from the garden.

Is it time? he thinks, turns and looks out the kitchen window at the unkempt garden beds in the back yard. Yes. There's only a slight hesitation as he reaches for the phone. He sets an appointment with his lawyer for tomorrow and calls his accountant. His plan is made. Melanie's gardens will bloom again.

#

The door chimes tinkle his presence. He pauses while taking it all in, conscious that Melanie is not out back. The Blue Aster wraps him in with its perfumed energy. It doesn't feel like he's been away for a year. A teenager looks up from the counter, gives an awkward smile and rushes out to the workroom. Brewster greets a couple looking around the wood panelling he'd installed, lovely old greying timbers from an ancient barn. That had been Melanie's idea, like the name. Right now he'd give anything to walk with her and see the widespread blue asters they both loved. He looks through the shop windows into the plaza parking lot, gazing through an art school student's rendition of the aster's pale purple petals painted on the glass some eight or nine years ago. It was Melanie's world: bright, happy, friendly. He dreamily fancies Melanie stepping out of the cool room.

"Hello, Brewster. Boy are we glad to see you," a young woman says, wrapping her arms around him.

"Hello, Jo," he says. "I'm sorry I've been away so long and left all this to you. But I, well, I just couldn't …"

"No worries. Everything's been great. I totally understand." Jo laughs and sparkles, just like she did the day before Melanie officially opened the store. "You're naughty, though. You could have just come by to say hello."

He looks into her hazel eyes and remembers her answer when Mel asked why she wanted to work in the shop. "Oh, I like flowers." A pause. "My husband's been laid off, and I need a job."

"Well, that's three reasons," Mel had said, ushering her into the cool room out of Brewster's way while he stacked vases, flower holders and picture frames on the shelves.

"You haven't changed a bit," Brewster says. "How's that little boy of yours? And Danny—how's he doing?"

"We're all good. That little boy, Mikey, is seven now. Danny is part-time in school upgrading from an electrician to an instrument tech. He's doing really well."

With that, she steers him round and out to the back of the shop to meet a couple of new floral designers—asterettes, she calls them. The teenager is taking the new customer's order. "We've got two weddings this weekend, and there's a funeral tomorrow. We have a lot of walk-ins these days; people just want flowers to take home. You know: tulips, orchids and roses are always popular."

Although Jo is a few years older than Hannah, she is like a daughter. In fact, the two girls had been like sisters in the shop during their school years.

"Somebody giving you grief?" he says.

"Yes. I'm so glad you've come in. He likes dealing with owners, not managers, and I had to convince him that he'd get paid for his stock. I've always paid him on delivery and yet he's threatening to stop selling to us. He prefers owner-operators. I explained the situation to him—you know, about Melanie and all that. Maybe you should give him a call. He's a really good supplier."

"Come," Brewster says. They walk out of the work room, through the shop and out into the parking lot. "I've decided to part with The Blue Aster and wondered if you have time—say, early next week—to come to my lawyer's office to begin the formalities to take it over."

"What are you saying? Danny and me—you want us to buy the store?" Jo is shaking. "Impossible."

They walk across the parking lot to the plaza's treed boundary. He's glad they're outside. He puts his arm on her shoulder. "No, Jo. Don't worry. I'm not selling out from under you. Maybe that came out all wrong. I want you and Danny to have the shop. We'll just transfer the ownership, and then your supplier won't have an issue!"

"Oh, Brewster, your family has been just great to Danny and me, but we don't have that sort of money. We're week-to-week now, with Danny in school. We're trying to get ahead."

"Jo, you've worked hard here since the day we opened. You've looked after and run the place for this past year. Melanie and I are giving you the shop. There's no debt—you're turning a good profit, and I'm sure the future is good for the business. You've helped make it part of this community. It's yours. If you and Danny decide it's not for you, then we'll just keep going like we have this past year. You guys are family."

"Giving? You mean you're *giving* us the shop?" Jo looks back across the cars to The Blue Aster. She turns to Brewster, her eyes glistening.

"Yes, that's what I said. There will be some financial stuff around stock and assets, figuring out any receivables and payables, the lease, the phones and the bank. But don't worry; we can sort through that. That's what my accountant said yesterday. And if money does have to change hands, we can work something out. I talked with Hannah last night, and I got an email from Harris this morning, letting me know that this is what they want too. It's what their mom would have wanted." He chuckles. "And what's more, they're glad I'm taking a bit of action."

They saunter back to the shop, and no words are needed. At the doorway, to the surprise of customers ready to walk out with their flowers, Jo flings her arms around Brewster's neck in a tight hug.

Later, Brewster sits alone at a pizza house, happy that the decision has finally been made to quit the store. He's confident the exchange of ownership will go as he's planned. His phone buzzes; there's a text: "Danny thrilled, scared stiff, excited. Bless you."

Chapter Four

Blackness settles over Brewster as he begins his morning rituals of showering and shaving. His night has been troubled, as though mites found comfort in the wooliness of his brain and have slowly developed nests cell by cell. He stares at the strange face in the mirror, mowing his shaver over an anger, a storm and a pestilence destroying yesterday's pleasure. He refrains from lashing out and smashing the face looking back at him.

Punished. Yes, he's being punished for his stupidity in thinking that his closet doors had all been closed and locked long ago, that his mistakes sealed away forever. Is this the price he pays, spending the rest of his days alone? Why, why, why has she been unceremoniously ripped from the face of this earth? Is this what God does?

Sure, he knew there'd been a couple of years when he was an utter idiot, and when ego and whisky almost cost him his marriage and threatened his thriving business. But Melanie was goodness itself. Her forgiveness, his remorse and their love enabled them to work it out and renew a commitment that lasted for 30 years. But to wrench her out of existence was wrong. That it happened when it did was a mockery of every beautiful blue sky day forever after.

This morning's sun shines on his bowl of cereal. The brown flakes glare up at him. Perhaps today he should walk out in front of a bus. Maybe that way he'll see her again. All those people have paraded around him, saying she was in a good place now, saying they would pray for him, saying Jesus will heal, saying Jesus will give peace. *Yeah, yeah. Blah, blah blah.* He remembers the day, after watching his wife for almost two years and seeing a change in her, that he too prayed with a footballer to become a child of God, to give his life to Jesus, to become a follower of the Way. Yes, he'd believed. Oh, how he'd believed and knew the changes he'd experienced in his own life, knowing that someone out there was for him always and forever.

He abandons the table and his cereal bowl, yanks the toaster cord from the socket, picks up his coffee and walks out the door, not bothering to close it. He heads out like a dark cloud moving down the street, sunshine in front of him and sunshine behind him. *Why all this sunshine? Why not black skies—moody, tortuous skies? Get me outta this half life.*

Brewster reaches the intersection, dumps his coffee cup into a garbage container and stares over four lanes of destruction at the crosswalk. Morning traffic zips by—*whoosh, whoosh,* rhythmic. A fall, a winter and a spring, and all trace of her smashed body has gone. It's like it never was. What brings him to this place today? He's avoided it for a whole year. She's not here, she's not coming. She was put in a box and scorched out of existence.

He thinks back to that day. Just as he's imagined many times before, he sees Melanie walking up the boulevard, stopping to tap the crosswalk signal and then walking across two lanes to the median. She walks in front of a stopped pickup, and then *wham,* tossed and crushed, her life gone in an instant. His Melanie, a gentle, loving, happy woman lifted from amongst the spilt milk, broken eggs and crushed bread and taken away. He cries as his picture fades. He taps the signal button, pauses for the orange crossing lights to flash, gathers a deep breath and steps out. The cars stop today. No one is out to beat the system. There's no idiot whipping out from behind a stopped pickup to drive through and move him to eternity. Once across, he waits for the traffic to be rushing both ways again, and he pushes the signal button just as she had. The pedestrian light flashes, the traffic stops both ways, and he walks back to the south side. He crosses over and back three more times. He stops between lanes and glares at the bewildered drivers. He sees them wave at him to hurry across.

"There is no God," he yells at the traffic. "There is no God."

#

Miserable as all get out, he steps through his open front door and pulls the phantom screen across. "Hi, Dad. Where are you?" He looks at the phone on the hall stand. "C'mon, Dad. I know you're there. Pick up."

He strides through to the hall table. His hand shakes as he reaches for the phone. Anger—so much anger and bitterness.

"Hello, Hannah. I've just come in from a walk." He takes a painful, deep breath.

"Dad, you okay? I had this awful feeling that something might be wrong, so I'm just between classes and need to hear your voice."

"Yep, just great," he lies. "Gorgeous morning here."

"I got an amazing email from Jo last night, and I think it's just terrific what you are doing for her and Danny," she says. "Mom always said she'd like to do that one day, and I agree that the timing is perfect. I'm glad you dropped in on her."

Hannah's the very image of her mother. Her voice has a nice calming effect, and he looks back to the front door. The sun has moved across the threshold and spreads its warm glow into the hallway.

The bubbliness of his daughter slowly reaches across the country, and his rage subsides. *A pinprick releases the air in a balloon.* He listens to her chatter, mostly about her studies, her excitement and her travel plans. "I've got a break coming up and will be home for a few days next week. Must go—have a class." With that, his spirited daughter is gone.

He sits in the warmth on the front step and wonders what "be home for a few days" really means. He guesses the detail will come later in her promised email.

As with most mornings over the past year, Brewster has woken in time to see the sunrise, but nevertheless he has shed the sheets without a plan. The house is a mess, and there's always laundry to be done; newspapers have to be picked up, and the garbage and recycling need to be sorted. He looks in at Melanie's empty office. He's barely set foot in there since the funeral.

He tackles housekeeping, motivated not only by the thought that Hannah will be home soon but also because he doesn't want to show her what a slob he's become. He realizes he's been living like a hermit, leaving the house simply to escape and avoiding people at all costs. Very few people call him these days, and he's long ago discouraged drop-in visitors. He feels some sort of sick glee that his church friends now leave him alone. "Never want to see you again," he'd said to a couple of persistent types. He's slowly isolated himself, preferring his own miserable company.

Melanie's magnet on the washer control panel tells him, *As for me and my house we will serve the Lord.* "Is that right, Mel?" he murmurs as he sprays a stain on his polo shirt. He stuffs the laundry into the machine. "Jesus, you're not real. And all this time, I thought you were. It's what I really believed, until—but now, no matter what anyone says, you're just not." He forgoes sorting into lights and darks like Melanie always insisted. As far as he's concerned, it's all just dirty washing.

If there was one chore that Melanie did not like, it was vacuuming. The cleaner was too heavy for her to haul around, she'd say, so as encouragement he'd printed a colour picture for her on the computer. She'd stuck it to the hall closet door. The picture showed a blue aster overwritten with, "Jesus loves me!"

Not true, he tells the vacuum cleaner. The vacuum whirls around the lounge. On the way to his office, he looks into Melanie's work room. The busy clutter is just as she left it. He's not been in there for some time. But today? He warily takes two steps in and looks round. Sewing, mostly; a closet of her fashions through the years; boxes and shelves which he only knew as her stuff, the things of her private and personal world.

Her desk is littered with his wildflowers photographs. He looks at two pinned on the wall. One, a globe cornflower, has a bee hugging the fluffy, thread-like, deep yellow petals. Across one corner, Melanie has scrawled, "I am with you always." The other shows a gaillardia face up to a brilliant blue sky, its yellow and purplish-red petals arms up to the sun peeking from behind a dazzling, fluffy cloud. Melanie's neat printing reads, "I will not leave you." "Bible stuff," he murmurs, looking at the open notebook with its simple notations of where and when to find her precious plants. They'd been planning an excursion down to the park when, instead of finding a sparkling woman with a new hairdo at the front door, he'd been confronted by a man and a woman dressed in black greeting him with bad news. Brewster shudders as he recalls the sombre-voiced police. He's not been this close to her workspace since that black day.

The walls echo. *Accident, tragic, died instantly, paramedics, hospital, some things we collected, can you come with us?* Her Bible lies open beside another notepad. Her morning quiet time ritual is forever in the past.

Brewster backs out of the room, trips over the vacuum cleaner and goes sprawling over and over down the stairs. He lies there. His head hurts from crashing against the banister post. Pain shoots from his knee; a foot is twisted.

"Are you happy, God? Are you happy?" He tries to roll over to sit up, but an excruciating pain pins him to the floor. His world goes black.

#

Postie sees a bare arm and blood on the floor as she drops the day's mail into the box to the side of the open door. She peers in. "Oh my goodness. Sir? Sir? Oh, no." She pulls out her cell phone and dials 911. "Oh, no."

She's been walking this route for a couple of years now, and she often stops to exchange a few words with Brewster; she knows he lives alone, quiet and reserved. She tells the operator what she sees: a man sprawled on the floor, a vacuum cleaner humming upside down at the top of the stairs, blood on his head, no movement. She reaches down, lifts his wrist and checks his pulse. "Beating fine," she reports. She shuts down the vacuum cleaner and waits beside Brewster.

An ambulance announces its arrival, paramedics take over and an unconscious Brewster is packed away to hospital. She talks to the police, shaken, telling them everything she knows about the man. Then she heads off to complete her deliveries. She smiles at the people who linger on the sidewalk.

The police stay on and walk through the house. One of the officers notices the phone message and picks it up. She organizes a call trace and is soon telling Hannah the events that have taken place. Hannah recaps the conversation she'd had with her father just a couple of hours earlier. The house keys, she tells them, should be hanging on a hook near the door.

Chapter Five

"So what happened to your Dad?"

"Funny, really," Hannah says as she trims a fern stalk and places it in a new arrangement. She's spending the evening helping Jo at The Blue Aster to prepare the flowers for a wedding the next day. "Well, not so funny. He just freaked out when he read some verses Mom had written on a couple of his photographs. He tripped over the vacuum cleaner in his rush to leave Mom's room, went head over heels down the stairs and crashed into the open front door. He blacked out, and Postie found him and called 911."

"And now he's got a broken arm, a sore head and a twisted ankle," Jo says.

"Yep, not to mention a bruised ego."

Hannah loves the fragrance of the flower shop. Tonight she's enveloped in the heady sweetness of daffodils, the lucky flower, in yellows and whites that will decorate the church and reception.

"I'll add some gypsophila with the quad-coloured roses for the bouquets," Jo says. "The five bridesmaids will be in cherry red, so it's a very colourful wedding. Your dad's okay, though?"

"Oh, yes," Hannah says. "Just as well I came home the day he got out of hospital. Because he lives alone, they kept him in for observation for a couple of days to keep an eye on his head injury. He's still struggling over Mom. Know anyone who can help in the next couple of days to sort through her things? You've made a lovely job of that bouquet, you know. You're so talented."

"Your Mom taught me," Jo replies. "I think there's a couple of women at the church who might be able to help. They're used to this sort of thing. I'll call them when I get home."

Over breakfast the next morning, Hannah talks about her university studies and the planned trip to somewhere in Europe. Brewster senses there's something else. "Let me freshen your coffee, and then you can tell me what's on your mind."

"Well, Dad, it's been a year now. I think we should put away some of Mom's things," Hannah says. "I know what you're gonna say, but you have to. I'm here for a few days so we can get through this together. It's tough, I know. You could just leave it to me too, y'know."

Brewster loves his daughter. She's calm and matter-of-fact, and she likes to get things done. He stands and looks out the window. "People walk their dogs, and they all pee on those front plants," he says. "Pretty rank when I have to weed around them. Not that I've done that this year. What about Harris?"

"He's okay. I talked to him last week and we reckon it's just something we all have to do to move ahead."

"You mean that's why you came home?" Brewster tenses.

"Kinda yes and no," Hannah says. "We are on a break this week, and I wanted to see you because I won't be home this summer. We wanted to bring this up when we were home at New Year's. Please don't get mad, Dad."

"Not easy," Brewster says. "I don't want to talk about it. Been here a lifetime. Look at all her knick-knacks. Place is full of them."

She watches her father leave the room. Discussion over. Hannah is stunned. There's seemingly nothing she can do. She clears their breakfast dishes. The bond, the joy of being home with her Dad, is temporarily adrift. She shakes her head in disbelief as she sees their car driving down the street. She didn't hear him go out. This is a mood she has not seen before, this inner turmoil. "Dear Lord, what shall I do?"

She heads to her room, wondering how she might work through the day, thinking about what her father would do next and how long he'd be gone. She needs to talk with someone, but whom? She's spent most of the past three years in Nova Scotia, away from home. Her closest friends have gone on with their lives: university, travel, marriage and relocation to other parts of the country. Jo is the closest now. "You're like sisters," her mother always said.

She scribbles a note and leaves it by the phone. "Dad: Helping Jo. She has a big wedding. Love ya."

The previous night's work has left a pattern of greenery, petals and leafy bits around the workbench. As she sweeps, Hannah opens up to Jo. "Mom's clothes and underwear are still folded on the shelf in the laundry, where she put them from the dryer a year ago. I guess I just don't understand what's going on, this grief. What happened when your dad died?"

"Little bit different in our house," Jo says. "The boys kinda took over before they headed back up north. What say we add some of these lovely soft pink tulips with the arrangements for the front of the church? Mom sat with us and reminisced as we sorted through Dad's life. She enjoyed the memories. We'd cry a bit and then laugh." She holds up the greenery. "What do you think? Makes a nice display. "Look at the time. The bridesmaids are due any minute to pick up the flowers.

"The toughie was his closet and drawers," Jo adds. "Packing the clothes suitable for reuse and bagging the rest for pickup. Didn't take long, which was good. I'll be going to the church. Wanna come?"

#

Brewster limps with his cane along the path. He doesn't hear the cyclist come up behind and swish past. He wobbles to the side in fright and yells at the speedster, who turns and gives him the finger. "So much for having a quiet time in the park," he says. He smiles at the oncoming young woman jogging behind her large, three-wheeled buggy and its sleeping passenger.

"Wish we'd had those things around when our kids were that age," he says to the imaginary Melanie at his side. He doesn't want to go home; he's upset. He knows his daughter is only trying to help. Now he's mad at himself for being such a twit. "C'mon, Mel. You've gotta help me out here."

The park trails and pathways have been his place of peace ever since the accident. It's where they'd spent many happy hours walking, talking and finding the hidden gems underfoot. Having left the house in a snit, he's embarrassed to return. He hears his wife telling him, "Suck it up and get over it." The familiar gravel path crunches with his clomping. "We came a long way, Mel. Why did you go so soon? We came through all those troubles so long ago, enjoyed a life with our two amazing kids. We had a wonderful future ahead of us. We were in a new time together, like we were one."

He's so busy with his crowded mind that he doesn't notice the woman in the wide-brimmed, floppy straw sunhat until it's too late. He swerves to avoid her. With his arm in a cast and resting in a sling, he unsteadily bumps against the red backpack slung casually over her left shoulder. He reaches out to steady her and apologizes profusely. She doesn't speak and stares at him, shocked. He hurries on, embarrassed at being so clumsy. He half turns to look back, but the woman is slowly walking along the side of the path, looking into the underbrush as if she has lost something. She appears unfazed.

"Selfish," he says to a chickadee ducking and diving from branch to branch in the aspens. "Hannah has a point. Perhaps she doesn't like coming home to the house so full of you, Mel, with all your things about as if you're still here. I know you're not going to walk through the door one day, but I just can't erase you."

Brewster's cell phone buzzes. "Helping Jo. She has a big wedding. Hugs." His eyes water.

The water ripples over the rocks and deadfall from the spring floods. It's a peaceful place on the bench he and Melanie shared so often, eating their lunch during their flower expeditions. He looks up as the woman in the hat walks by. Beauty in the woods. He gives her a smile and waves as some sort of consolation for crashing into her. *Thankfully, no harm done*, he thinks as the woman nods an acknowledgement. He enjoys the sun, takes off the blue beanie covering his bandaged head, closes his eyes and feels a comforting warmth as he dozes until the sun makes way for shadow from the trees.

Brewster sighs, rolls the stiffness out of his neck, stands, stretches and limps his way to the parking lot. *The woman in the big floppy hat—I wonder if she found what she was looking for. Flowers, perhaps?*

Chapter Six

Louise Reverte enjoys her late morning starts. With summer approaching and evening study groups, she knows that for at least a couple of days a week, she has the pleasure of walking to work. Living close to the park has its advantages. This morning she starts out in plenty of time thinking about the main part of her day: she has a monthly management meeting followed by a quiet afternoon that will allow her to finalize her materials and thoughts for her first volunteer get-together of the season that evening.

"Who's the guy sitting out in the Jeep?" she asks the conservation officer as she plonks her briefcase at her desk. "He's in the visitor spot. Are we expecting someone?"

"I don't know who's out there," Calvin says, "but the Jeep has been there maybe half an hour or so. I didn't know there was anyone in it. We do have a guest for our meeting today. José has set up a photographer to give a presentation on a possible wildflower project."

"Sounds interesting. I for one would like to see a few of our park flowers on the walls around here. Our offices are a bit barren for an urban park. Our meeting still scheduled for eleven and over lunch?"

"Correct. Couple of managers in from Edmonton to review our plans for the summer—and of course, budgets," Calvin says. "I certainly hope they're not asking us to cut. We're pretty bare-bones now."

Louise laughs. "I think you'll be okay. It's usually the education budget that gets whacked first. I'm so glad we have such an enthusiastic

31

and knowledgeable group of volunteers. They've been with us for years now."

"Maybe the fellow out there is one of the head office types, waiting for the rest of his group to turn up. Anyway, gotta check the room setup. See you in 30."

#

Louise welcomes the extra time she has to prepare given the agenda, which includes visitors from head office, department managers, budgets, summer program approvals, her wish list and the coordination of park volunteers. She piles her folders together and looks up in fright as a man crashes into one side of the double doors before opening the other.

"Oh, dear," Louise exclaims. "Are you okay? You look as if you've been in the wars. Perhaps I should unlock that door as well—it catches a lot of people. Must be something to do with being left- or right-handed."

Brewster waves at a chair and sits down to recover. His head hurts, the arm in a cast hurts because it carried his brief case and the extra wobble on his leg has jolted pain into his ankle. He feels flushed and removes the knitted beanie, revealing the bandage.

"Oh, my," Louise says. "Look at you. How can I help?"

Brewster introduces himself, smiles and allows Louise to carry his briefcase as she ushers him into the meeting room. He scans the faces: four women and two men. No José.

One of the women steps forward and hesitates about shaking hands when she sees one hand and arm in a cast and the other hand propping him up with a walking cane. "Welcome," she says with a smile. "You must be Mr. McWhirtle. So glad you could make it. My name is Tanya, and I'm the senior education officer." She introduces the others, adding, "José can't be here because he's dealing with a situation down at the other end of the park."

Smiles around the table follow the warm welcome. Brewster looks toward the exit as Louise tells the group about him crashing into the door.

"Good morning." He coughs. "About all this. I can say that tumbling down the stairs and ending up in the hospital is not a good way to start the week."

"José has told us so much about your work and the interest you have in the flowers found in this park," Tanya says, drawing his attention back to the group. "We're rather keen to have these walls covered in good pictures of what can be found here. There's always lots of attention to the obvious stuff like the animals and the trees and the bugs, and why we protect the ecology. But not too many people know about the flowers. So, over to you. We're keen to know about your work."

Louise connects his laptop to the television monitor. Brewster clicks open his file and stumbles through his pictures, displaying the brilliant colour the many orchids and flowers he and Melanie have catalogued during three years of park visits. He pulls plaque-mounted pictures from his briefcase and passes them around the group. He feels like an uneducated idiot for not knowing enough about the flowers he's featured in his presentation.

The room has been very quiet. Are they bored to tears? he wonders as he seeks to fade out of sight. Then it seems like everyone present wants to ask questions. Where did they find the flowers? What section of the park? What camera does he use? How about the lighting for the close-ups? How does he print and get the plaques made? What other flowers does he have? Are they all Fish Creek Park pictures?

This back-and-forth goes on for a good half hour. Brewster relaxes and enjoys the conversations around the table.

"What sort of costs would we be looking at for you to decorate our walls, and to possibly allow us to use some images in our printed materials?" Tanya asks. The woman who brought him into the room—what is her name? Louise. Brewster looks to her. The others fall silent—an almost deafening, expectant silence.

He's tongue-tied and stumped. José had mentioned costs, but he'd put it aside, not thinking the issue would be raised. He looks beyond the group to the treescape out the window. He knows that as soon as he speaks, he'll choke. Just thinking about what to say brings moisture to his eyes.

"Well, I, er," he says, trying to control his emotions. "Let's see. This project started with my wife. With Melanie. She was the brains behind it, and we did it for our own fun. I'm not able to readily identify the flowers, though I can help find them. Um, because Melanie is no longer with us, I can just let you have what you want for the good of the park and the pleasure others will get from them. She really wanted the kids to know about the flowers and why we have flowers. 'Beyond decoration and honey,' she used to say.

"So there's no fees. I'll finish what we've started, and I'll seek your advice in locating any missing plants and when to find them at their best. I know Melanie has left a list of the flowers she wanted to document this year."

"Brewster, we're not quite sure how we want to use your material," Tanya says. "We wanted to see what you have and how we might be able to use it in our programs. No need to worry about names— there are lots of people around here who can jump in with that. Your photographs are amazing."

"Melanie has compiled a lot of information, like where and when we found many of the flowers," he says. "I'm sure I can work most of it out and attach it to each picture."

Louise helps him leave the room and head through the main doors to his vehicle. He's flushed and sweaty. Maybe he overstepped the mark in suggesting they might consider a park bench in memory of his wife, overlooking the river in the place where they'd often stopped for their snack in the sunshine. He didn't know how to read their reaction, the quiet hush. Perhaps he said too much, choking on emotion. Why did that have to happen?

"Well, Melanie," he says in his Jeep. "I've gone and done it. I've given your project to the park. I think they are very excited about it and the material we collected. They wanted to pay me, but that doesn't bring you back. It's better that they just have the pictures so that maybe your love and fascination of the flowers will transfer to others, just as you always wanted."

#

José calls a couple of days later. "Well, Brewster, you certainly know how to win friends," he says. "The team loves your idea, praised your offer, and took the plan to the administration, who said to go for it. I knew they would. You are so generous, and they couldn't believe it. Are you sure all you want is a bench in the park in return for all that work?"

Better than an illegal rock, Brewster thinks as he hangs up the phone, feeling much better with himself. He goes to his computer and thinks about how it will come together. Back upstairs, he looks for Melanie's list of the missing flowers. He tenderly approaches the untouched materials on her desk. *Hmm, bit dusty.* Hannah wanted to tidy it up, but he'd not allowed her near her mother's things. He tenderly explores, knowing that the to-do list will be on a scrap of paper, as per her style. But where would she have left it? He rifles through the many Alberta plant books and thinks back to their last outing. They'd made plans for the very day that she …

Brewster stops. The thought scares him. Now he knows where the list might be. His camera bag? No. Maybe her shoulder pack, hanging on a peg near the front door. Like most of her things, it's been untouched for a year. Her field book is there, and so is her camera. His eyes water as he lifts the field book and leafs through it. Her neat, precise printing. He recalls how he's never really had a look at her notes before. They'd always exchanged things verbally, working on accurate identification from the back-and-forth conversations, checking their pictures. He does not like what he's doing. It's like looking into her soul, the very things that were Melanie. He picks out the day's to-do list, carefully closes the notebook, snaps the green band around it and drops it back into the bag. *Maybe Hannah will want to have that.*

"Well, Mel," he says, "I've found your list and am glad to have the expected dates to find these missing ones from our collection. I'm sure the park people will be able to help me locate them. But your eyes were so special at spotting. That was surely your gift. I know we'll find the striped coralroot this summer, and perhaps a reshoot to get the perfect shot of a bracted orchid, or frog orchid as you called it, just to confuse me.

"Now, Mel, I wonder when I'll get to see your bench? Will you mind me sitting on it?"

Chapter Seven

Clotilde Chiasson is in the garden clearing the beds of the leaf clutter her mother had spread before the winter snow. This is the first time she's tackled the yard work alone. It's always been the two of them, mother and daughter, preparing the soil and planting out new annuals amongst the perennials to bring newness and colour to their private oasis. Now it's just one more thing she has to get used to doing alone. She's trying to reorder her life around her home, her hospital visiting and her pursuit as a self-taught botanical artist.

Sunny spring days lure her to her gardens and the garden centres as the days advance in this seasonal renewal; buds begin to swell on the branches, the promise of leaves and blossoms. She watches a robin bob over the grass, stop, tilt his head, *et boum*, beak down into the green to land an early lunch. A couple of chickadees make their nest in a garden post, and finches flit through the trees as she dethatches the lawns. Tulips and daffodils bravely poke their way through the soil to daylight. They're always ready to get out and about following the hardy, furry little prairie crocus into the sunshine, its purple flowers a herald of spring. She enjoys digging in the damp, dark, rich-looking earth and is glad her mother insisted they develop a gardening habit together.

"A garden is a treasure," her mom had always said. "For out here among the plants, you see life. If it wasn't for the plants, you wouldn't be standing here."

Her mom's passion has become her own. "Yes, Mom. I get it. We see plants for their beauty here in our garden, but all living creatures on this planet depend on plants and flowers to survive."

It's this thought that drives Clotilde to pursue perfection in drawing the flowers of the forest, the wildflowers that few people get to see in the park's understory. Her favourite pastime in the warmth of summer days is to spend time in the nearby Fish Creek Provincial Park finding and drawing the flowers, petals, stems and leaves in every detail. Flowers might be lovely for the human eye to appreciate, but to the plant they are all about reproduction. The design, colour, size and shape of flowers attract many species of bugs and insects just so they can repopulate. *So really, I'm an artist whose subject matter is sylvan sex!*

The pocket of her jeans vibrates: a new text message. Her lifeline.

"Hi, C. We have a new young patient, Anil, who'll be with us a while. Totally deaf. He's so desperately alone. Can you help the little guy?"

It's late evening by the time Clotilde gets back home. She luxuriates in the shower, the hot water smoothing the fatigue from her body. It has been a long day, yet she's happy that she's made a small difference for the young boy.

Severe burns to much of his 10-year-old body, immense pain and his big brown eyes showing another silent pain. He mostly nodded as she patiently worked with him, telling him through lip-reading and sign language what the nurses and doctors were doing to help heal him. It's been a tough day, especially with police quietly hovering and trying to piece together what had happened in that south-east townhouse.

The boy's aunt is also in hospital with similar injuries. All Clotilde knows is that there'd been a fire, an explosion at a backyard barbecue. Anil did not want to say much; he was tired, very scared and hurting. Her job is to befriend him, calm him, gain his confidence and allow the medical team to ease into their care and treatment. Tomorrow she'll tell Anil about her garden. Maybe he'll be well enough for a wheelchair tour of the hospital where she can, in their wordless world, talk about the nurses and the doctors and what they do. It's something she's always done with other patients, young and old.

She sips her lemon and ginger tea at the drawing board, and she looks over the work she's done, detailing the tiny, delicate, star-shaped flower of the blue-eyed grass. Though inconspicuous, she is always delighted to spot this perennial in the grassy meadows and along the edge of the pathways. Even when in bloom, blue-eyed grasses are hard to find, and it depends on the time of day because the flower tends to open in the early morning and close at noon. She looks at the watercolour she'd painted a year before and reads the lines her mother wrote.

> In sunlit meadow by the lake,
> A tiny flower cheers the morn
> And sways to the quiet breeze.
> How lovely is this blue-eyed bloom,
> A frail splash of prairie wealth
> That shyly eyes the passer-by.

Clotilde smiles at how her mother often created a verse to celebrate the beauty of the landscape. She loved flowers, wildflowers especially, and when things had been good, they'd spend hours searching in the woodlands. She'd filled notebooks of where and when she'd seen the plants. and she'd often take Clotilde and her dad back each year to make sure they were thriving. The flowers were family to her.

It was because of her mother that she'd pursued her private study of botanical artistry. Her illness and sudden deafness might have closed the door on her nursing career, but it had fully opened her eyes to the world of plants. She'd moved from nursing people to health, to valuing the dependence of all living creatures on plants and their flowers. She makes a mental note to chat with her son Ben. Would he have the environmental interests of her parents or is he more inclined to follow his dad's interests in politics and law. She looks forward to their next FaceTime rendezvous when she'll be updated on all the family adventures he has with his dad.

While her teenage days were filled with the wonder of medicine and caring for the sick and injured, her midlife days are filled with the silent wonder of the botanical kingdom. One day her drawings, the detail of individual structures, might stimulate someone's interest in the real value of a healthy ecosystem.

Tonight, stroke by tiny stroke her pencils create the yellow throat of her blue-eyed grass illustration. There are many hours still to be spent bringing all the parts, the veined sepals and petals, to an exact and true picture of this native perennial that's found across Canada. Clotilde enjoyed the watercolours she'd painted in the past, but once her passion moved to botanical illustrations, she got a little frustrated, partly because of constant interruptions caused by her father's and then her mother's illnesses. This reawakened her interest in the world of the colour pencil, which she could pick up and put down at any time. The wax-based pencils and their rich pigments allow her to build a depth of unique colour for the flower and its parts. Layer upon layer, shade upon shade, dark to light—and a true, larger-than-life image emerges. One day, perhaps her talent for colour and detail will result in something more than an absorbing pastime.

Anil is waiting for her. His sad little face lights up as she walks into his room, her smile and her hands saying good morning. He sits up, gives her a salute, palms his two hands and put his fists and two index fingers up. With an even bigger smile, he moves his open hands upward and over, lightly touching his chest. "Hello, nice to meet you. Happy," she translates.

She is a nurse again, assisting in the care of a little boy, changing his dressings, checking his fluids and helping him with snacks and lunch. She leaves him to sleep in the afternoon and enjoys the familiar sights, smells and bustle of the wards. She helps him with his supper and chats in sign about his family, telling the police later that his parents, a brother and his two sisters live in British Columbia; he lives in Calgary with his aunt, who is best able to help him with his deafness. Darkness settles on the room, and Clotilde tucks in Anil. She looks into his quiet dark eyes, strokes his brow, and signs, bringing her right hand to her mouth and then palm down to the back of her left hand. "Goodnight," she murmurs. She smooths his bed and promises to be back in the morning.

These hospital days encourage the lonely Clotilde. She's still not over having to live alone now that her mother has been gone these past months. She loves being back at the hospital and caring for a small boy, and all the while fascinating a growing group of youngsters with stories of Winnie the Pooh. She sees the smiles on the faces as she both reads and signs the adventures of the bear and his pals in the Hundred Acre Wood. Occasionally she has to stop and check with a volunteer about what the kids are saying. These are wonderful, interactive times. On her way home, she stops to visit with the boy's aunt, who is recovering well from her severe injuries, and updates her on Anil's progress.

#

"Where's Anil?" she says a few days later to the charge nurse. "Is he off playing somewhere?"

"He's gone—left early this morning. His aunt was discharged yesterday, and she came by with her relatives from BC and picked up Anil."

"What? No." Clotilde asks her to repeat to make sure she's read her lips correctly.

"He was a happy little fella," the charge nurse says. "I guess the doctor cleared him after you went home last night. I was here when they left. The family appreciated everything we've done, especially you. They were so sorry and very apologetic to have missed you."

Clotilde is stunned. She knew this day would come; it always did. "What's it been?" she asks. "Three weeks?" She heads past the day room and looks inside. A small girl comes to her and pulls her dress. She sees the girl's lips move but does not read her.

"She wants a story," says the hospital volunteer who is new in the day room. She speaks while looking at the girl and away from Clotilde.

When she does not get a response, the volunteer looks up. "She wants a story. She says you are the story nurse."

Panic for Clotilde. Her unmodulated voice squeaks. "Can't," she says. "Can't. Not today."

She hurries off down the corridor.

Chapter Eight

Clotilde's throat tightens in panic and frustration. "Please look at me," she says to the check-in agent. "I'm deaf. Je suis sourde. I can't hear what you say. I read lips."

The woman looks up from her computer, smiles and looks back at the screen. Clotilde sees her mouth move.

"Please!" Her voice is rising and loud. "I need to see your lips when you speak."

"Ms. Chiasson, I've told you several times already this is not your flight gate. An announcement was made on the PA almost an hour ago that there'd been a gate change." The woman smiles and hands the boarding pass back.

All Clotilde can read of what she's being told is "gate change."

"What am I to do?" Clotilde's voice is uncontrollably loud. "I've been sitting in that seat right in front of you for more than an hour, waiting. I showed the person before you my boarding pass and was told to wait. No one told me about a gate change."

The agent looks up and then back at the computer screen. She's talking, but Clotilde cannot see a word she's saying. Clotilde rests her handbag on the counter. "I'm deaf—look at your screen." She knows she's shouting now. "It tells you I cannot hear. Look at me, please." She feels her voice rise out of control. "Je suis sourde, regardez votre écran, il vous dit que je ne peux pas entendre. Je suis sourde. Regardez-moi, s'il vous plaît."

Waiting passengers nervously watch what's going on.

"I told you, this is not your gate," the agent says. "I don't have your flight information. Please be calm."

Two uniformed people quietly step up beside her. Security. Clotilde shouts and waves her arms, in a total panic that she's missed her flight. "Just help me," she says. "Please!"

The security man grabs her bag from the counter and begins to open it. She lunges at him, wanting to retrieve her bag. "What are you doing? That's mine," she says in a high-pitched voice. The other, a woman, quickly moves to her, and before she knows what's happening, Clotilde is in handcuffs, her arms behind her back. She sees a man trying to move toward the check-in agent. He's saying something, but he's pushed away by the dark-bearded, turbaned security guard. Clotilde is pulled away and led, shouting and wildly resisting, to a joyless, glassed-in room on the concourse. Her bag is in the hands of the security man.

"What is this?" she says. Through her tears she asks if she is under arrest. "Why, why, why? I just want my plane so I can go home."

The security woman waves at her to sit down. The man stands guard at the door. The woman is talking at her, but Clotilde cannot follow her lips. The woman has an accent—not Canadian, not French.

A police officer enters. "Please help me," she says. "I'm profoundly deaf, je suis sourde. All I want to know is how to get home to Calgary. Where's my bag? Where's my boarding pass? I'm not a criminal. Am I in custody? Why am I here?" She's uncomfortable and in tears.

The police officer holds her handbag and talks with security. He does not look at Clotilde. She cannot see what they are saying.

A tall, dark-haired woman in a smart navy blue business suit walks into the room. She ignores the security and police and goes straight to Clotilde, turns abruptly to the security woman and tells her to go get a bottle of water and a glass.

"My name is Alison," she says, speaking slowly and quietly and looking directly at Clotilde. Her glistening brown eyes and warm smile are calming. "I'm with the airport authority, and I'm here to clear all this up and see what I can do to help." She turns to the young fellow coming through the door. "Were you able to talk with the passenger?"

"Yes, and all he could say—he was very angry actually—was that he wanted to tell us that the woman is deaf and to stay calm, face her and listen. He says a deaf person who speaks has trouble controlling their voice levels when they get excited or frustrated. This is always seen as violence and anger. He's very, very mad at us though for treating the woman and him so roughly and uncaringly. He catches this same flight each week out to Calgary."

Alison turns to Clotilde and quietly asks how she is feeling.

Clotilde looks at her closely, watching the words form on her lips. She's terrified. *Is this woman here to help me?* She breathes softly to calm down and to speak in an even voice. "T-tissue," she says. "I n-need a tissue. My bag."

Alison heads to the door, says something to the security guards and speaks with the policewoman who'd remained outside. Clotilde rubs her wrists as the handcuffs are removed. Through the frosted windows, she sees the shadows of her captors leaving. She sips her water and has no idea what is happening to her.

Alison returns, and Clotilde knows she is talking, but the woman is not directly facing her. She sees the lips moving but cannot see the words.

"Please," she says, "let me see your face, and then I can see what you are saying."

Alison faces her, apologizes at length and asks if she is feeling okay.

"What's happening?" Clotilde asks, her eyes watering. "Am I in trouble? Am I going to be charged with something? I don't know anyone in Toronto, and now I don't have a ticket to Calgary. They took my boarding pass. Where's my baggage? It's on that plane."

"No, no. Don't worry, Ms. Chiasson. Everything's going to be okay. A few people just got things wrong and overreacted. When you're ready, we'll go over to the airline folks and see what we can arrange. It's been one huge, embarrassing mistake, which I will personally deal with later after you are all set. There's no need to worry further."

She pulls a small silver case from her jacket pocket, takes out a business card and prints a phone number and email address on it. "That's my private line and email, if you are ever in need of me at this airport again." She smiles. "Let's go find someone with the airline."

Clotilde takes out her iPhone and taps a note to her travel agent explaining what has taken place. Two hours later, after coffee and a snack with Alison and an airline supervisor, Clotilde finds herself at another gate waiting for a new flight. In her hand is a business-class boarding pass, and in her handbag an open business-class ticket to fly anywhere in North America.

She'd apologized profusely for causing the ruckus. The airline official assured her she was in no way to blame. "We've learned a great deal through this experience and will be briefing all staff on the challenges faced by the deaf and the hard-of-hearing. Most of all, agents must take notice of personal comments in the customer file. This should not have happened to you, and we are extremely embarrassed by this morning's events."

On board, she sinks into the wide, soft leather seats at the front of the plane. This is a first. She tries to relax but is all the more aware that she's alone in life. Her parents are no longer around, and few people bother to call on her now. She lives without people and wonders what the future holds.

She smiles at the attention she's given. Every now and then, a cabin attendant sits beside her and faces her squarely, and they chat and even laugh about the incident.

"It went round the terminal quicker than a grassfire," the attendant says. "A lot of people thought you were some kind of terrorist being marched away by security. Some wondered about that man who came over and was yelling at the desk as well. They thought he was part of it and that you had a weapon or something in your handbag."

This puzzles Clotilde. She'd forgotten about the man. She'd only been concerned with why they were going through her carry-on and her handbag. And then she was handcuffed when she tried to get her bag.

The whole experience leaves her extremely troubled, and even though she has an open ticket in her bag, she doubts she'll ever fly again.

Back in the secure, comfortable surroundings of her home, she writes an email about her experience to her relatives in Cape Breton. The journey to Nova Scotia had been taken at the insistence of her mother, who made her promise she'd go visit her relatives. She'd put off the visit for months, never wanting to get on a plane on her own. Aunts, uncles and cousins on both sides of the family have been badgering her to return and embrace her heritage, where relatives can be the best company for her now that her mother has passed.

Clotilde does not see the sense in this argument, though she appreciates their concern for her well-being. All things being equal, she is happy in her familiar surroundings, near the hospital, near the park and closer to her son. She's determined to make it on her own.

#

A month has passed since the airport debacle, and Clotilde is surprised one day to open her email and find a message from Alison, a name she'd all but forgotten.

> Hello Clotilde,
>
> I do hope this message finds you well, happily back in your Calgary lifestyle. I took control of your case and encouraged the airline to implement procedures and specific training similar to ours for all front-line staff. This sensitivity training has since extended to other airlines operating through here, and I fully expect it has been implemented at all airports across Canada.
>
> Anyway, enough of that. Now for the surprise and the real reason I'm writing to you.
>
> The agent you had difficulty with at the gate came up with a suggestion that we adopted. The agent was extremely upset with herself for her complete lack of understanding, believing that if you could speak, then you could hear. She shared this with her colleagues, and they approached us, the airline management and

the security company with the idea that we give you a new companion, a hearing service dog.

We have been in touch with the organization to find out the procedures and requirements. You fully qualify. We went ahead and ordered a dog on the basis that even if the idea is not to your liking, we will donate our dog to another person. This idea and our actions have made a big difference here in understanding the challenges some people have.

Do let me know what you think, and if this is something you would like to do. Our understanding is that a fully trained dog will be available in about a month. There is a white poodle that has not yet been placed, and we have a reserve on him. The airline will fly you here for a two-week training period at our cost.

This project has brought a ton of meaning to our organization and is a tangible reminder that all who work in our industry must be aware of the specific needs of all travellers. Once you and the little fellow are comfortable, we'd like to introduce you both to the staff as a follow-up to what we've been saying.

Please let me know your thoughts about having a dog in your life.

And one last thing, the dog's name is Bibeau. French, I think.

Warm regards,

Alison

Clotilde bursts into tears.

Chapter Nine

"Sushi night," Brewster calls from the doorway, and Hannah appears at the top of the stairs.

"Sushi?" she says. "I didn't think you were into that, but I'm definitely a starter. Now? It's only about five o'clock."

"Yep, I'm hungry. Skipped lunch."

He allows Hannah to order, and when the food comes, he admires her chopstick dexterity. They talk about her day, the wedding and the flower arrangements at the church, and his afternoon at the park: being almost bowled over by a cyclist and then bumping into the woman with the red backpack slung over her shoulder.

"I apologized to her, but she didn't say anything. Smart-looking woman. She was slowly walking along and staring into the grass and clutter beside the path. Bit like your mother used to do when we were looking for flowers. The park helps me think about things," he says, breaking the soft tension. "Your mother's things. We can do this. I'll try to be a little more positive. Big question for me is the how?"

Hannah smiles. "I know, Dad. But I'm sure Mom would want us to forge ahead. The chaplain said something like, 'Yesterday is history, and tomorrow's a mystery.' Today we have the present, and that is the gift."

"Sounds like you're the wise one here," Brewster says. "What have you got in mind?"

Over green tea ice cream, Hannah gives a shrug and says she'll look after things. Providing he was okay with it, Jo would call up a couple of helpers from her church.

"You mean have some outsiders come in and clean out your mom's things?" he says. "Not sure I like that. It's private."

"I'm sure it'll be fine, Dad. They've done this sort of thing before, in their own lives and while helping others."

Truce.

Later, they meander through the house, opening and closing closets, cupboards and drawers while quietly assessing what needs to be done. It's sobering for Brewster, who wants to pull away. He joins his daughter as she chats on FaceTime with Harris, knowing deep down that his children are right.

"Okay, enough of this," she says suddenly. "Scrabble. Let me beat you again."

He yields the whole matter to Hannah after she beats him twice on the Scrabble board. She's always been the family wordsmith, quick and witty.

#

Two women with a pile of boxes and bags arrive at the front door as he leaves the house for the coffee shop and then his lawyer's office. It's better if he's out of the way, leaving Hannah and her church mice to the task. He knew he'd miss seeing his son again. Hannah arranged to FaceTime Harris on her iPad as she sorted through Melanie's jewellery, personal memorabilia and papers. "I think there are too many memories, and it's making a mess of Dad," Harris had said to Hannah. "Call me anytime, and you can show me and talk about things." In spite of the time difference between Alberta and Australia, he'd be on standby because he very much wanted to be able to contribute to this very necessary business that had been left far too long.

Brewster's lawyer laughs at the story of his broken arm, shaved head where the stitches had been and the walking cane to support his ankle. "Sure glad the mail lady came by," Horton says, "otherwise I might have been talking with Hannah today. You haven't been in to see me for a few months, and now you waltz in with a broken arm and a cracked head."

"So this is the price I pay for keeping you in business for 16 years?" Brewster shoots back. A lively round of legal humour? He smiles at his friend. "I've left Hannah and a couple of helpers sorting through Mel's belongings. She'll get Harris online too. Best if I keep out of the way. I'm grumpy enough without all that."

"Relax, Brewster. Hannah is her mother's daughter. Now, to business. I have all the papers drawn up for the transfer of The Blue Aster to Jo and Danny as you directed, and I've some other matters relating to your business interests that we need to go through."

Two hours later, Brewster grumps his way across the parking lot. He doesn't do too well sitting around talking legal stuff. While driving into the southeast of the city, he realises that being out of circulation for several months brooding about his loss may not have been the best thing for business. Still, he has confidence in the people he's relied on over many years.

A carwash sign encourages him to do something he hasn't done since the funeral: check out the true colour of his vehicle. It's very dirty, and with a good half hour before any lunchtime crowd, the car wash may well be empty.

There's no answer when he tries Hannah on the hands-free as he drives his shiny red Jeep to his office. He's talked with his accountant by phone, but he hasn't been near his office for months. Is he up for this visit?

Alone in the elevator as it whirrs its way to the third floor, Brewster is curious about what his accountant might have in store. He's not sure how he'll handle himself, and more out of habit than confidence, he whispers, "God help me now."

"Good to see you, man." Ever the effusive greeting from the man who is not only his accountant but also his company business manager.

"Hi, Joel," he says. "Yes, good to be here—though I rather thought you might be saying something like it's about time I got back here."

"Ha! Good one, but not quite true. Sure, I've missed your happy, smiling face, Brewster. You've had a lot to deal with, and I certainly haven't anything of an urgent nature to bother you about. Need some signatures today, though."

Brewster looks at his tall, grey-haired friend. They'd grown up together and had reunited 20 years ago after being separated by school and careers. They've enjoyed a very successful and profitable partnership. "You mean to say we've got nothing to argue about today?" Brewster says. "Let's get a coffee. I guess everyone knows I'm here?"

"Not unless you told them," Joel says.

And with that, Brewster opens the door to the main office.

"Hello, you're a new face," he says to the receptionist. "I'm Brewster."

"Hello, Mr. McWhirtle. I'm Jane," she says. "This is my second week here."

"I'm just Brewster," he says, shaking her hand with the fingers protruding from his arm cast. "None of this Mister stuff. Who's all here?"

"Eleanor's in her office, Gavin's out on an inspection with a contractor, Devi's meeting with a possible new tenant and Brian is … well, he might be back. He had to go over to the printer's."

"You have a good team here," Brewster says as he and Joel settle in to the boardroom with their coffees.

"It was sad to lose Wilf from the front," Joel says. "I tried to call you to say he was going; an opportunity in his wife's family business out in Medicine Hat. Jane is a good find, though. She's also well-qualified to handle a lot of the financial accounting. Bright as a button and just amazing with people, especially the testy kind. You noticed she's in a wheelchair?"

"Yep." Brewster says. "Glad you hired her. How did you find her?"

"Just word of mouth, I suppose," Joel says. "She came in because she'd heard we had an opening. I hired her on the spot. Gotta like that sort of initiative. I had Gavin handle the necessary changes to make it easy for Jane to move around and do her work."

"Okay," Brewster says. "Let's go through everything and see where we're at. And thanks for always being here for me during the past few months. You've been a great help. I do apologize for the extra stress I must have caused. I see we have an empty suite on the ground floor, where the gift shop used to be."

"Mavis decided to retire and closed her business out when the lease expired two months ago. Devi has been shopping the space, but no takers as yet. Lots of interest, though."

"What about a coffee shop?"

"Devi has a potential there," Joel says. "Not sure of the progress on that one."

Brewster senses that Joel has something much bigger on his mind. "Let's cut to the chase, Joel. What's up?"

"I've had a couple of offers for the building, and one of them is really interesting. You'll do well financially if you consider it—maybe a couple of million over what you bought it for."

"So what's the 'but'?"

"One's a national with deep pockets. We have a number of leases up for renewal, and I can only see major increases for those tenants— people who have established businesses here over a long time. Any new owner would be jacking rates up, and I foresee some tenants on the upper floors having to move because the company wants to put its regional offices here. I think that's their main interest."

There's silence as Brewster looks at Joel. The plumber and the accountant; the Christian and the Jew. Joel reviews the letter of inquiry along with all the other business of tenant leases, maintenance and capital needs. The afternoon is busy. Staff come and go, some adding their contributions and concerns. He feels the weight of being *in absentia* for far too long. He'd taken a huge risk several years ago in buying the building and everything that went with it. Now there's a new decision, and he didn't have Melanie to throw around ideas.

His cell phone dinged with a new text. "Terrific sorting day, Dad. All well. Heading out with a couple of old school friends. See you later."

"Hannah," he says, and he explains the disagreement they'd had over Melanie's belongings. "I hadn't changed anything or moved anything. It was just as it was when she went to get her hair done. Hannah reckons it's time to move on. Hard to do."

"I bet," Joel says. "Let's go find something to eat. Anna's taking the kids for swimming down at the centre tonight. I told her you were in, and we'd look after ourselves. She'd like you to say hello. You know, you've been too long the stranger."

"Let's head to the centre, then," Brewster says, reluctant to be out in public, eager to get home and worried about the changes he will see in the house. By the time he reaches the first set of traffic lights, second thoughts float in like clouds on a sunny afternoon. *Too late to bail, and anyway, Joel is on my tail.*

It's all go at the Jewish centre. It is quite possibly the most people he's been around for some time apart from the mall. Joel ushers him to the cafeteria, past the glass-walled mirrored gym full of fitness fiends. They find a spare table, and he sizes up the organized chaos. People are moving in all directions. Joel looks after coffee and a sandwich. Brewster shrinks as far as he can into the wall, intimidated by the couples and families and the low hum of mixed conversations.

Anna bursts in, hugs him and offers cheerful banter. Then she's gone back to the pool and the swimming lessons. A whirlwind of beauty, inside and out, Melanie used to say of her always-on-the-go friend. She exuded life. For Brewster, now there's no life without Melanie. He sighs deeply, and Joel senses his slump. He brings their conversation back to the safe territory of the business topics of the day: their shared success and outlook.

Brewster drains his coffee, fiddles with some crumbs left on his plate and politely listens. He's had enough, pushes back on his chair, stands and thanks Joel for his time and attention. He turns to go and realizes that perhaps there is still one outstanding issue of their day together. "Let's not look any further into that offer for the building. I'm not ready to sell and have no need to sell."

Joel nods and suggests that maybe they sit on the offer for a while. They hug. As Brewster walks to the door, he sees his friend head off to be with his wife and children at the pool.

Chapter Ten

The woman in the large, floppy sun hat kneels on the grassy bank overlooking the river and slowly unpacks her red backpack. She flicks out a large blue and green tartan rug, sits, closes her eyes and breathes in the fresh, late-morning air. She unpacks a little plastic box of sandwiches, opens a thermos of coffee, smooths a fresh page in her sketch book and lays out her colour pencils. She enjoys the peace where she can sit out of the wind and be wrapped in sunshine. It is a place where she can lose herself and be absorbed in a very natural part of her tiny world. What's extra nice is that it's only a short walk from her home to this broad sweep of a park, which spans rather like a smile across what used to be the southern part of the city. Where life will take her now, a deaf woman and her dog moving from one day to the next. A few friends might drop by, but not many and only infrequently. They're at work, and after the years she spent caring for her parents, she slowly became isolated. Communication has become difficult. There are days she hopes the hospital will call with a need for her nursing skills combined with her lip-reading and sign language abilities. Otherwise, the park is her escape, her art, her joy. She hopes that one day she'll learn how to capture an online market to liberate her pictures from sketch pad and easel.

"Okay, Bebo," she says to her quiet, four-footed companion. "Today we have to find a bracted orchid." She saw one a few years ago, before she had the idea of cataloguing the flowers of the park into a small handbook, though she isn't sure the hand-drawn artwork is a seller anymore. At this stage, she simply gets a lot of pleasure creating the botanical drawings of immense detail and colour.

They sit there, a woman and her dog. Clotilde is pleased she changed the spelling of his name from the French Bibeau to Bebo, the name given to a special part of her park. She watches the ripples on the river as it meanders across and around the rocks, shallow and clear now after the spring thaw. A couple of mallards paddle their way along the river's edge, and mergansers bob in centre stream. It's a tranquil spot, and there is no one else around. The first of the picnickers will not be through for at least another hour. By that time, she'll be ready to go look for her flower, when the sun is at its best angle to beam through the aspen, poplar and spruce canopy.

Mmm, these cucumber sandwiches are good. Next time, perhaps I'll add some crumbs of blue cheese as an outdoor treat. Clotilde takes off her jacket and relaxes with the sun's warmth on the olive skin of her arms and neck. She dares not look back these days on what her life might have been. She's now on her own and knows she must look forward and make out of life what she's been given. Her time now works around her artwork. If only she could build the words to go with the drawings. That is her weakness. With today's emphasis on social media, she considers some continuing education classes in the fall. She watches kids arriving to play in the river, maybe to build a dam, and she hears the bygone laughter of her friends splashing around, moving dam-building rocks only to be washed out in the next freshet.

Time to move. She packs up her things, slings her backpack over one shoulder and pushes her way off the trail through the raggedy tangle of the undergrowth, crouching and shuffle-stepping under the low branches spruce and aspen until she reaches a boggy depression where her orchid might be. She is now in the territory of her archenemy: mosquitoes. She walks slowly along the ditch, moving plants with the tip of her walking pole. She knows the mozzies will zero in on her as soon as she stoops to check a plant. She is wrapped neck to toe, with no flesh exposed. A net hangs from her floppy hat, and she hopes the surgical gloves will enable her to sketch with ease. First she'll take photographs. Only then will she outline the plant in situ. She'll use her lighted magnifying glass to begin to capture essential detail within the flower itself. She will only pick the flower if conditions are too wet or the mosquitoes too nasty. The orchid she seeks is beautiful, and with its shades of green, it's no bigger than a fingernail. The flowers spread up a slender stem.

Bebo follows quietly on the end of his leash. Clotilde loves her little friend, who is thoroughly trained to warn her of any noise or intrusion into her space. His white poodle paws will soil in the mud, and twigs will knot in his coat. His red uniform jacket protects his middle.

"Well, Bebo, I don't see any here," she says. "Strange—I'm sure this is the spot I saw them last summer. Let's try over by last year's washout. Might be some there."

She enjoys the solitariness of the pathways today. She's on a quest and likes to work while the sun is directly overhead. Too often she meets well-meaning park-goers who want to stop and check out the dog in his little red coat. Others stare as they walk by. Today's bonus, the reason she comes midweek, might well be a lack of bicycles threatening her little friend with their speed. Bebo warns her when he hears a bike bell or just the thrum of tires on the pavement or gravel.

She finds the plants in the soft ground under a spruce tree. No flowers yet, but when she's on her hands and knees, she can see that in a week or two, she will have everything she wants. She pencils the location in her notepad.

"C'mon, Bebo. Let's call it a day." She feels the slight shift of the gravel under her shoes as she moves along the path. A light wind ruffles the new leaves in the aspens, squirrels dart here and there and a chipmunk scurries for the shelter of a log. Around her she sees chickadees flitting back and forth and she breathes in the new earth smell of the forest.

Once home, she washes the legs and feet of her young friend, pulls some twigs from the fur on his rear end and ears and takes off his coat. With that, Bebo jumps and runs around the lounge. As far as he's concerned, he's off work, finished for the day. He looks at Clotilde. *Is that a smile?* she thinks as she goes to her computer.

Email—her lifeblood connection with a chattering world. Still, she longs for that human contact, to be able to look a person in the eyes, see their lips move and watch words form. Instead, she is comforted by Facebook and items of interest posted there by people she knows. It's been more than half her life since that strange and sudden turn of events altered her forever.

She scans her inbox, hoping for a contact that will elevate her spirits. She's disappointed that the orchid was not ready for her to complete her outside plans for the day.

Emails from the east, the Cape Breton homeland of her parents. Regular messages from relatives wanting her to fully discover her Acadian and Mi'kmaq roots. Aunts, uncles and cousins suggesting she pack up and move out there, where she can be cared for.

The constant flow of kindly family jabber annoys her because somehow her deafness seems to make her less of a person. "I'm deaf, not stupid," she tells people. There's a note from a favourite cousin extolling the wonderful, quiet life she could have in Cheticamp. Clotilde is reminded of the property she inherited there from her grandmother. No mention of her dad, though; he came from the Eskasoni Nation of Cape Breton.

"Oh, cousin," Clotilde says in her reply. "I like it enough here in Calgary. My parents are here. Why would I move?"

She works through her other emails: a bookstore, Air Miles, an art supplies newsletter, a gardening magazine, and the Spruce Meadows Equestrian Centre newsletter. By the time she's done with that, a new email bounces back from her same-age cousin.

"So we could look after you, silly. Now that Aunty Helene has gone, you are all by yourself, and I'm sure having family around would be the best thing for you. And you've got your dad's family over in Membertou. Your roots are here, in Cape Breton."

Cousin Ruth is a busy woman: wife of a fisherman, mother of four and a quilter who's found a ready market for her creative designs at craft outlets along the Cabot Trail. Clotilde taps a reply.

Dear Ruth,

    I know you mean well, but I'm comfortable here. Benny comes and visits me when he can during his school breaks. I have a lot of work these days with my flower drawings. I get called in to the hospital to help deaf patients. It's good. Bebo is wonderful company. Thanks for your concern, but as I've said before, I'm only deaf, not incapacitated.

                                    Clotilde

Clotilde can almost hear the tut-tuts from her relatives around their kitchen table. She's typed this same message before and knows without a doubt she'll be typing it again. Maybe she'll have to take another trip out there. It's been some time since that last disastrous trip, before Bebo brought new meaning to her life.

She looks across the room where her little dog is busy gnawing on his furry, rubber plaything that, as a service dog, he's only allowed to have during his non-working time. The western Canada violet draws her back to the drafting table.

"This is such a lovely little flower," she tells Bebo, who, tired of his toy, trots over to sit near her on the window seat. "It tells us spring is really here and summer is just round the corner."

She works on the detail of the charming white flower that's easy to spot in the woods and along pathways. She's already happy with the way she has depicted the heart-shaped, finely toothed leaves and the slender purple stalks of the flower. Today she continues her work on the petals, gently stroking in the purplish veins that emanate from the yellow throat on the lower three of the five petals.

Bebo jumps from the window seat and softly paws Clotilde's shoe. She looks down at him and sees that it's time for an outside break. "Okay, mon petit," she says. "Out it is, and a good time for me to work this cramp out of my thumb."

Chapter Eleven

"Look, Dad, just let go. Things will get better." Brewster closes the tailgate, steps on to the sidewalk and holds his tearful daughter in a fatherly hug. "Don't come in," she says. "I'm just going to the check-in and then go straight to the gate. We agreed." She picks up her backpack. "Be on your way, and don't stop till you get to wherever you're going." Hannah smiles, gives Brewster a loving shove and heads into the airport terminal.

He watches after his daughter as she disappears through the double sliding doors. "'Scuse me, sir. You'll have to move. No waiting here," airport security said.

"Just going," he says. "Just going."

No looking back, Hannah had said repeatedly. She'd even helped him pack a bag this morning to go on a road trip to get himself together. "Not a time to be at home worrying about what we've done with all Mom's things. You and Mom used to get away, so go. Get some wind in your hair."

Out of the city, the Trans-Canada Highway is welcome after the stop-start, whizz-whizz of city traffic. He doesn't have a plan. It's early morning yet, and something will come to mind once he gets into the mountains.

The miles slip by. Brewster is mesmerized by the fleeting landscape. These might be fantastic mountains he's heading toward, the gateway to the Rockies, but who cares? He stares at the grey-black ribbon stretching out in front, one long, wide line etched between the trees, fences and farmland. Cruise control takes care of the speed; he just steers.

He's not really aware that he's even travelling. The wind through the sunroof and the thrum of it on the bug catcher keeps him alert. The calming of an open road—there's nothing like it to brush away emotional cobwebs in his stubborn subconscious. What was it Hannah had said yesterday?

"Look, Dad. I know this is tough for you, but really, it's time you conquered these thoughts that drag you down all the time. Mom was a fantastic person and a big loss to us all, but I know she'd be pretty upset at you moping around the place all this time."

"Too true. I'll work on it," he'd promised.

"Why don't you get in the car and go somewhere you like?" Hannah said. "Get outta town. What about going over to BC?"

"Well, Hannah, my wise and wonderful daughter, that's what I am doing today," he says into the car. "Trouble is, I don't have a plan yet."

He bumps through the quick lane at the park gates because he does not need to go into the town of Banff or Lake Louise; he'll just keep the wheels rolling. The morning cloud burns off, giving way to piercing sunny blue skies.

Stunning stretch of highway. The folded multi-tones of rock rise skyward on either side. Cars and trucks zip by on his left, their drivers showing little regard for the reduced speed through the national park. Ninety is fast enough, anyway. There's a wildlife overpass up ahead, and he smiles as the thought springs to mind of how cool it would be to see a bear or two looking down at the crazy humans in their crazy cars.

With Castle Mountain shaping up in all its magnificence to his right, Brewster knows he'll need to make another decision very soon: swing off and head to Radium Hot Springs and into the Kootenays, or head on through on the Trans-Canada to the Okanagan. In his hesitation, the off-ramp to Radium blips by.

Springtime in the Rockies, he thinks with a smile. A movie and a song that attracted and meant much to his immigrant parents. His wannabe cowboy father sang Gene Autry style, "When it's springtime in the

Rockies, I'll be coming back to you ..." He gulps and thinks, *But Melanie will not be coming back* ... "Little sweetheart of the mountains, with your bonnie eyes of blue."

He's surprised the words come so easily to mind. He's not heard the song for many years, perhaps since he moved out of Grande Prairie way back when. The band was Peace River Riders, maybe. Something like that. He slows and pulls in behind a line of vehicles parked on the shoulder still some distance from Lake Louise. Wildlife. People are out of their cars and pointing. He joins the mob at the railing. Sure enough, down by the sparkling Bow River is a young grizzly meandering along the riverbank quite unconcerned about the crowd he's attracting.

"Sorry, Mel. You're not here this time. He's a real beauty. I can see the silver fur on his hump rippling as he walks," he says. "You always had your eyes out every time we came through here. So here's the one that got away."

Brewster considers the colour of the river. "Really, what is the colour?" he says, still thinking that Melanie is beside him. He smiles at the woman a couple of paces away. She's dropped her binoculars and looks questioningly at him. "Ah, just thinking aloud," he says. "Is the river green, green-blue or turquoise perhaps?" The woman turns away, and he looks back at the bear. Does it have a mate somewhere in the woods? Or was it like him, mateless and alone?

He leaves the bear and its crowd of onlookers and eases back into the traffic. He murmurs for the cars to slow down. This marvellous highway through breathtaking country is not a place for speed. *Slow down and smell the roses.*

He sighs deeply and pulls into a rest area overlooking the river. Time for a stretch and a nature break. The mountain air is gorgeous, and he sits on the rock wall enjoying the coffee and granola bar courtesy of his daughter. He recalls Melanie's antics at this particular stop, running back and forth with her camera, bending over to get a shot of a nicely arranged twig in the grass, a flower, a mushroom or toadstool. That was the energy she had, taking delight in anything that in many ways seemed out of place.

"Incoming call," the car announces as he pulls back on to the highway. He pushes the hands-free button. "Hi, Dad. Lunchtime here. How ya doing?. Where are you?"

"Hi to you, missy," he says. "I took your advice, and here I am on the highway, just passing Castle Mountain. You should see it. I think it looks different every time we come through."

"Great. You feeling okay?'

"You betcha. Couldn't be better. Springtime in the Rockies. Think I'll head to Kelowna or somewhere along the way, and then I'll spend a few days meandering back home along the border and through the Crowsnest."

"I'm so glad, Dad. You need that. We're kinda in the last stages of the term, and I've got a couple of exams to get done later this week. Then we'll work on getting stuff ready for Europe."

"Well, good luck with your exams. I'm sure you'll do well. I'll send you an email when I hole up somewhere for the night," he says. "You're so very right, Hannah. This is good for the soul, and the weather is making it even better."

As Brewster disconnects, he nears the top of the Kicking Horse Pass and pulls off into the Spiral Tunnels viewpoint. He shuts off the car and addresses his wife. "Hey, Mel. I'm back at this amazing place. You'll remember the last time we were here, maybe just a couple of weeks before, before …"

He chokes back his emotion, and gets out of the car and stretches. He saunters over to the panels to once more acquaint himself with the engineering involved in cutting the highway and railway through from its highest point at more than 5,000 feet down to the valley floor. He thinks of how railway and highway broke through the wall of mountains to get people and freight from the prairies to the Pacific coast. To him, the massive cuts through rock, the spiral railway tunnels needed to provide easy grades up and down and the super sweeping bridges that cross the rivers are breathtaking in their enormity.

This surely is a country of contrasts, Brewster thinks. The viewpoint is a popular place as travellers read the information panels and take photographs, waiting for a train to show from one of the tunnel portals while its tail end is still entering the spiral. He's glad he missed the highway to Radium. The Kicking Horse is a triumph of highway and railway engineering, of man against the mountains.

"Riveting," he says to the woman beside him. "Just riveting."

"I think of all those men who came here to do this job," she says. "And they didn't have the equipment we have today. I wonder if they all made it home again. Coming all this way to labour hard to earn a dollar."

He and Melanie often stopped at this point. Today as he rereads the information panels, he sees what it cost: one death a week as men laboured for $2.25 for a 10-hour day. If they took two years to build, that's more than 100 people who didn't go home. He watches a big diesel power out from the upper portal of the Mount Ogden lower tunnel; the back end enters the portal, a half-mile spin for a 50-foot elevation gain. A politician's impetuous promise 140 years ago to bring British Columbia into confederation, and a ploy to keep out American branch railroads, is now a national historic site that moves millions of tons of prairie cargo daily to the port facilities.

Brewster sees the tunnels, the railway and the highway as a memorial. Though men died in rock slides and explosions and derailments, they live on in the recreation and economy of today. He swishes down the Trans-Canada, dropping rapidly in elevation in the run through Field to Golden. It's a ride like no other as he eases down and around the well-tailored curves, past a runaway lane and down to the Kicking Horse River smashing its way through the gorge. In the opposite lane, heavily-laden 18- and 22-wheelers grind up the Big Hill to the Prairies.

Chapter Twelve

"Thank you, Tom, for that very flattering introduction. This is the first time I've been an after-breakfast speaker, and I hope and pray that what I'm about to say is a good beginning for your day."

Clotilde holds the podium with both arms outstretched and looks out at the 100-plus men and women who have gathered in the conference centre for what is termed an in-house training seminar.

"I am a registered nurse, a graduate of the University of Alberta. I find it interesting that you invited me to speak on a subject that is not connected to my training and yet is totally associated with who I am today. I always wanted to be a nurse; it's a career I pursued from the day when I first entered the hospital in Fort McMurray and worked as a candystriper. I loved that uniform and caring for the patients who were always glad to have me around. I was a small teenager who smiled at patients, listened to them and found out what they needed. They were enjoyable times. Even the grouchy ones couldn't dissuade me from pursuing nursing as a career."

Clotilde looks out across the room. She looks to her side at the company president, who made her introduction, and at those with whom she shared her breakfast. Though she can't hear any noise in the room, she senses a stillness and feels her audience waiting.

She looks out, smiles and continues. "What most of you don't know is that I'm profoundly deaf. Two years after graduating and working as a fully bilingual nurse at the Rockyview Hospital in Calgary, a disease took me away from patient care. Somehow I'd contracted meningitis. I didn't take any notice of the symptoms until it was too late, and I ended up as you see me today. Je suis sourd. I am deaf.

"But I didn't have time to think too much about being deaf because I was also pregnant, entering my second trimester. Would our baby suffer the same fate as me? It was a worry, but I had excellent care. As much as my sorrows would allow, I tried to be a model patient. Benjamin was born happy and healthy, a beautiful boy. My wonderful husband and I were relieved and felt like we could take on the world.

"That's when the threads started to unravel. Pierre struggled as I tried to come to grips with new forms of communication. I speak two languages, sure, but I cannot hear. I could not hear our baby cry. I could not hear him gurgle with the happiness of a growing newborn. I could not hear father and son.

"I was alone, locked up in a silent world, speaking but not listening. My unmodulated voice made me sound angry. To tell you the truth, I *was* angry and bitter. Poor Pierre. I could not understand a thing he was saying. I was struggling to learn to read lips.

"My parents moved to the city and bought a house nearby. My mother would come help me during the days. In the evenings at home, Pierre was the nighttime watchman, helping me as much as he could. His work as a young lawyer began to suffer. He tried to learn sign language with me. He did what he could to encourage me, but it was tough because he was also continuing his studies to build on his law degree. We'd leave each other notes. He'd wake in the night to the sound of crying, get me awake, and indicate that Benjamin needed attention. His pointing became shouting I could not hear, but I could see his anger and frustration. His eyes and his face showed it all. I would cry.

"Yes, the inevitable happened, and Pierre had to move. I think it was my suggestion. I could see his pain, and he could see mine. My silent world was slowly closing us down. His notes became hurried scribbles, sometimes half words. Then one day I threw away all the notes. We had been recycling our stickies: yellow for me, orange for him and blue for Benji. I threw them on the floor and burst into tears.

That's where he found me. We hugged, and Pierre left. He is still my dearest friend."

She pauses, frightened that she is not adding interest to their seminar, but stillness is still palpable in the room.

"My mother did what she could to help me. Eventually both houses were sold, and I moved into a larger home with my parents. They loved Benjamin, and it was like he was their child. I was the big sister. When Benjamin turned three, I wrote to Pierre and his new wife, suggesting that perhaps it might be best for our darling boy if they took care of him. They jumped at the idea because it would reduce travel and visiting time, allowing Benjamin to grow as a normal and healthy boy. Perhaps even a hockey player.

"I was still struggling with sign language, and lip-reading did not come easy to me. It's a practice-makes-perfect art, and it was very difficult for me because I was essentially housebound. I was used to expressing myself in French or English. In fact, I was used to being told I talked too much. Waving my hands, remembering the signals and learning hand, arm and finger positions was difficult.

"The hard decision was made, and Benjamin moved. My heart broke, and I could not understand why my life, so full of promise, had cratered to where I saw myself as a deaf old maid living with her parents. I did not know what to do.

"I'm not going to say what happened over the next few years because it would evoke the wrong response. Yes, I tried returning to the hospital, but I could not work with patients. I could not return to my old position in ER. I was no good in surgery. Filing was not my thing. I could not answer the telephone. My supervisors tried to place me, and I'm forever grateful for their efforts. They even tried me in triage—you know, getting the vitals—but that was a bust. My lip-reading skills in those days were not as polished as they might have been. I'd learned from speakers with a French accent: my mother, my husband who grew up in Montreal and my relatives.

"My dad, the best grader driver Calgary has ever known, came down with terminal cancer. I became his caregiver. He'd been given six months, but his treatment improved his general condition, and he remained with us for four years. I was able to care for him at home—a true blessing for both my mother and me.

"During my nurse training and hospital employment, I'd become totally fascinated with medical drawings. The detail is remarkable, and I discovered in simple, easy terms what lies under our own skin—where it is and what it looks like. Check out the artwork on your doctor's wall. You will see what I'm getting at.

"My mother loved plants, and we had a fantastic garden each summer. She saw me looking at a drawing of the inner ear. I was ever hopeful that perhaps one day, someone or something might happen that would allow me to hear again. 'Why don't you draw my flowers like that?' she said. 'A flower can't speak, but it still shows its beauty to the world.'

"My dear mom. She barrelled through my protestations, took me to the art shop, talked with them about what a beginner should start with and bought a box of colour pencils and a sketch pad. Well, Mom put these things in my hands, but it took some time that summer to bring myself to imitate the precision of medical drawings with flower drawing. Come to think of it, is that even possible? When I did start, I even tried tracing around the edge of a petal or a stalk or a leaf to get it onto paper. Try it sometime; it doesn't work. But as I dissected Mom's plants, I did get drawn into the world of a flower. So moms are never wrong! I was hooked and read as much as I could to get to where I'm at today as a botanical artist.

"It was Mom's idea that I get down to Fish Creek Park and take a look at the flowers there. Little did I know when I started that I'd become so preoccupied, or that I'd be able to at least recover a portion of my costs by framing and selling my work. Those walks to the park that we took for as long as we could sustained Mom as she developed early onset Alzheimer's. It was sad to see, but the flowers kept her, and regardless of what else happened, I could almost count on her to find some of the treasures I drew.

"There were tough times: she'd forget she was in the park, why she was out walking or even who I was. Then suddenly out of the blue, she'd spot a flower, even the tiniest one that I would have missed. Yet she'd ask me why I needed a pencil. It was hard to stand by and watch her always active mind take sudden turns. In a blink she could tell me the stamen I'd drawn was not correct, or the petal did not show true colour. The mystery of her mind gave me courage.

"That dear lady died almost 18 months ago. This one thing she gave me will always stay with me. My illness affected my father, my mother, my son, my husband, and his new wife. There's no 'why me' in this. Mom showed me hope. She was a very spiritual woman. She was always at her Bible, especially after Dad died. She would always tell me to never lose hope, to have faith in the things unseen.

"And even at her lowest point, not long before she died, she quoted me this passage from an Emily Dickinson poem."

> Hope is the thing with feathers,
> That perches in the soul—
> And sings the tune without the words—
> And never stops at all.

Clotilde looks across the room and takes a sip of water. "Enough about me. I want to introduce you to a new and very special friend of mine. He's special because of the generosity of the industry you all work in, because of the generosity of you people and your colleagues here and in many places across Canada, and because of the staff at Toronto Pearson International Airport. I want you all to meet Bebo."

The little white poodle bounces to her side when she gives a simple hand signal. He'd been sitting nearby with Alison. Though she cannot hear a thing, Clotilde looks out on a crowd of people smiling and clapping, and she feels a new energy. Everyone loves a spirited, faithful dog.

"Yes," she says. "He's a lovely companion and has made a massive contribution to my life in the six months since Alison arranged to have me trained and partnered with him. He's a treasure for sure, but I must remind you that he is a working dog. When he has his jacket on, he is working, and he knows it. I can take if off, and he knows that is the time when he can play. I'm sorry that I cannot pass him round. He cannot and must not be petted during his working hours. Watch him now as Alison texts me on my phone."

Bebo, sitting upright at her feet beside the podium, hears the phone signal, looks to her and pats her leg. "Telephone, microwave, oven, doorbells, alarms, bike bells on the pathways, traffic and yes, even people calling me. Bebo is my ears and has given me a new life. He carries his service dog licence and other credentials in his backpack. Most times people are very positive about his presence.

"My final comment here this morning is around me speaking. I'm constantly asked why I can speak and yet cannot hear. I spent 22 years speaking two languages every waking moment. I've had to get used to speaking evenly, as I have done today. My problem comes when I get frustrated, upset or anxious, and I lose control of my voice levels. Because I'm deaf, I have extreme difficulty controlling my voice levels. It goes up when I'm anxious or frustrated, and this is always interpreted as me being angry and out of control. That is how I ended up in difficulty at Toronto's airport.

"It is Alison, of the Airport Authority, who has been my guide here today. I thank her for her attention to my problem and taking it forward to help others understand that among the travelling public, there are many who require extra consideration. I'm sure you are all aware of this. Our occupations—me as a nurse and you folks in the airline industry—are confronted daily with how our actions affect people in different ways.

"Thank you so much for your generosity in giving me Bebo and in listening to me. I wish I could have heard what I said."

Clotilde smiles and steps back from the podium, Bebo's leash in her hand. Her audience stands, and she can see them clapping. She waves and leaves the stage with Alison, finds a chair and collapses, flushed and near tears.

It's just a pause, though; Alison beckons her to get up. "They want to see you again," she says, looking directly at Clotilde. "They are still clapping. You have to go out again."

They walk hand in hand to the podium, and partway Alison stops and ushers Clotilde and Bebo forward. Clotilde sees the audience still standing and clapping. She's totally lost on what she should do. She smiles, waves and notices a young man walking forward, wending his way through the tables and seats to stand on the opposite side. He looks at the audience; she sees him speak, and the crowd sits. He turns to her with the room in total silence, and with absolute dexterity he signs, "On behalf of my colleagues, we want to thank you for your time and for your quiet words of encouragement to us. You have brought new meaning to us in both our work and personal lives. You've told us about people who live in a world of silence, and who face many challenges. You have showed us much today, and for that we are truly grateful."

He steps toward her and presents her with a new leash for Bebo, all leather and featuring the airline's logo. Tom comes to the podium and, with the young man signing as he speaks, presents Clotilde with a company blazer.

"Clotilde, you are now an honorary member of our airline. Thank you for enlightening us all and sharing your world with us, and for encouraging us to think of the public we deal with every minute of every day and how we can try to make a difference."

Chapter Thirteen

Golden is truly golden in the midday sun as he pulls off the Trans-Canada into Tim Hortons. Time for a bathroom break, a refreshing splash of water on his face, new coffee and maybe a bowl of something—chilli or soup, maybe. Uh-uh, wrong time to hit Timmys. The line-up is out the door. He excuses his way past to get to the washroom. There's the usual line-up for the women's, and he hovers to wait out the couple of fellows inside the men's.

Brewster spends 15 minutes in the food queue and with nowhere to sit he takes his lunch outside hoping for a spot on the grassy verge. That too is crowded. He looks around and finally makes himself comfortable in the sun on a concrete parking barrier. A busload of tourists pulls in to add to the congestion. A fully leathered biker draws up, lifts his shiny silver and black Harley onto its stand, takes off his helmet and leather jacket and drapes them on the seat of his bike. He nods at Brewster and joins the line-up outside the door.

The chilli is good. Brewster soaks up the sunshine, feeling the soothing heat on his arms and through his blue polo shirt. He enjoys the happy buzz of the crowd. As the level drops in his bowl, so does the upbeat feeling he had when he first pulled in.

Motorbike Man emerges from the human crush with his coffee and doughnut, goes to his bike and turns up the speakers. The country music punches out over the parking lot, and a couple of women laugh and joke in an impromptu line dance before joining the queue. It's happy times in the sunshine.

"How's it going with you?" Motorbike Man asks. "You look as though you could use a friend."

Brewster looks around and realizes he's being spoken to. "Oh, me?" he says. "Going good, just got a lot on my mind."

"Pardon me for saying," Motorbike Man says, "but you look a bit like a flea on a hairless dog—and on a brilliant day like this. You travelling?"

"Yep," Brewster says, wishing this really chatty fellow and his country music would quietly disappear. He does not want to get into small talk. "Just bit of a road trip for a few days, and then back to Calgary."

"Yeah. I was in Banff last night, and with this weather, I decided to take a long ride. Might go south to Invermere, or I might go on to Vernon."

"You're pretty trusting, leaving your stuff on the bike with all these people," Brewster says, hoping to keep the conversation away from himself.

"No worries, really," the man says. "Funny thing is not many people would rip off something from a parked Harley with the music playing, 'cause nobody really knows who's watching."

"Good point," Brewster says, draining his coffee. "I reckon I'll get on my way now; heading to Kelowna for the night. Enjoy your ride, whichever way you go. And it's supposed to get hotter as the day wears on."

Brewster saunters over to the garbage and drops in his lunch packaging. A squirrel squeaks across the grass, and crows hover around hoping for a morsel here and there from the crowd on the grass.

He's glad he's taken this journey through the mountains. Hannah's words come back to him: to move on, just like she and Harris have done. He's already aware of one thing: it's up to him to make the change.

"How? How? How?" he says, stepping into his Jeep. The sun has warmed his spirit, and the unplanned jaunt through the mountains has softened his soul. The kids are grown and have gone on with their own lives. He's proud of them for what they are doing and how they have handled the sudden, tragic death of their mother. He should take heart from that, learn and adapt. Back home, the Fish Creek Park project has offered him an opportunity to complete the one thing that he and Melanie had so much enjoyed together.

"Trouble is, Miss Melanie, you were the brains of the outfit," he says, checking his side mirror as he merges back onto the highway. It's as if his wife is in the car with him. "All I did was follow your lead and take the pictures. But you knew what we were looking at, and looking for."

As he picks up speed, he allows his thoughts to drift back to the park project. He's concerned about how he might complete the hunt for any remaining wildflowers now that he's made a semi-commitment to the park people. Surely they will know where he might find the plants on Melanie's checklist.

He went past Golden and on through highway avalanche tunnels. In one side into darkness, and out the other into sunlight. Is this life? Is this *his* life? Is he trapped in a tunnel? The train tracks move along, always not far from the Trans-Canada. The long tunnels are maybe the longest in the country. They're so long that air holes have been drilled, and huge fans circulate air to let the diesel electric engines breathe. Without that, they'd die, trains marooned in a dark tunnel. Even trains have to breathe, have to escape the darkness.

Where will he find his new breath, new light, new life?

The mountains stand out in all their glory against a radiant blue sky as he winds through Glacier National Park and the steady rise to the top of the Rogers Pass. He thinks about the rise and fall of the highway, from 5,400 feet at the top of the Kicking Horse, down to 4,100 feet at Field and then on down to something like 2,500 feet at Golden. The sign at the Rogers Pass summit reads 4,300 feet above sea level.

The route through these mountains, the up and downs, curves and flats, and asphalt and steel winding through avalanche country match his own emotional geography. This rugged country, bathed in brilliant summer sunshine today, recovered from last winter's avalanches. *Am I still deep under the avalanche of Melanie's death?*

Nearing Mount Revelstoke National Park, his thoughts drift to horses and wagons, men and shovels, the early road builders and their toil, a sharp contrast to the highly powered, motorized road maintenance crews he slows to pass. The tree-cloaked ranges reach into the blue, his red vehicle less than a speck in the grand scheme of the mountains.

The Jeep shudders and coughs, and he feels the engine gasping. "Rats," he says. "She's sounding very rough, kinda like stalling or misfiring." He slows, looking for a safe place to stop. The instrument panel shows the temperature at max. The engine trouble light is on. The squawking electronic alarm fills the interior. He pulls over, cuts the engine and gets out. There's nothing to see when he flips open the hood, but there's plenty to smell: a sickly sweet odour that to him spells doom.

"Well, this is just plain crazy," he yells, kicking a tire in frustration. He's grateful for the extra wide verge where avalanches have been cleared away. He's alone, miles from anywhere, and nothing has passed him either way since he pulled off. He sucks on his water bottle and scratches for the owner's manual in the glove compartment. This has not happened to him before, never in his 40 or so years of driving. *And this is just a 2-year-old vehicle!* He's plenty mad because he's just had it serviced. This should not be happening.

The manual says to call Roadside Assistance, but he also has Alberta Motor Association coverage. What to do? Either way it takes a phone call, and he worries if there's a signal this far into the mountains.

He leans against the vehicle, reading the manual. A motorcycle barrels past. Then it slows, swings round and pulls up in front of him. The rider noses his Harley into the bank, slowly gets off and walks to the Jeep to peer into the engine.

"Phew," he says. "With a stink like that, I reckon you've lost your water pump."

Brewster recognizes the Motorbike Man from Golden. The speakers on his bike are blaring some song from the Man in Black.

"I thought you were going the other way," Brewster says. "Thanks for stopping. Not much traffic today. I'm just about to call Roadside Assistance. I think that's the best call to make, rather than AMA in these circumstances."

"True," Motorbike Man says. "I've heard Chrysler is pretty good about that. I'll wait till you get through."

"Oh, don't do that," Brewster says. "Don't want to put you out. I'm sure I'll be okay. How far do you reckon we are from somewhere?"

"I'd say about 30 clicks to Revelstoke," he says. "Not sure if there's a dealer there. Give it a try."

"They seem to have everything under control," Brewster says after he gets off the phone. "A tow truck will be out to get me and the Jeep and take it in to the nearest dealer at Salmon Arm. I'll just wait here in the sun."

Brewster offers to share his freshly filled thermos coffee with Motorbike Man, who does not appear to be in a hurry to be on his way.

"I'm glad this little turnout showed up just when I needed it," Brewster says, looking round the rock walls of his mini gravel pit. "Just as well this didn't happen further up the road, like in the snow sheds."

"Might say someone's looking out for you. By the way, name's Jess. I live in Okotoks. You?"

Just as Brewster is ready to identify himself, the haunting song "Hallelujah" comes through the bike speakers. A big and sudden change from the Man in Black. The men are quiet.

"That's neat," Brewster says. "Who's singing?"

"It's kd lang. She's big now, gone all the way from small-town Alberta to the world stage," Jess says. "I just love that version. Written by Leonard Cohen. He's Canadian too. But kd lang sings it to perfection. Very moving."

"Got that right. Didn't she sing that at the Olympics?"

"You got it—opening ceremony in Vancouver couple years ago. Billions of people heard it that time. Song's been around a long time, since the eighties I think, but she brought it back to the top. Never get tired of listening to it myself."

Silence.

"Um I was gonna say, I'm Brewster. Live in Calgary; been there most of my life. Wife and I had a business for about 10 years until …" He chokes.

"Lose your wife, eh? Sorry to hear that. Recent?"

Brewster stands up from where he's been leaning on the Jeep. Jess stays half seated on his bike and watches Brewster move to the back, lift the tailgate and pull out a folding lawn chair. He returns to where Jess is, arranges the chair into the sunshine and sits. He's not sure he wants to open up to a stranger, but the fellow seems pleasant enough, even though he's dressed in black leathers and rides a Harley.

Jess pulls a couple of chocolate bars from his pannier. "Let's enjoy these, and I'll be on my way. Tow boys'll be a couple of hours getting here, I reckon."

Blue jays and whisky jacks cackle in the pines. Chickadees flit through the aspen across the highway. Every now and then, there's a burst of traffic in either direction, and then there's quiet. The only sound now is the crinkling as both men unwrap their chocolate bars.

"Thanks, Jess," Brewster says. "This is good. Melanie died a year ago. She was killed on a crosswalk."

"Oh, man. That's tough. Sounds like you two were pretty close. Funnily enough, I think I remember that. Someone from Okotoks, wasn't it, or Black Diamond?"

"Yeah, somewhere south of the city. Poor woman. I lost my wife, and the kids lost their mother, but she has to live with it. Got a young family too. Even though the orange overhead pedestrian light was flashing, she didn't slow down after changing lanes and didn't see my wife in front of the stopped car. Ploughed straight into Melanie, killing her instantly."

Brewster scuffs his shoe in the gravel. Jess looks across the highway. The awkward silence of two men not knowing what to say to each other.

Why did I tell him that? Brewster argues with himself. *It's bad enough without blabbing about it.*

"I guess that's why you're out here on the road," Jess says. "I thought in Golden you were doing it hard. Ah, how are the kids?"

"This excursion is my daughter's idea," Brewster says. "She says I gotta get it together like they have, instead of moping. She figured a road trip might help, to see the places where Melanie and I visited and enjoyed. Now, this. It makes me out a double loser."

"Hey, don't go down that road, man. It's a dead—um, I mean, no exit. My wife, Janey, is a counsellor. She knows how to put up with me."

"I really thought Mel and I would grow old together. Y'know, that Rockwell image of holding hands in our rocking chairs by the fire?" He smiles at the thought of it. "Our son and daughter have dealt with it well. The oldest, Harris, headed back to his sailing school in Australia right after the funeral. Hannah is so like her mother, and she's at Acadia University in Nova Scotia. They both called me on the anniversary, and we had good talks. I was the wimp and couldn't stop the tears. They're good kids, doing what's in them to do and pushing ahead, growing into their unique lives. Of course they want me to do the same." Grinning, he adds, "And they are very blunt about it!"

Jess stands and stretches. "Sounds like you're getting good advice there. You'll be fine. If you're ever in Okotoks, you can always find me at the motorcycle shop." The starter whirrs and the bike growls to life. He revs the throttle, drowning out John Denver's "Annie." "Tell ya what. Wherever you are tonight, you should write your wife a letter. My Janey would suggest that, I know." He wheels his bike around, smiles and idles out to the highway. With a short skid in the gravel and a wave, he is gone.

Brewster catches a glimpse of the big logo on the back of the leather jacket. Something about Christian Riders Association surrounding a big blue cross. "Hear the Angels Sing" blares from the speakers.

Happy man, Brewster thinks. *Christian riders, eh? He didn't say, "I'll pray for you," and he didn't preach at me.*

He just listened.

Chapter Fourteen

Waiting around is not as bad as he thought it would be. Brewster delights in the silence between the swish of vehicles and the rumble of the diesels. In spite of his engine failure, he's in a happy zone, far away from the things that pull him down. It's like being on holiday.

The cell phone buzzes, announcing an email. *Maybe Hannah or Harris,* he thinks.

> Hello Brewster,
> I've been trying to get hold of you for a few days. You away again? Anyway, contact me because we have some interesting news and developments for your photographs.
>
> > Cheers,
> > José

He drags it into the trash can. *Not now.* He looks out on the road, wanting to regain the peaceful solitude of just moments ago. *The tow truck must be close by now.* He gets up and wanders around; out of habit, he checks the ground along the tree line. As he turns back to his chair in the sun, a blue aster nods its head in the soft breeze. He stops and stares at it. This flower, his blue aster, is out here—and it's just a single plant.

The roadside chat with Jess has him thinking about the driver in the accident. He speculates that she could be a client of Janey's because of Jess's almost immediate recall. He wonders how she is doing, how she is handling her life. It must be awful. After all, she didn't set out that morning to be involved in such a tragedy. He did get to meet her at the court hearing. He'd suggested leniency to the judge, and although it now surprised even him, he'd expressed forgiveness in his victim impact statement. He considered then, and still does, that she's suffered enough and that the ordeal and memory would never leave her. How had she been able to deal with it? How about her young children, her husband? *Funny how life can change in a heartbeat.*

Why is that blue aster over there? I'd have thought it too early in the season for them to be in bloom. Why does it show itself to me, here and today?

It's late afternoon, and the sun is arcing to disappear behind the spruce- and aspen-covered range. Brewster sits in his chair, moving every now and then to catch all the sun he can. Opposite him the mountains are in darkness. His side is still golden.

Finally, the tow truck passes him and turns around at the Parks Canada Mount Revelstoke National Park information turnout about a kilometre down the road. He'd walked down there while he was waiting and enjoyed reading the information panels encouraging visitors to "wrap your arms around the ancient trees in the world's only inland cedar rainforest."

The young driver jumps from the cab. Big brown work boots that are unlaced, baggy denim shorts and a grubby T-shirt. He's maybe in his early 20s with tattooed biceps. "Yeah. Gidday. Got a bit of trouble here, eh?" he says in a very heavy accent. He walks to the Jeep and peers into the engine. "Whoa, that's a stinky one you got there, mate. Definitely a water pump, I reckon. No worries. We'll get her safely hauled away and into the dealership in Salmon Arm. Trevor," he says, extending his hand. "But call me Trev."

The young man's chatter hasn't allowed Brewster to get a word in. *Definitely not a local,* Brewster surmises. He watches his jovial rescuer unhitch all his chains and tip the deck of the tow truck to winch his Jeep up for the journey.

"This is a rare one, I reckon," Trevor says. "Not heard of a water pump failure on these chariots before—not this model, anyway."

"Where you from?" Brewster asks.

"I'm a genuine Kiwi. Ha-ha, bet you thought Aussie, eh? Just helping out me mum's Canadian cousin for a few weeks before I go climbing around the Rockies. Want to knock off a few of those peaks over the summer before I have to head back home."

Trevor's a welcome companion as he wheels the truck out on to the highway. One of those never-stop-asking kinda guys. For Brewster, it's an ideal way to pass the time.

"Me uncle says you want to stay in Revelstoke while they fix your wagon. Didn't mean that—fix your wagon. Just an expression. Well, I can drop you there, okay? No worries. It's where we're based. Suits me too. I'll deliver this first thing in the morning, y'see.

"Funny. Y'know, I had to haul a Chrysler van through just the other day. Not sure what the problem was there. Some electrical thing, I reckon. It'll take a few days for them to find out how serious things are, what parts they'll need. You might have got it in time, so that could be helpful. Uncle says the impeller inside might have jammed, causing it to stop circulating. Good news for you, though: me uncle says it's a warranty job."

Brewster smiles. So much information from this chatty young man, and he doesn't even work at the dealership.

"Yeah, I just come to play in the mountains. Love the climbing and tramping—you call it hiking I guess. I'm a mechanic back home. Work on all sorts, even Jeeps, but mostly Japanese stuff. Or Ford."

Chapter Fifteen

"There's a spare seat at the table I'm using over by the window." A slight woman, her soft brown hair pulled back in a ponytail, spots him hovering at the entrance to the dining room, plate of pancakes in one hand and balancing orange juice in the other. Brewster waits while the woman picks up a muffin, reloads her coffee and follows her to the table.

"Very nice of you to offer," he says. "I was just about to head upstairs to my room. I've never been one to just occupy an empty seat, thinking that people always like to be a bit private at breakfast."

"Ha, no worries with me," she says. "Company is good. I'm here often in my job. I'm Irene Steele."

"Good morning," he says. "Brewster McWhirtle. I'm from Calgary." He munches through his pancakes while watching the sparrows and crows outside finding morsels around the swimming pool and on the gardens.

It's been some time since he's eaten breakfast with a woman. Now he starts to internalize, wondering what he might say without sounding like some predatory male. He sees from her finger that she's married. *Good*, he thinks, making sure she might spot the ring on his finger.

"These automatic pancake machines they have here are quite good," he says. "I usually avoid things like that, but I'm glad I cooked one today." *Good grief, that's so lame*, he thinks. *She probably doesn't even want to talk.*

He scoops a forkful of pancake and bright red strawberry topping around his plate. He gets the feeling she is looking at his every move. *Mmm. I should have gone to my room.* He watches the workmen out the window—changing light bulbs, he thinks, or cleaning the glass covers.

"Would you like a coffee?" Irene says, getting up from the table. "I'm in for seconds with a muffin."

"Oh, um, sure. That'd be great. There's milk here on the table. Yes, that would be great. Thank you."

Brewster smiles at her as she walks back from the coffee station. She's wearing a dark sweatshirt and jeans and what looks like safety shoes, brownish with black toes. Same as he's seen on road workers. She can't be much over five foot two and maybe 60 kilos. *Nifty little figure.* He looks back out the windows as she reaches the table, suddenly bothered by the way he assessed her.

"There you go," she says. "And these are the first mugs out of a new brew, hot and fresh."

"Thanks so much," he says. "What brings you to sunny Revelstoke?"

"Work. I'm here for about three days this time, I think. Came in last night from Calgary." Her smile is enough to light up Calgary's Saddledome. "I'm spending today and possibly tomorrow in a dark tunnel, though," she adds. "No sunny Revelstoke for me."

Irene describes her work as a consulting engineer on what is a routine inspection of the ventilation systems in the Mount Macdonald railway tunnel.

"Fascinating," he says. "I'll be going over to the Railway Museum a bit later. I'm not what you call a railway buff, but I'm fascinated by the tunnels and the way this all happened after starting out as a political confederation strategy. Besides, I've got nothing else to do."

"Are you visiting here just to go to the museum?" she asks.

"Nah, my car broke down about 20 miles east. I had it towed to the dealer in Salmon Arm, so I'm here till the repairs are completed. A water pump issue, I believe. I could have gone there but chose to poke around here for a few days. Revelstoke's a very historical place."

Irene nods as her cell phone buzzes. "Oh, the crew will be here in about 15, so I'd better be ready for them," she says. She stands and offers her hand. As they shake, he mumbles a thanks. She turns to leave but adds that perhaps they'll see each over the next few days. "Have fun with your day," she says. "Think of me in that dark tunnel while you sit in the sun."

She loads her dishes on to the trolley near the kitchen. Although it's been a long time since he's relaxed in a woman's company at breakfast, he thinks over how she sparkles just like Mel. Then he frowns because he's comparing again. *Why?* he wonders. *That's not fair to Mel or to this woman.* He sighs, collects his dishes, sorts them at the trolley and picks up an apple, orange and banana from the fruit bowl.

"Don't get lost in downtown Revelstoke."

Irene steps from the elevator, hard hat in one hand and wearing the yellow-brown jacket favoured by outside workers. He waves and smiles as she heads to the lobby, and he climbs the stairs to his floor.

As he steps up each tread, he considers the options for his day. Nothing in mind except the Railway Museum and the rest of the day to wander.

Brewster fires up his iPad and tells Hannah all about the journey, the vehicle breakdown, his unplanned holiday and his breakfast. He has to think twice about the breakfast because he's not sure how his daughter might react. He tells it anyway. After all, he figures it was just a chance meeting, some friendly chatter with a person who knows nothing about him. Cathartic in a way—a pleasant change for his inner being. He's been forced to participate in human contact outside his deepening insularity.

The guest folder contains a couple of sheets of hotel letterhead and an envelope. Should he or shouldn't he? He thinks Jess's suggestion to write his wife a letter might have some merit.

He looks at the blank white page with the blue and yellow hotel logo across the top. He sits back then leans forward and writes down the date on the page. New line. "Dear Melanie." He doesn't like that, so he scrunches it up and starts on the second sheet. "My Dearest Melanie." Better. New line. Now what to write? Slowly he starts, and with tears that at times drop onto the page, he writes about where he is and why. He reads it through and thinks it a bit whiny. He turns over the page and fills the back of the sheet. He doesn't read that through again, merely folding it in three, sealing it in the envelope and hiding it in a pocket of his backpack. He escapes the hotel.

#

The floorboards creak as he moves from exhibit window to exhibit window in the quiet, austere, cavernous railway museum. Black-and-white pictures, maps and the faces of politicians, surveyors and engineers credited with the marvel of the Spiral Tunnels. Their ingenuity and political smarts are documented in the solutions to get the wheat and coal off the prairies and down to the waiting ships in Vancouver. The big link to make confederation real, from sea to shining sea.

There's more than a hint of cynicism in Brewster as he views each panel. The government promises to make it happen. The cost? Major. The strategy? Justified. The locomotives and semis on road and rail today illustrate that boldness more than a century later.

He moves to a small alcove. More black-and-white photographs. Models of the tunnel structure and excavations. The faces of men lured to the task with pick and shovel, muscle and sweat to hack and dig and die, to scratch a living to keep their wives and children, many with their families in some distant place.

And the Chinese: Far from home and eager for a new life. Eager to meet the challenges in the hopes of sending money to their homeland far away. Eager to bring wives and children to the brave new country. There are no smiles in these pictures, which Brewster predicts were carefully posed. How many in that picture, or this one, did not make it home, did not make it out of the pit? How many succumbed to accident or utter despair in the substandard conditions and lesser pay and food than their white counterparts? *One person killed per week, the records show. How many more were there really?* he wonders. *And who kept the tally?*

As he strolls through the museum, these deaths keep surfacing in his mind. Who told their wives and children, "Daddy won't be coming home"? Did the police turn up at their door like they did for him? "Sir, your wife won't be coming home."

"I bet some families were never told. The money dried up, and they had to carve out a new life, never knowing. At least I was told within minutes."

"Were you talking to me?" a woman asks, standing with her children near him.

"Ah. Um. Sorry," Brewster says. "I guess I was just thinking aloud."

"Easy to do when you see these pictures," she says.

Brewster nods to her and takes himself upstairs, past the amazing model railway display. He walks out to the balcony and admires the old poster pictures and paintings around the walls depicting train travel, the age of the locomotive and the glory of rail travel to the retreats in the Rockies. He bypasses the opportunity to "drive" a loco or watch a video, and he heads into the open air, breathing in the freshness of the present.

He sits in a small park, intrigued by the architecture that's more than a century old, and he considers what this community had been before technology, highways and modern transport slowly scuttled its economy. Freight locos three kilometres long rumble through the town at all times of the day. A stone cairn tells of Walter Moberly, the British Columbia surveyor who found the Eagle Pass for both railway and the Trans-Canada Highway.

#

There used to be days when he wanted to stomp on his cell phone. Every time he thought like that, it would buzz. Generally it was something to do with his business or a call from Melanie. He's become addicted to its beeps and bells. This time, far away after a brilliant sunny day, his connection with the world rings through. Hannah, he expects, checking up on him. *She's just like her mother.*

Dear Mr. McWhirtle,

My name is Clotilde Chiasson. I live here in Calgary, and I've been given your name about the possible collaboration of a wildflower book project that you are working on for Fish Creek Park. I am a botanical artist, and when they found me drawing in the park recently, they suggested you and I might combine our talents for a useful book, for the better understanding of the flowers that bloom in the park.

They tell me you are an excellent photographer and have produced some captivating images of the rare, the common and the beautiful. As for me, I am an artist. I draw the parts of the plants in minute detail, from flower to stem to leaves, and in some cases to roots.

Please let me know when we might meet to discuss. It sounds an intriguing project, and it's one of which I'd like to be part. I'd like people to see what I do.

I should tell you too that I am profoundly deaf, the result of an illness that invaded my life in my 20s. I do speak though, both French and English, and I lip-read as well as sign.

Regards,
Clotilde Chiasson

Brewster sits back in his hotel room easy chair. He's uncomfortable. Any contribution he makes is on behalf of his wife, not this deaf lady. *I bet this is what José was getting at in his note the other day—"some news and a new development." This must be the new development.*

He feels a big grumpiness coming on. "So they've decided I have to share this," he mutters. "Well, they can jolly well do without me."

He shuts down the iPad with a pouty flourish, tosses it under his pillow and escapes to the elevator. His mind is on a nice, satisfying dining experience, being waited on hand and foot. "After all, I am in this luxurious place."

He closes his door and heads to the stairs, once again avoiding the elevator. He pauses, rethinks and returns to his iPad.

Dear Ms. Chiasson,

Thank you for your inquiry. Your work sounds interesting. At this stage, photographing the park's wildflowers is only a potential activity that I may undertake on behalf of my wife, who died a year ago. I'll be meeting with the park people in the next few days and will advise them accordingly.

Brewster McWhirtle

On a whim he reckons that if Irene is back from her day, they could find a restaurant together. He writes a brief note, puts it in an envelope and heads to the lobby, asking them to slip it under her door because he does not know her room number.

Chapter Sixteen

Compared to yesterday, the dining room is almost empty this morning. Brewster finds a table in the corner and looks out over the patio at the sparrows circling the tables, pecking at anything that might resemble breakfast. He wants to share his cereal with them but remembers it's not a good idea to ladle out human food to the wild birds

"Mind if I join you?"

Irene doesn't wait for an answer and puts her muffin and juice down. She heads back to the servery to collect her toast, yogurt and coffee. "Sorry about last night," she says. "I got your note okay, but I didn't get back till after 10:00. We had a few issues in the tunnel and I had to spend time at the office with my crew. Your idea sounded a whole lot better than my takeout pizza."

"No worries," he says. He is about to add something more, but Irene continues.

"Hope I didn't cause you any stress, and that you didn't wait too long in the lobby."

"No worries," he repeats. "I guessed you must have got held up somewhere. I did the same thing: ordered in pizza and read a book."

He finds it easy to talk with this happy woman sitting opposite him, but he soon runs out of things to say, gets a bit tongue-tied and leaves the conversation to her. He's happy to respond. He watches her butter her toast, load on marmalade and slice the piece into quarters. Precise, just like an engineer.

"More coffee?" he says, getting up. "I think I just spotted a fellow putting out fresh."

He takes his time wondering if he should again invite her to dinner tonight. Is that what people do? This is new territory for him, and it's something he hasn't done since he first invited Melanie to coffee all those years ago. Melanie. What will she think of him now, finding company with another woman?

Irene looks up at him, smiles, thanks him and shatters his nervous tension with plans for the day.

"I have to go to the office for a bit this morning to finish off yesterday's inspection. I've got my car, and if you don't have anything planned, I could show you what I know about this remarkable town."

Brewster is flummoxed. *How should I react? And why so jittery?* "Um. Sounds good," he says. "Um. So, right. I'm not doing anything except ambling around."

He looks at Irene and sees the light fade from her brilliant brown-black eyes. "You took me by surprise," he adds. "I'd love to hang out and check the sights of this area with you. Maybe I could get some sandwiches and a pop at Subway, and we could lunch in a park somewhere."

With all the poise a woman can muster with a mouth full of toast and marmalade, Irene grins. "Great. I'm glad you like the idea. What about Meadows in the Sky? Going to be a brilliant afternoon."

"Never been there," Brewster says. "If you say it's a good place to visit, let's do it. It'll be fun. It's the sort of thing I haven't done in a long while. Thanks for the idea."

They agree to meet at the Grizzly Plaza in the midtown Heritage Walk. After swapping cell phone numbers, Irene packs up her dishes and heads out. Brewster remains at the table, lost in his thoughts and mixed reactions of sadness and delight at the opportunity to spend an afternoon in the mountains with a beautiful, vibrant woman.

He pulls up his iPad and taps out a message to Hannah and Harris. "This is what is happening in my day here in Revelstoke. The breakdown with the Jeep has a good side." He writes about Irene and her friendliness, and he emphasizes that the afternoon trip to the

Meadows is not a date, just a small adventure in a picturesque place on a picture perfect sunny day. He finishes breakfast with a marmalade-loaded croissant and returns to his room.

The city has made a big deal out of its heritage legacy, and in spite of its changing fortunes, it has revitalized many of the original buildings in the downtown core. It's a history town, and it's this history that holds a fascination for Brewster. He likes the architecture and takes his mind back to the days when settlement was based around building the railway and its operation in an area that knows more about winter snow than probably any other region along the railway's length from coast to coast.

He walks along the streets of historic commercial buildings and houses of a bygone era, and he is saddened by the fact that he is without his lifetime friend. They'd long promised each other a visit to this railway city, but they had never made it past the Tim Hortons on the Trans-Canada Highway as they drove through from Calgary to the fruit stands of BC's interior. He gets to thinking about all the times he's foregone something because it took time, because it wasn't on the schedule or agenda, because he had something else to do, because he thought Melanie was busy. So many excuses, and he's reminded that he almost did the same with Irene a couple of hours before. Spending the afternoon together was all she suggested. Visiting the Meadows was all she suggested. What is he so antsy about?

There's still some time before he's to meet her, and he finds himself walking toward the Columbia River. A spur line used to run down here from the railway to bring cargo and people to the sternwheelers. He tries to imagine the noise of people and machines; sniffs the air for any telltale signs of coal and wood smoke and loses himself in an imaginary time warp from his rest stop on the cedar seat of a paddlewheel sculpture. It's a city that has matured beyond the rush and crush of developing the railway, sternwheeler traffic up and down river, electricity and the construction of one of the largest hydro dams in the province, the logging in its heyday and today, the enduring aboriginal people's love of the land and its abundant resources and yes, even farming—dairy cows perhaps on this very piece of land.

The history and the industriousness of a community named after a London banker have combined to give him something to think about besides himself. *Sure, I can feel sorry for myself, but I can't bring her back. No one can. She's conquered this life and gone. Just like the pioneers of this town. They worked it, developed it and left a legacy for others to enjoy.*

Hannah was right to tell him to get out of town. It was right that his vehicle had an inexplicable breakdown seemingly in the middle of nowhere. Here he is, sitting quietly, listening to the voices of days gone by—people who lived and died. They are surely the faces in this town.

He finds he's looking forward to his trip up Mount Revelstoke to the Meadows. This is good bear country, and the area shares a reputation with *ursus arctos horribilis* and his sidekick the black bear. He engages in an imaginary conversation with Melanie from where he sits on the kerb near his meeting place with Irene. A crow looks at him and contemplates a raucous reply when Irene walks up.

"Were you talking to that crow?" she asks.

"Too right, but he's not listening," Brewster says, thankful that Irene did not hear his conversation. "I hardly recognized you all dressed for the outdoors," he says. "I've really only seen you set for exploring tunnels."

She's dressed in an easy-fit floral top, light khaki walking shorts and hikers. Her tanned legs and arms show off her slender, athletic frame.

"I'm parked just over by the visitor centre," she says. "I love this country, these mountains. I get out whenever I can. There's a group of us who hike and bike most weekends during the summer. In the winter we snowshoe or cross-country ski."

Brewster picks up his daypack. "This is lunch," he says, hefting a large plastic bag. "Don't ask me what it is, because I don't have a clue. I was walking past the coffee house just down a block or so and asked them to put together a lunch for two up at the Meadows. All I had to do was pick it up on my way back from being down at the river, where the sternwheeler dock used to be."

"Sounds like a man's approach," she says. "I'm all for that kind of surprise. Knowing that foodery, it'll be good."

"Hey, same as mine," he says when she points out her forest green Jeep Grand Cherokee. "Except mine's red and is now happily being repaired in Salmon Arm. I love it—well, until the other day anyway."

He recounts his reason for being in Revelstoke. His chatter masks his schoolboy nervousness at being alone with Irene and the strange feelings that tell him he's being unfaithful.

Her Jeep is a true engineer's vehicle, and he scans the array of gear stowed in the back: shovel, hard hat, boots, Carhartt overalls and jacket, a level, stakes, orange tape and spray cans.

"I like to be self-contained," she says, noting Brewster's interest. "I dunno. It might be my size or the fact I'm a woman, but a lot of the guys must think I'm a delicate, desk-bound, corner-office type. Having a trunk full of gear lets 'em know I know what I'm talking about even if it's never used. Anyway, let's go. Meadows, here we come. I'm more than ready for this adventure."

They head out to the Trans-Canada Highway, turn east and find themselves in the heavy mix of midday traffic with semis hammering along in both directions.

"Busy highway," she says. "Always is. I'm glad there's a good looping off ramp just up a bit to get across to the Summit Road. Have I told you I love it here?"

Brewster's lost his voice. *How can I keep up with this person? She's like a hyper alpine guide. I haven't climbed around mountains since my early 20s.* He smiles at his host and bends to peer out the windshield at the tree covered rocky bulk towering ahead.

"Now we're through the park gate, we've got 26 kilometres of paved road that will take us up about 1,000 metres from here," Irene says as she pilots the Jeep around a tight, rising curve. "Sixteen switchbacks. Great views."

Chapter Seventeen

It's a hurried and unexpected start for Brewster. His morning email includes the good news of his Jeep being available for pickup around noon at the Salmon Arm dealership. He stops by the front desk after his leisurely breakfast to inquire about the best way to go the 100 kilometres west to the lakeside town.

"We're heading that way in about an hour," a voice beside him says. He turns and is greeted by the middle-aged couple who'd been sitting behind him at breakfast. "We can drop you there—only about an hour or so trip."

"You sure?" he says. "That's a wonderful offer. My Jeep broke down on the highway and had to go there for dealer service. I only have a small backpack, so I can be ready to go anytime you want."

"Done," the man says. "I'm Jim, and this is my wife, Doris. Let's meet here at, say, 9:30?"

"Boy, don't get that very often these days," Brewster says to the young woman at the desk.

She smiles and adds that the couple often visit the hotel on their way through to the Okanagan. "They're good people," she says. "You'll enjoy their company."

#

An hour later, Brewster waits in the lobby and covers business and pleasure on his iPad.

Hello Harris and Hannah,

On my way to Salmon Arm to pick up the Jeep. I met some people here an hour ago, and they offered to drive me through. Very nice of them. Not sure what I'll do when I'm mobile again. It has been very restful here in Revelstoke. I might head back home because the park folks want to talk about what they say are exciting new developments with our project. I'm not sure I'm fully on board. What do they want? I'm still a bit reluctant to part with the photos even though I'm sure your mom would be tickled pink that our pastime might benefit park visitors.

I spent a magic day up at the Meadows in the Sky in Mount Revelstoke National Park with Irene, the woman I mentioned the other day. Over dinner last night, she talked a lot about grief. In a very nice way, she challenged me to get over it and accept it as one of those unexpected life events we're actually quite powerless to control.

As I say, she was quite frank and said a few things I really didn't need to hear. She asked me if I believed in God, and I said rather bluntly, "No, not anymore." I emphasized that I didn't want to talk about it. After a bit of a sticky silence, she opened up about her own circumstances. You won't believe it, but her husband went overseas about 20 years ago as an aid volunteer and has never come home. She hasn't heard from him—doesn't know where he is or even whether he's coming back.

She's reconciled to that and enjoys life to the fullest as what she terms a "volunteer widow."

Hannah, I expect you are through your exams now and getting ready for your time in Europe. You'll have an awesome summer, I'm sure, and I long to hear all about it. Not sure what's happening in your world,

Harris, except that you're into winter, and I wonder if that is a good tourist time.

A car has just pulled up at the door; it's my ride to Salmon Arm. I'll check in with you later.

Blessings,
Dad

#

"I'm all set, Jim. I can't tell you how much I appreciate your offer," Brewster says, packing his iPad and picking up his daypack. He settles into the rear seat of the Subaru Outback and greets Doris, and they're on their way. As usual, he's a bit lost for conversation.

"Takes about an hour," Doris says. They talk about the weather, the pending rain showers and the promise of sunshine when they reach the Okanagan. "How long will you be in Salmon Arm?"

"I'm picking up my Jeep from the dealer there. It broke down the other side of Revelstoke, and because this is a warranty fix, it had to go to the nearest dealer. Then I'll head back to Revelstoke because I've left my room open there. I'll head back to Calgary tomorrow."

"You must like Revelstoke, then," Jim says. "We do. We always find it nice to stop there on our way through. It's pretty regular because we have family over this side and like to check up on the grandkids. Every now and then, I'm called upon to speak on a Sunday at one of the churches."

"You're a pastor, then?"

"I'm a teacher at a Christian school in Calgary. What about you? How do you fill your days?"

"Oh, just a businessman. I sold my sheet metal and plumbing business a few years back and bought some property and a multi-storey commercial building in the southwest. That keeps me fairly busy, and my …" He hesitates, his voice breaks and his eyes sting. "Ah, well, we own a flower shop too."

A discomforting silence fills the Outback.

"Looks like we'll be in Craigellachie soon," says Doris. "Historic little spot once we're through the Eagle Pass. Ever stopped there, Brewster?"

"Matter of fact, I haven't," he says. "One of those things that was always on the to-do list but never happened. Always wanting to get from A to B in one day."

They stop at the rest area and walk across the large parking lot toward the cairn marking the completion of the transcontinental railway in 1885.

"This is an interesting place to me," Jim says. "It is said that maybe British Columbia might not have joined confederation without the railway. I connect the last spike driven here, that uniting of Canada, with the last spike driven in the hands and feet of Jesus as he was crucified. So you see, the last spike fulfilled Canada's promise to unite this great country, and so too did the nails in Jesus fulfil God's promise to unite us by grace with Him."

Awkward. Brewster watches as young Chinese spill excitedly off two tourist buses in the parking lot. He fiddles with his briefcase. *Should I just let that go, say nothing?* "I've not heard it put like that before," Brewster says.

Camera-laden boys clamber around the caboose at the stone monument, taking their photographs, while several chattering girls head to the gift shop. Some young guys mimic driving in the last spike nearby as others stand at the mural, excitedly pointing out the Chinese faces.

"I can imagine the hoopla and rah-rahs here when they connected the lines from east and west," Brewster says. "I wonder if they thought about the human cost, especially amongst the underpaid Chinese? Their deprivation, substandard facilities, no food or clothing provided as in the 'other' camp, segregated, abused, fall sick or injured or dying. I wonder how uniting that was."

"Serious thinking there, Brewster," Jim says. "And we must never forget that cost. All the more reason to know the Gospel, to have faith in God's promises and the hope that we have in Christ."

"Didn't do my wife much good," Brewster says. "Killed on a crosswalk just a year ago. She put Christ first all the time, loved the church—an ardent volunteer always. And then bang, she's gone, and I'm still here alone. It should have been me. She had so much to give. Where is God in that?"

The tourist shop is full now of the Chinese visitors looking for treasures and memories to take back to their homeland. Their enthusiastic chatter floats out the door. Their brief glimpse at history ends as the coach drivers and guides wave them to reboard.

Doris looks at him, steps up and says, "May I?" She holds him tight. His body quivers, and he's near to breaking. *Why, oh why did I say that about Melanie?*

"I knew something was troubling you about your wife," she says. "I'm so sorry. Don't give up."

Brewster mostly listens as they cover the miles to Salmon Arm. He changes the conversation to his children and answers Doris's questions about their career choices, and finally how they had accepted their mother's death.

"All I can say is that they have done much better than me," he says. "At least, that's what I see. Sure, they've talked to me about it, but they share the faith of their mother. Me? I thought I did too, but now, not so much. I don't see God around at all."

"Just remember, Brewster, the Word that God has planted in you," Doris says. "I can assure you that God is as near to you as the breeze on your cheek."

There's a departing awkwardness in the parking lot. They exchange smiles, shake hands and hug. Jim and Doris decline his offer to pay for his ride, and with a wave they are gone.

Brewster heads into the dealership, and an hour later, he turns out onto the highway. He's grumpy and ticked off that it took so long to get his Jeep, and that he had to sign too many pieces of paper. On top of that, he's wrestling a negative attitude on his parting conversation with Jim and Doris.

He doesn't want to talk to anyone, ever again.

#

The intermittent *slap-slap* of the wipers clearing the light drizzle from the windscreen reminds Irene of life itself, the contrast between yesterday and today, last night and this morning. Magnificent views in brilliant sunshine and light breezes on the mountaintop unfolded into late evening thunder and lightning as a prelude to grey skies, morning showers and drizzle.

She loves this drive through the mountains and through the Rogers Pass to Golden. Today the clouds seem to hang like giant veils. The light drizzle beads on the windscreen, catches light in vein-like rivulets. *Whap!* The wiper blades swish across, and they're gone. Start again.

Life is about starting again, sort of every day. *Why doesn't Brewster get this?* He's the sort of fellow she'd like to get to know, but he's so self-absorbed. If he could just pull himself out of this, he'd have a lot to offer. She admits he did come out of his shell up at the Meadows, but he turtled when she raised the issue of what was so different about his loss compared to what others experience, herself included.

She wonders if he'd continue to head west or turn around and return to Revelstoke for another night before the trip back to Calgary. An odd but nice fellow, thoroughly depressed and so full of a pain he did not know how to handle.

"At least you know where and what happened to your wife. Tragic, yes," she'd said. "Me? My husband just did not come home. I've no idea where he is, what he's doing or even if he is still alive."

Mark had wanted to do more than work in the oil sands, and that was what led him to find a six-month assignment as a volunteer with an international agency after an earthquake in Asia. Letters, cards and even photos had populated her mailbox weekly. With her tacit approval, he'd renewed his contract and stayed away.

"'This is my life's work,' he told me in one of his last letters. Slowly his letters became less regular. After five months, my letters were returned, address unknown. I panicked," she'd told Brewster. "I called embassies, politicians and agencies, and then: 'Don't worry, Irene. I'm okay here. Mail and stuff is very irregular. There's a big call on my engineering and communication skills here. It's what I need to do.'

"He never came home. He never wrote. Eighteen years or so now, married to the only man I've ever loved, ever wanted to love. Yet he left. As our savings dwindled, I sold the house and went back to university.

"So, Mr Brewster, what's different? I had to make a new life all the while thinking that maybe one day he would come home. I made sure—well, at least I thought so—that he'd always be able to locate me. I kept in touch with our mutual friends, our university, our neighbours. But nothing. I always prayed for his safety and his return."

It's like Brewster is in the car with her. She'd suggested over dinner last night that he should get counselling. It is how she herself had overcome her own misery and made the decision to get on with her life. Mark was not going to control her. Armed with a master's degree in geologic engineering and her undergraduate civil engineering degree, she said goodbye to the oil patch and focussed her expertise with a consulting engineering firm based in Vancouver. What's more, she loved her work with the railway from her new home in Calgary.

Her work and her life with the church were more than enough for her, she'd told Brewster. "I love being on my own, independent and fulfilled. Sure, I've thought often about whether Mark would walk through that front door, and whether life would ever be the same again. I supposed I could have got some legal advice, but I never bothered. I enjoy the life of a bachelorette. I have a great circle of friends."

Funny thing, he didn't ask her about children. Just about anybody she came across asked if she had children or had counted down with her biologic clock. Might have been different if Mark was still around, but in her heart she'd never considered a need, want or desire to be a parent. Her times with children revolved around her friends. She got her enjoyment as aunty or godmother. She even had some of these youngsters stay over when their parents wanted a time out. She'd happily built a life without her own children and without Mark.

"I haven't altogether been a saint either," she told Brewster. "Yes, I've enjoyed some special relationships, but I prefer my own life. There's a richness to it that few people recognize. It was tough for me until I completed my master's. Then I became involved with the church through a recovery program, and through Christ I was able to work through my grief. I quit drinking and discovered myself."

The rain eases as she reaches Golden, where she turns off for a coffee and lunch. Relaxing in the restaurant, she reflects on how she'd opened up to Brewster after he'd told her about his journey through AA, and how he and Melanie had rekindled a new life together. He'd volunteered something of his past, but she could tell he was withholding huge parts his story, especially his marriage. She guessed that he'd only volunteered this because she'd put the wine list aside and asked for a tonic with a lime twist.

It was odd that he, a first-timer to Revelstoke, had found what must be the most exquisite restaurant in the town. It was one that, in spite of her many visits, she had never encountered. He chose wild salmon and she chose wild sablefish. They'd shared a delightful dessert platter, enjoyed good coffee and talked until they were the last to leave. Who knows if they'll ever make contact again?

Irene checks her fuel before swinging out into the traffic to climb the big hill and enjoy the run through to her next stop at Field for a review of some remedial work she'd initiated on the Spiral Tunnels tracks.

Chapter Eighteen

Hello José,

Sorry it's been a couple of days since you emailed me. Yes, I am away. Drove west through the Rockies for a bit of a change of scenery and a holiday. My car broke down last Monday, and I spent a relaxing time in Revelstoke. Nice place; lots of history. Give me a couple of days, and I'll call you.

I'm heading home today, and I'm keen to learn what these developments are that you talk about. At the same time, I'm very hesitant that you might be wanting more than I can give. It's possible you might want to do more with Melanie's project than what we originally agreed. It sounds like there's a change in the air.

Looking forward to speaking with you directly about any future plans.

Cheers,
Brewster

He deliberately avoids any mention of his distress over the email he received from the artist. He trusts his park contacts and wants to give them the benefit of the doubt. Through his trade and business interests, he'd become a stickler for agreements and contracts, whether on paper or with a handshake. And who knows, this deaf woman might be just trying him on. Now that he'd put that aside, he was confident the issue was out of the way.

He updates Hannah and Harris and gets a note off to Joel and Jo because he realizes he'd not told them about his sudden plan to disappear from Calgary for a while. He reminds himself to be more diligent—to get with the program, as the kids would say. He used to always be on the ball, but since Melanie, he'd withdrawn into himself. From his time with Jim and Doris, he recognizes his unsociability is an expensive by-product of his grief.

Out on the highway, heading east, he watches the heavy grey cloud draped across the mountaintops and mulls Jim's bluntness. "Just remember, Brewster, it's not your friends who have forgotten you, as you say. I think you bailed on them whenever they reached out. Look at it that way: Jesus hasn't left you either; you've just pushed Him aside."

Jim had certainly offered a new perspective. Trouble is, he's not sure if he's really in the frame of mind to accept it. "Yeah, sure, Jim. I hear ya," he says to the Jeep. "But I don't feel or see anything. I still wake up on my own in the morning. I still don't have the thrill of spending my day with a truly exciting person."

"But I think you have to turn it around, Brewster. You are wanting to know what Christ might do for you."

"Jim?" Brewster says. "Jim? Where are you?" He is alarmed at hearing the voice. It's as if Jim is beside him in the car. He turns and looks out each window, checks the rear view mirrors and tries to focus on the road ahead.

"How about asking what you can do for Him? You know where Melanie is; you know that. Now, what is it that Christ has in mind for your life? You're in the middle of a battle. Jesus is Lord. Do you agree? And if He is, then there is no other—it is not me, it is not you, it is not money. Trust in the work of the Holy Spirit. You and I speak on the surface, but the Holy Spirit goes much deeper. People are not the enemy. I know you can figure that out."

A sermon in the car? But I'm all alone in here. What is this? Did I really just hear that, or is this some sort of divine extension from what Jim, or maybe Doris, said in the car after Craigellachie, when he'd conveniently tuned out of the front seat conversation.

The voice has faded and Brewster calms down. He understands what Jim said. It's straightforward, probably the best words he's heard since the accident. No hedging.

"What do you think, Melanie? Am I losing it, or are you trying to tell me something?"

He slows to the loss of daylight as he travels through the first of several avalanche tunnels in the Rogers Pass. Then another, and another. *Is this the analogy? Out of the darkness and into the light?* There's another couple of tunnels. Out of the darkness and into the light, out of the darkness and into the light. "I get it. I get it already," he yells. "I get it."

The radio offers mostly static. He switches it off. He doesn't have a CD either. He tries thinking about the railway, the engineering and surveying to forge a way through these mountains. The men, the cost, the political gain. And always he thinks of the ones who didn't make it home.

Around a couple of big bends, the sky opens, and he finds himself with the wipers full on, trying to cope with a driving rain squall ripping through the valley. He pulls his speed down to match the flooding asphalt. The mood changes, and he's in a hurry to get to Golden for a coffee, a bowl of chilli and a chocolate donut. *Change the subject. Give me light.*

Then there's a small sound deep within his subconscious, feeding a different hunger. "Jesus loves me, this I know. For the Bible tells me so." He used to sing that to Hannah and Harris. Now they sing to him. He hears their little voices as if they are in the car, like when they used to go on trips—camping, perhaps. "Little ones to Him belong. They are weak, but He is strong. Yes, Jesus loves me ..."

By the time he reaches Golden, the skies have opened to blue. He lunches at a picnic table outside the restaurant. Jet-black crows sneak across the grass scavenging as usual. *How would they get on if humans weren't so messy?* The gutsy throb of a big diesel loco pulling westward drowns the voices he heard in the car. The trains—they pick up, they put down, they haul in, they haul away. Moving, always moving. Was this the expectation those 100-plus years ago? The lost men, their breath is in the tunnels and their sweat on the rails.

#

Modern engineering, machinery and practices have carved a smooth and fast thoroughfare through the wilderness. He winds his way through the Kicking Horse Pass, passes Field and overtakes the semis hauling their laden trailers up the Big Hill. It's such a giant effort, just like having to go home. He doesn't want to be there, or to have to part with his photographs or work with the park.

He follows the lead of other travellers and pulls in behind a stream of vehicles parked along the shoulder. Beyond the wildlife fence, a black bear wanders along the meadow, minding his own business. This is his second bear sighting; Melanie would have been thrilled. He regrets the many times he got frustrated with her, having to stop to check on whatever she might see—bears, moose, elk, deer or even a flower. The bear stops, turns and looks up to the road. Brewster has the uncanny feeling that the bear's eyes are on him, singled out from the crowd of shutterbugs.

Do their eyes meet as Brewster hears the voice of the bear in his head? "You are watching me in my life," the bear says. "What are you doing in yours?" Brewster groans, startling the excited young Asian couple next to him. The bear stands and puts his nose on the wind. "Yes, you," it says. "Think about it."

Across the fence where the ground drops away from the highway, a small blue flower bobs in the breeze. The blue aster.

Rattled by this encounter, Brewster gets back in his car, grabs a chocolate bar from the glove box and swings wide to miss others pulling onto the highway, almost clipping a big motorhome bearing down in the inside lane. The kilometres slip by. Is that Melanie's voice he hears, or the bear's? The stuff that has happened to him in the past few days alarms him. It seemed to start with the tunnellers and the history of human triumph and human loss. Then the motorcyclist's company, Irene's bluntness, Jim and Doris and what Jesus had to say about the whole business of life. And who was it talking to him about "out of the darkness into the light" as he passed through the avalanche tunnels?

The rest of the drive is a blur. Traffic is heavy, yet he stays quietly in the right lane, leaving the speedsters to do the braiding back and forth, as if the horizon will disappear before they get there. The thrill of the westward journey has left him. He feels as though he is heading into a fog. The radio catches an Irish Tenors song, ordinarily one of his favourites, but it doesn't push him above the take-home voices of his get-away-from-it-all trip. He switches off the cruise control and slows as he enters the Calgary city limits. The stop-start, slow and go of the city traffic brings back the "out of the dark and into the light" chatter. *You're in the middle of a battle.*

"Too much, too much," he shouts as he pulls up at the traffic lights. He realizes that voices carry through open windows when he sees the alarm on the driver's face in the car alongside him. He lifts his hands, smiles, pulls ahead and decides he's in no mood to prepare an evening meal. It's a meals-to-go from the new supermarket again tonight— prime rib or turkey, he'll take what's on offer.

After the long journey with its manifold advice, he's simply had enough.

"You are watching me in my life," said the bear. "What are you doing in yours?"

#

He passes a swank hotel and immediately vetoes the supermarket. He's not going home to that awful, silent, empty house. He's not going home to Melanie's place.

"Is that one night or two, Mr. McWhirtle?"

"Just tonight, thanks," he says. "Just tonight. You do have a room available?"

"Let me check with housekeeping and see where we're at."

He turns and sees himself in a mirror to the side of the black tiled check-in desk. *Good grief,* he thinks. *No wonder she looked oddly at me.* He sees untidy haystack hair, wild and stressed eyes, chocolate stains and coffee drips on his T-shirt, shorts and beach shoes. He's only carrying an overnight bag. He's near some sort of breaking point as he taps his credit card on the counter. The young woman returns with a man dressed in a white shirt, tie and black waistcoat. He watches them peer into the computer screen.

"Mmm. We don't have a standard room available, Mr. McWhirtle, but we can upgrade you to a king bed room with a Jacuzzi. It's all we have left for tonight, and the room rate is $300. Let me see if I can get a reduced rate on that. Busy time of the week for travellers. Is it just yourself, sir?"

"That will be fine," Brewster says, looking directly at the young man. "I'm sure that will be fine."

"Just yourself, Mr. McWhirtle?" he asks again.

"Yep, just me. I don't really need all that, but if it's all you have, I'll take it."

The man keeps looking at him while the woman processes his Visa and readies his room key. Others are waiting to check in—travellers. He can hear the rolling suitcases clicking over the brightly tiled floor.

Brewster slowly puts his credit card back into his wallet and stuffs it into his back pocket. He forces a smile, picks up his key and listens attentively as he's given directions to the elevators. "Welcome, Mr. McWhirtle. We trust your stay with us will be restful."

The man nods to a valet who wants to carry his bag.

"Thanks all the same," Brewster says. "I think I can manage this just fine."

The valet escorts him to an elevator, and all the while he feels the eyes of the man at the check-in following him.

"I guess I don't look like your average guest," he says to the valet as the elevator door closes.

"You have a lovely room, sir. I'm sure you'll like it," The valet says. "Where've you come from today?"

"Revelstoke. Feeling very tired and in need of a shower. Thank you."

The room is pure luxury. Guilt again. *Why did I never treat Melanie to such opulence? She would have loved this but then she would have said, "Why spend that much money to sleep in a bed?"*

He drops his bag on the bed and inspects the bathroom and Jacuzzi. Should he or shouldn't he? Ah, why not. He's paid for it. He sets the taps flowing and watches the water foam. He listens to the water pouring into the tub as he strips to the nothing and pulls out a fresh shirt, underwear and jeans, laying them on the bed. He carries his toilet bag and shaver into the bathroom, adjusts the temperature in the tub and eases into the hot water. The jets are on, and he lies back into the bubbles as the high-pressure streams attack every fibre of his skin. The day slowly fades, and he imagines his guilt, grief and grumpiness being pulled from his body by the spontaneous miracle of bubbling water. After 20 minutes in the foamy warmth, he figures it's time to get out before his skin wrinkles all away and he falls asleep.

"I haven't felt this good for a long, long time," he says to the mirror as he puts on his fresh polo shirt before giving his hair a brush and a shake to end up with the clean, tousled look Melanie enjoyed. He can't find any socks in his bag, so he slips into his loafers and then takes them off. It's too early to go down for a meal. He powers up his iPad. *Better make contact with a few people.*

> Hello José,
>
> I'm back in town again, and as of this moment I have the rest of the week open. What did you have in mind? Should we just meet down at the park—say, Thursday around 10:00? Intrigued by your note and what you have in mind.
>
> Brewster

#

> Hey H and H,
>
> I had a very interesting time in Revelstoke. Nice city, lots of history. I love the early 20-century style of architecture; it tells a story. The old buildings have been restored and lend a delightful air in the mountain town, as if time stands still. The buildings, many of

them privately owned residential and commercial, have revitalized the town core. Concrete and glass towers have not invaded the beauty of the place.

The trip up to the Meadows in the Sky was a miracle in itself. Most enjoyable day, and I did have great company. My only regret is that we never visited that place as a family. Your mother and I always said we would, but I always wanted to get to our destination and didn't like stopping to take in the sights.

He shuts the lid on the iPad and opens the venetians to look out over the balcony at the city skyline. *Quite the scene,* he thinks. *Wonder who the main customer is for a place like this? Businessmen? Tourists en route to the mountains?* He looks in the desk and is thrilled to find letterhead notepaper and an envelope. *Maybe a letter to Melanie, later.* He sees a couple of postcards and regrets that he didn't send a card to the kids from Revelstoke. He thinks he should finish his note to Harris and Hannah. He likes his comfortable den for the night and smiles at the sudden flash of humour that he's as hungry as a bear.

He opens his iPad on the mahogany desk and resumes his letter.

The flowers were remarkable: views across meadows of red paintbrush, blue Arctic lupine, bushy hairdos of the western anemone, piny subalpine daisy, knobbly white-pink heads of Sitka valerian, carpet after carpet of pink and white heather, yellow arnica, and white rhododendron bushes. Imagine how your mother would have reacted at seeing the last of the season's golden glacier lilies. Now, don't laugh. I only know all these flowers from a brochure I picked up at the artist's cabin at the summit!

I expect the pair of you will give me an award for the stupidest man ever known. After years of insisting I take cameras everywhere I go, I did not take one on my road trip. You heard correct—not a single one. As a result, the grand array of blooms in the meadows go unrecorded. My only excuses are that the trip up there was totally unplanned, that your mom was not with me and I'm not that into the job right now. On top of that misfire, I saw a grizzly between Louise and Banff.

I wonder how you are both doing. How does winter affect your business, Harris? Being so close to the tropics, it must still be a terrific escape hole for sail and sun. We're in for a fabulous summer this year, and no doubt Hannah's Nova Scotia will be awash in colour come the fall.

I have a meeting later this week with the park folks to go over our earlier discussions for the wildflower project. Even though I have most of the photos ready for them. I continue to have reservations about it. They say they have some news for me and new developments. I wonder where this will all lead?

A lot happened to me on the trip these past few days. and it will take me some time to process it all. I met a lot of people who reminded me over and over that I am not alone. I did get a lot of advice on how to move on. So stay tuned on this front.

I love you guys and do love to hear of your adventures. Stay calm and stay cool, and I promise I will too!

Dad

He reads through his email, checks his spelling and does a couple of rewrites where he sounds a bit negative. He figures his message will ease the minds of his worried offspring; he's aware his moods have caused them concern. He presses send. The email is now in cyberspace. Time for food. He's expecting the best in this luxury hotel. *Mr. Bear, let's go eat. Who knows what tomorrow will bring?*

Chapter Nineteen

Brewster unpacks his computer on the park's boardroom table. He's the first to arrive for the requested meeting, and he assumes its purpose is to roll through plans to possibly extend the scope of the project to pictures on the wall and education materials.

"Hello, Brewster. Good to see you this morning." A happy José comes into room followed by Louise and Tanya, who chairs the meeting. Brewster's had enough experience with meetings like this that he has the feeling he's being set up for something, but what?

After a good bit of idle chit-chat across the table, Louise leaves the room and returns a minute or two later with an attractive, middle-aged woman leading a little white dog dressed in a red coat. "Brewster, we'd like you to meet Clotilde Chiasson. We understand you've already exchanged emails."

"I met Clotilde in the park one day, working at her sketches," Tanya says. "She's a very talented botanical artist, so we invited her here to meet with you and to move our joint wildflower project up a notch."

"Hello, Brewster," she says. "I think we literally bumped into each other one time, in the park. It's nice to formally meet you. I've seen your pictures, and I think they're the best close-ups I've ever seen."

Brewster knows he's staring at Clotilde. He watches her arrange herself directly opposite him. The dog sits quietly at her right foot. Tanya coughs. "Thank you both for freeing up your time to be with us, and on such a beautiful day. I'm sure we'd all rather be out in the park. Louise, over to you."

Clotilde looks over at Brewster, who quickly turns to face Louise. "As the education group here, working mostly with very keen and knowledgeable volunteers, we feel we can expand on our original thinking and create a thoroughly informative and interesting book combining Clotilde's botanical art with your photographs, Brewster. We see you both selecting the flowers, and Melanie's notes will form the background with our added technical information."

"We don't have anything like this, so specific to the park," Tanya adds.

Brewster feels trapped. His initial reaction is to pull back, to walk away, but Melanie's bench is already installed. *Will they take it away?*

"It sounds a good idea, but it's gone beyond what we agreed on," Brewster says, avoiding eye contact with Clotilde.

Tanya senses the awkward moment and suggests Clotilde pass some of her artwork around the table.

When he looks back to Clotilde, he's immediately taken in by her beauty. He watches as she removes her folio from a red backpack and passes samples of her detailed drawings across the table. Maybe he has seen this woman before. There's even music in her voice. *She can talk,* he thinks. Is she really deaf? What's with the dog?

"These are really good," he says as he views her work. "Louise, you mean we put these with the photographs. Isn't that doubling up a bit?"

Tanya retells his comment to Clotilde, who nods. "I'm sorry, Brewster. I could not see what you said."

"People will most likely first identify the flower from the photograph; they will be drawn to it," Louise says. "We see the artwork describing the parts of the flower without the flower having to be picked. One complements the other."

He nods in tacit approval of their new plan, though he still fails to grasp how he can work with a deaf artist. Tanya senses his hesitation and suggests they work through her and Louise, though they do encourage collaboration to coordinate their contributions.

Tanya closes the meeting with a request to have all the material to her before the end of August, so that design work can proceed on the final format of the book.

Brewster suggests he meet with Clotilde in about a week. He will email his selections in batches.

As gets into his car, he worries that Melanie's concept has been hijacked.

#

"Irene? Hi, it's Brew …" He coughs, covers the mouthpiece with his hand and splutters and coughs some more. "Irene. Hi, it's Brewster. Sorry about that. I must have something stuck in my throat." He splutters again. Nervous tension. "Um, I have a couple tickets to the show at the Jube at the weekend, and I wondered if you'd like to go?" There. He'd made the invitation. He wipes the sweat from his eyes and listens to the quiet at the end of the phone. "I've had the tickets for a while; we have a subscription," he adds, breaking the silence.

"Well, hello to you too, Brewster," Irene says. "I really didn't think you'd be calling me up, but yes, I'd love to go. Why don't you email me with the details and arrangements, and I'll get back to you? I'm in the middle of a conference call to Vancouver. I'd love to go."

He slowly puts the phone back into the silver charger unit and sighs with relief. He feels all clammy after the call, at having taken this major step to invite a woman friend out on a date.

It's not a date, he reminds himself. *Just a couple of friends going to a show together.* Harris and Hannah would say it's a date, though, and they'd probably laugh at him. He really feels like a schoolboy now, like when he was 15 and invited one of the girls in the swim club to go to the movies. It wasn't really like that with Melanie. No ice to break. They'd met by chance at a Christmas party and spent the evening together— and then the next 34 years.

Now, although he's made the effort and extended an invite to Irene, he's not sure he wants to go through with it. Sure, they'd enjoyed each other's company at Revelstoke two weeks ago, but this is different.

Why? *Well, not sure. Just different.* She'd done the inviting to her breakfast table, and she'd initiated the sunny eye-opening afternoon up to the Meadows. He'd simply gone along with the whole idea. Yes, a night at the Jubilee will be different. Now, what is he to do? Does he take her to dinner and then the show? Does he pick her up, or meet her there? What about afterward? Do they go for coffee? A late-night supper, perhaps? Will he have to take her home? Maybe he'll call the whole thing off. She's given him an out.

It's Monday night, and Hannah usually calls. Should he tell her he's invited a woman to a performance at the Jubilee Auditorium? What will she have to say about that?

"Dad, that's terrific. I'm so glad. Now tell me again, where did you meet her, and what's her name? I hope she's older than me." Hannah's voice leaps down the phone line as he mumbles his way through.

"There's nothing in this, Hannah. Nothing. We met at the hotel in Revelstoke. I had this season ticket and thought she might like to go. Nothing to get excited about."

"Oh, tosh, Dad. You like her," Hannah says. "This is really good for you. You do need to get out and find yourself again. I'm sure she— what's her name? Irene?—is a lovely person. You'll have a wonderful evening. Now, this is what you do...."

On Friday afternoon, Brewster picks up his cell phone.

> Hi, Brewster. Sorry to be a nuisance, but I have a late-afternoon conference call with a client in Portland, Oregon. Is it okay for you to meet at my office here in Quarry Park—say, at 7:00 p.m.? I'll leave a message with security. I'm looking forward to our evening. See you then.

Brewster is stunned. *Is this woman always like this? She is so tied to her work. It's like 24/7. Oh, well. No worries.* At least that covers the pre-show dinner—which, he quickly realizes, he hasn't made any arrangements for anyway.

Irene talks a mile a minute when he meets as arranged. She is ready and waiting. "I just told the client—he's a philanthropist based in Portland—that I was heading to a special concert tonight and had to leave. He laughed and said, 'We all gotta learn there's more to life than work,' and he asked that I get back to him early next week on what we might suggest in working with local companies there on development plans for the fossil beds. Interesting project."

Irene slips her arm through his as they walk from the parking lot to the auditorium. "Long time since I've been here," she says. "If you have a subscription membership, you must come here a lot."

"Melanie and I often came, but it's really a company thing. On one hand I'm supporting the place, and on the other I usually give away tickets to clients and visitors to the city. Sort of my own little PR thing, and a thank-you to tenants and staff in my building."

Brewster feels the awkwardness disappear as they settle into their seats, the curtain goes up and the orchestra sweeps them into a new land. It's a dazzling opera with captivating theatre and music, and they're totally engrossed in the magic that rolls across the auditorium. They sit close together, slightly leaning toward each other and caught up in the emotion. Brewster feels her gasps of delight as the sopranos and tenors release their rich voices.

Tension melts, and for the moment Brewster forgets his grief as Irene looks at him. He smiles and remembers how Melanie used to do the same thing. He's pleased at this escape into a creative world.

He doesn't want to stand at the encore. He doesn't want to leave his seat. Irene grabs his arm, lifts him up and claps vigorously, swept up in the audience's adoration. She resumes her chatter as he pilots his car through the traffic. He doesn't have much to say, leaving it all to her. He doesn't want to lose the moment and suggests they stop someplace for a late-night snack to close out a successful evening.

"Not sure what we can find," she says. "Let's just go to my place, and I'll make you a decent cup of coffee."

Brewster doesn't know how to read this. Hannah's tips for a successful evening disappeared sometime earlier as the evening took control of itself. "Um, well, that sounds good, but I thought we'd just go to one of those places around 17th."

"That would be very nice," she says. "But after such a magical evening, I'm not sure I can handle a noisy crowd."

Brewster finds himself without any conversation as they drive south across the city to Irene's condo, just blocks from her office. Irene is quiet. "It was a lovely show," she says. "I think I should go to the theatre more often. A wonderful, refreshing escape."

She offers directions to her condo and the parking area and overrides Brewster's protestations and stage fright. "Maybe I should just leave you here and head on home," he says. "It's almost midnight."

Irene laughs. "Are you're embarrassed to be out with an unattached woman? Come on in. You've only got yourself to go home to. Make this your night out."

He's blown away at the interior of her ultra-modern home. "It's just new," she says, watching him look around the living room as he walks to the windows overlooking parkland to the river. "It's big for just me, but I often have friends or family staying over. I work a lot from here too. It's more of an investment, really. The security is handy because I'm frequently away, in exotic places like Revelstoke."

She busies herself in the kitchen, all part of the big room. "I'm making you a flat white, an espresso style I picked up in New Zealand when I was on cycling holiday there a couple of years ago. Just like a cappuccino, but you steam from the bottom of the jug, and it produces a nice micro froth."

Brewster is quite uncomfortable, not knowing what to say or even what to do. She puts the coffee mugs on the table near the white leather sofa, sits beside him and produces a silver bowl of dark chocolates from the shelf underneath.

"There," she says, settling back. "This is much better than a noisy, can't-hear-yourself-think restaurant. The square ones are caramel, the ovals are generally nuts and the swirls are cremes. Well, more or less."

"That Mark in the photo?" he says as he picks out a caramel.

"Yes. A picture of him working in Africa. That's the last picture he sent me, and that was maybe 20 years ago. I was frantic for a long time, trying to find him and thinking the worst. It turns out he went to Africa after his time in Asia. Then I heard he'd gone to South America. I've lost track of him, and after my last discussion with the Canadian authorities, I gave up trying. They told me they'd been in touch with him, and he'd said he would make contact, but there's been nothing."

"That must've been tough on you," Brewster says. "Really tough. Years of not knowing."

"You bet. I got really angry, but blamed myself. What had I done wrong? Was I a bad wife, a lousy and insufficient lover? Did I want too much? Was I overbearing, too busy with my work? I hurt a lot, and in many ways I still do. I keep a wall up around me and have deliberately not allowed myself to become too involved with any man. It grew into an easy pattern. I love my work, I love what I do, I love the outdoors. I have good friends, guys and gals, and I love my solitude. I read a lot, travel when I can and stay busy."

"You've obviously found a lot in life, and I wonder if I can do the same now," he says. "I'm kinda surprised that you've avoided any serious relationships, though. You're bright, attractive and busy."

"Ha-ha. That's why I keep my wedding ring on. It scares them away and keeps my work and life in balance. There was one time that I was really hurt. In a way, I overreacted after I realized that Mark would not be coming home anytime soon. A guy I worked with in Fort McMurray became more than a shoulder to cry on. He lived in New Brunswick somewhere but would fly in for work on rotation. He quit the camp life and would stay at my place. I thought there was a chance we'd end up together. He was special and caring.

"Then after a couple of months, one of my associates asked me how I felt about him—and about the fact he had a wife and family back home. I'd never suspected anything. I was a naive Prairie girl. I finished early that day, went home, packed all his things into his suitcases and left them outside the front door. I've never seen or heard from him since."

"Certainly an interesting life," Brewster says as he reaches out and touches her hand. "I guess that's when you sold up and headed back to university, as you told me over breakfast."

"So right. I had to, and before I got back to the lecture halls I had a lot of time with a psychiatrist. My parents were really grand and helped me back on the road. Completing my master's degree was the best thing. It gave me a great change of pace and time to heal. "But enough about me. What you see is what you get," she says as she gives his hand a squeeze. "You've done very well for yourself after starting out as a tradesman and getting to where you are now, financially secure and with what sounds like two great kids. Sad thing is losing your wife. But grief won't change that. Staying miserable all day and every day won't alter that. That's what my shrink told me, or words to that effect. Even now, I still expect Mark to walk through that door. What would I do?"

He leans over and kisses her on the cheek. "You'd think of some—"

Her lips meet his. They're warm and soft, tender. She pulls away and strokes his hair. "And so will you," she says.

Chapter Twenty

"Hiya, Brewster. Irene. I have an environmental pre-assessment to do on an old oil well site and need some pictures. You in for this? Call me."

Brewster's thrilled to hear the message. "I'm not a commercial photographer, but if you just need a few shots taken, I'd be happy to help."

"Thought you might like a run out into the countryside," she says. "Tomorrow looks good. We don't need anything fancy, just illustrations for a report and a bit of a benchmark to begin. This is not normally my area, but one of the field techs is down with the flu, so I volunteered to take a look at the site and get the project started. She'll take over from there."

It's a beautiful day as they head south through the rolling prairie. Brewster's conversation is reserved. He's not sure if he should apologize for walking out on her. Irene seems unfazed and chatters on.

"About the other night ..."

"No words needed," she says, taking her hand off the wheel and touching his knee. "I figured that was on your mind. We had a lovely evening together and made the right decision. I'm pleased the way our evening ended."

"You mean it was some kind of a test?"

"No, no. You're a good man, Brewster. After all, I am a married woman." She laughs. "Don't be so serious. Everything's cool."

With that out of the way, Brewster talks about his progress with the wildflower project. "I'm not really used to this sort of thing. I was a tradesman plumber who turned into a businessman, employing others to do the work and provide the information. We followed what the engineers gave us—and very successfully, I might add."

Irene enjoys his perspective and the relationship between engineering and the trades.

He confesses that reports have not been his strong point, and he's not sure how to present his material for the book. "I really don't know what they want," he says. "They just said they'd like my pictures, and they'd do the rest." He details how he's suggested profiling 100 wildflowers found in the park. He has that many pictures and more, although he and Melanie had still been looking for flowers, which they knew from historical documents had been identified but now proved a little more elusive.

"So you've just got pictures," she says.

"Pretty much. And I've got all of Mel's notes. The trouble is, I can't remember the names of the flowers; that was her thing. She could identify them easily and confirmed her labels with the help of several wildflower books."

"Here's an idea, then. Simply do what you can by adding her notes to your pictures. So what if you have some in the wrong place? The park folks will be able to verify and finalize. Your promise is to provide the pictures of your selected 100 with whatever information you have."

Brewster thinks about this and sees how simple the solution really is. "You mean just put picture and notes together, and submit them?"

"Yeah. Don't try to reinvent the wheel. You have the visuals as well as core information, which I assume includes location, date and time, as well as Melanie's observations."

"And then Clotilde does the rest?"

"Clotilde? Who's that? Not a very common name. Must be French."

"Yes," he says. "She was the surprise event when I got back from Revelstoke. I was called to a meeting at the park, and they introduced me to Clotilde, a botanical artist. They had the idea for her artwork to accompany my photographs and Melanie's information. Her work is the fine, descriptive detail of the plant as well as the flower. Our photographs and location help people to find and identify a flower, and her work examines its parts."

"How did you feel about that?"

"To be honest, I was very upset and felt they'd changed our arrangement by bringing her in, and that it would ruin Melanie's work and the intention I had at the very beginning. Yes, I was very upset and even said I wouldn't do it."

"But why would you do that? It sounds like a good idea to me, to make a complete and very interesting book."

"Clotilde is deaf, and she's probably in her 50s but looks 10 years younger. Her work is amazing, though."

They bump off the gravel road. "We'll have to walk in because I don't have a key for the gate lock. It's a nice day though, and only about half a mile or so," Irene says. "Do you mind walking? This is reverted farmland, so you might see a few flowers." Irene outlines her photograph requirements as he clambers over the gate. "This facility was decommissioned a couple of years ago, and now we are checking the site before a full reclamation. Your photos will help show what is here now and the work to be done."

The shoot begins showing the remnant of the original access road. He takes a couple of general shots before showing some detail in overgrown wheel ruts. He spots a blue aster beside the gate post. *Everywhere I go, I see this flower.* He says nothing to Irene and instead focuses on his unusual job, following after her across the access track. He's only brought one lens, a modest, wide-angle zoom to 85mm. Irene is keen to show any variation in the ground cover from the gate to the former well site. She explains that the field technician will do an actual audit while this visit is to get an overview of the site to discuss further with the client.

"All very thorough," Brewster says, and he begins clicking.

"Yep, have to be. Lots of regulations and money involved. Oil and gas is the lifeblood of this province, as you well know, and our work has to be done by the book. We fit between the regulators and the oil companies, though we are contracted by the companies to provide the reports."

He finds working with Irene very different from the work he's been used to. He's fascinated with her detail and holds one end of a tape while she measures, records and directs his picture-taking. He's made sure the date stamp is turned on in his camera.

They enjoy a burger in the village and head out on the highway and home. "Y'know, Brewster," she says. "When I was seeing my shrink after Mark failed to turn up, she said you never get over grief. To her, grief is not a process. Y'see, I really loved Mark. I thought—and in some ways still do—that the sun shone out of him. I was blaming myself, always wondering why he up and went away and never came back. I still think about that. The intensity lessens, like she said, but it stays in the emotional memory on my inner hard drive. I guess that's why I've found such joy in my work. I love what I do, the people I'm with, the travel and the times I can be on my own. I think it's the perfect life."

Brewster says nothing. He gazes out the window at the rolling countryside, millions of acres of growing grains and grass, beef herds and big round bundles of hay.

"I enjoy this country," he says. "We used to do a lot of this, head out on a sunny day and immerse ourselves in the landscape. Been in some real stormy times too, when we thought the big black clouds would drop on us."

"Sounds like a good memory to have," Irene says. "Reminds me of a poem my shrink had on her wall. I've never forgotten it—Longfellow."

> The holiest of holidays are those
> Kept by ourselves in silence and apart;
> The secret anniversaries of the heart.

There's the sound of the wind whispering over the sunroof. He enjoys the quiet, takes a swig from his water bottle and looks across at Irene, who is confident and assured at the wheel. She glances at him and smiles.

"Lot of nodding donkeys through here," he says. "All quietly doing their job. Been a few barrels of oil pumped from this part of the province. Bit like life, really. The pump jacks work away. Then the oil stops flowing, and the well dies and is abandoned, but it's never forgotten. It's life, no matter how brief or how productive, and it remains on the records that are kept while the site remains to be visited and checked over, as you have done."

"I suppose you could say that," she says. "Grief is always going to be with us. Certain things will trigger it, but we remember the good times, like high flow rates in your oil well analogy. Interesting way of thinking. Y'know, Brewster, I've come to realize that the best thing I can do is remember all the good things I did or had with Mark. I know it's a long time ago, but I still smile at some of the things he did, or we did. We graduated as young engineers and put our lives together to go out as Robin Hoods in hard hats and safety boots, to save the world. Oh, yes, we had huge dreams. Somewhere along the way, reality hit—mortgage, work responsibilities. Life took over, as they say, and we had trouble keeping up with each other."

They'd reached the outskirts of the city, and Irene suggests she drop Brewster at his house because she still has work at the office. "Perhaps I could tell you what's happening with me these days," she says as they wait for the lights to change. "Several months ago, an environmental company inquired as to whether I'd like to do some work on the geologic studies associated with the massive Nicaragua canal project. I expressed moderate interest then, but I hadn't heard anything further, and I thought the whole matter had gone away. Well, they've come back to me."

"Sounds pretty exciting," Brewster says. "Will it take you away for long?"

Irene talks about what she knows of the project: the controversy surrounding a link from the Pacific through Lake Nicaragua and on to the Atlantic, the cultural heritage, the $50 billion price tag, giant locks to handle giant ships unable to use the Panama Canal, lighthouses, a huge project.

"Wow. I haven't heard anything about it," Brewster says. "And China backed it, you say? For an engineer with your background, I'd say this is a startling opportunity, to be invited to join in what sounds like an extremely comprehensive study. You'll go for it, I take it."

She laughs. "That's pretty positive. I'd just be on contract for part of the study. Not sure yet what area they'd want me in, or for how long. I'll know more in coming weeks. Really, it is a good opportunity."

"Remarkable," he says. "Keep me in the loop. I'm fascinated."

That evening, Brewster takes yet another stuffed chicken breast from the freezer and puts it in his toaster oven to cook. He drops a cut up potato into a pot, and while that cooks, he pulls a few iceberg lettuce leaves from the fridge crisper. He thinks back over the events of the day, the conversations and his friendship with Irene.

"She's not afraid to say it like it is," he tells the chopping board as he slices a few raw carrots. "Interesting how she sees Clotilde. Learn to communicate, be excited for your project, honour your memory of Melanie—and the clincher, 'Why don't you learn to sign?'"

Chapter Twenty-One

Claire Rhodes walks slowly up the front path. She hesitates when she feels Brewster's eyes watching her from a window somewhere inside the house. She stops, closes her eyes for a second and whispers a soft prayer for courage.

The door opens just as she's about to press the bell. "Hello, Brewster. I'm Claire Rhodes, Melanie's friend."

"I know you're one of those church do-gooders," Brewster says. "What do you want?"

"I have to speak with you. Will you let me in?"

He says nothing and stands to one side, holding the door open. He watches as Claire walks in and heads toward the kitchen. *What's this all about?* he wonders, trying to recall if this is one of the women who visited just days after Melanie's accident, when it was all news in the paper. He shuts the door hard to let her know he's not in the mood for a social chit-chat, that she's in the house under sufferance.

He finds her setting the kettle on the stove. "Best to talk over a cuppa, I say," she says with a smile. She's nervous; he notes the tiny beads of perspiration on her upper lip and around her eyes. "I've made tea here many times with Melanie," she says. "We were together in a prayer group at church and often met here in the afternoon while you were at work. Melanie was my prayer partner, and I totally miss her, you know. So much wisdom."

Brewster says nothing. He sits at the breakfast counter and watches, allowing this interloper to prattle on as she gets cups from the cupboard and rattles the empty tea canister. She opens a pantry door and picks out a box of herbal tea bags. "Lemon ginger," she says. "That's a nice one. Okay for you?"

As she pours the boiling water into his glass mugs, he challenges her presence in the house. "I'm not in a social, tea-sipping mood," he says. "I'm sorry, but I think you should say what you came to say and leave."

Claire does her best to ignore his remark. She puts a mug in front of him and stands on the opposite side of the counter. She looks toward the lounge as if she'd prefer to be sitting there rather than standing in front of him. She seems finally at a loss for words. Brewster softens.

"What is it, Claire? Why have you just walked into my house?"

"Melanie and I were close—like sisters, we always said. We could talk about all sorts of things, especially my relationship with my husband. She helped me a lot; she had that way." Claire's eyes moisten, and she looks beyond Brewster to the window. "She loved you, you know. My, how she loved you. I did not know it was possible to love someone like that, but she did. But of course you know that."

Brewster rewinds 25—or is it 30?—years to when he sought Melanie's help to restore their crumbling, separating marriage. He wanted to stay with her, to acknowledge and keep the commitment he'd made in that church where they married: to love and to cherish. He recalled that troubled time and Melanie's forgiveness of his depression and his drinking.

"I'm not sure Heath and I would still be together if it hadn't been for Melanie. She talked me through that tough time, helped me to see life afresh, as Jesus sees me. I've changed, and Heath's changed. Our marriage is alive. Melanie was one special lady, and like I've already said, I've never seen a person love another as she loved you."

Brewster sips his tea. His mind's a long way away, barely listening, thinking only of how Melanie brought light to this house and his life. He wants Claire to leave, but she's barely started drinking her tea. She holds the mug and stares across the room.

"We've been praying for you, Brewster. We know how much Melanie meant to you; we know you hurt. That's why I didn't bring anything to eat this time."

"Oh, no," Brewster says. "Was that you?" Red-faced, he looks at her and calls to mind his shouting and hurling a cake to the pathway as a scared woman scurried to the safety of her car in the driveway.

"Yes, it was me. That was a jolly nice lemon poppy seed cake too. I made it specially, because Melanie told me it was a favourite."

"I hope, um, it wasn't one of your good plates," he says. "I really smashed it and kinda noticed it had flowers on it when I swept up the remains of your cake. I'm sorry I reacted that way. Um, you're pretty brave to come back again after that. Yes, I'm sorry I treated you that way."

"I was taken aback and very frightened," Claire says, "especially after all that Melanie had said about you. It took a while to get over it. I was so shocked that I've not been able to relate that to anyone, not even Heath. Both he and the kids have often wondered what happened to that plate. It was known in our house as the cake plate."

"My actions were uncalled for and very uncaring. I was distraught. I didn't even tell Hannah or Harris what I'd done. I wished they'd been home to receive you. So many people kept coming and offering food. All I wanted was for Melanie to show up."

"And you've been waiting ever since," Claire adds.

There's a long, drawn-out silence as they each hold and finger their mugs. Brewster coughs. *If this woman wanted to talk, she's not saying much.* She walks to the end of the counter and looks out the patio door.

"I always like the way you guys did the backyard," she says. "Melanie loved her garden and the flowers—a passion, I'd say." There's a long pause. "I've rehearsed this meeting a lot, but I don't know what to say now, Brewster. I struggled to come, but I just felt—well, I just felt that this is what God wants me to do."

Brewster is about to erupt. He's been waiting for more of the God stuff.

"You see, Brewster, Melanie came to me the other night and simply asked me to check up on you, and to tell you to get on with life, and to trust in Jesus."

Brewster looks at her, careful not to raise his voice. "Oh, come on. You have a nerve, telling me that." He begins to wave his arms around. "Saying Melanie came to you? What a lot of rot! Why hasn't she come to me? What do you mean to get on with life, to trust in Jesus? I'm sick of hearing that. Sick of it, do you hear? I've done that before and what happens. She goes, and I'm left. Trust in Jesus? Ha! You'd better go."

Claire stands her ground and whispers, "Lord, what do I do now?"

"I've got nothing more to say," he says. "You'd better leave. Melanie came to you? She's dead. Cremated. Her ashes buried. I know—I was there. Came to you? Ha."

Brewster is really disgusted with what he's heard. He leaves the kitchen and goes into the lounge. He doesn't want to be anywhere near this strange woman. He sits in his big, soft and comfortable chair that Melanie had bought for him. Her man's chair, she'd say.

Claire seems to be growing increasingly anxious. "Please, Lord, what am I to do? You asked me to come here, but I don't know what to do or say. Should I just leave quietly?" She is close to tears and seems embarrassed to be left standing there, holding her cup.

"Melanie told us about that chair," she says, walking softly into the lounge, "and how you could both fit in it and snuggle and pray together. She called it her wonder chair."

"You still here?" he says. "You should be gone."

But Claire wants to tell all of her message from Melanie. "There are no answers to all your questions," she says. "Jesus was with Melanie when she was hit by the car. She says her body was wrecked, but she did not suffer or hurt, and she's worried because she knows your pain. She says you promised to love her, and you did. Now it is time to move on, to trust Jesus with your pain and your days, just like you used to do. Jesus has not left you. You simply have to talk with Him."

He hears her words as she continues to talk about the faith and hope he'd shared with Melanie. Of how they'd read the Bible together and believed in the word of God, knowing that He was first in their lives and would always be with them. He could not get his head around the fact that Melanie had been taken from him. This was not the life they'd hoped and prayed for—just the opposite.

"Faith is not a matter of what you have," Claire says. "Faith is what you have not seen. Jesus gives us that faith and the hope of days to come. Melanie told me this not long after we met, and it certainly helped with me and Heath."

Her words reach deep within him and find all the times he and Melanie sat together in that chair. When they had argued and not talked to each other; when they'd hurt and come together; when they'd cried and shed tears for the love of Christ.

Claire talks on and off for a while. "The only answers we can get when we ask God questions or get angry are in His word."

Brewster breaks his silence. "Doesn't make sense—just doesn't make sense." He's pretty cynical about everything, but he keeps his words to himself. He says nothing, afraid he'll blow. He closes his eyes, not wanting to yield, only wanting to let go of the hurt.

"Brewster, you are a good man. Goodness, Melanie told us that so often when we met. Don't let bitterness rule your life. Let Christ connect your head and your heart and enjoy your fellowship with Him. Just remember what you have learned, and most of all the cross and what that means."

Claire tiptoes quietly from the room and without a sound leaves the house.

#

It's dark when Brewster opens his eyes. *Must've dozed off. Was all that a dream? But no, there are our cups. Yes, we had tea, and she told me to get my act together. Well, she reckoned that's what Melanie wanted her to say. And that God had somehow forced her to come here.*

He closes his eyes again, not wanting to get out of the chair that held so many dreams and so much warmth of a person with whom he once shared it. "I love you, Melanie," he says. "We'll always be together, but how do I continue by myself?"

Her Bible is still on the coffee table; Hannah and the packers had left it alone. It has not been touched since the day she left to get her hair done. So long ago. They'd even read it together that very morning over coffee. He reaches for it and thinks about their conversation about moving forward, knowing that they could not live in the past. Her Bible is bookmarked at the place the apostle Paul talks about reaching forward to the things that are ahead.

Was that prophetic? he wonders as he looks at the page they'd last read together. *That faith is a journey forward?* Claire's words push him to think of all that has transpired in his life since the accident. Anger, bitterness and isolation—and yet with all that, not a thing has changed, and certainly Melanie has not come back. He knows that will never occur.

What's a man to do?

Tears roll from his tired eyes. He's alone in the room, yet he feels a hand on his shoulder. His back and shoulders feel unusually hot, and he begins to weep uncontrollably as the tide of grief surges through him. Encouraging promises from the Bible come to mind. He hears Melanie reading them, and tears stream down his face. His mouth waters, and he cannot speak for crying. His body shakes, and he mumbles quietly the words of an old song, "O lamb of God, I come, I come ..."

Chapter Twenty-Two

They're in here somewhere. Brewster rummages through his drawers and then heads to the laundry room, searching for his long-forgotten jogging shorts. He finds them in a pile of washed, folded clothing left by Melanie. He realizes now how he's existed in a cloaked numbness. This morning, he's fresh and feeling a new energy, and he heads out for a quiet run just as he used to. Trouble is, he has only a vague recollection as to how he got through the night. Claire was here, and he fell asleep in the chair. But getting to bed, sleeping right through the night for the first time in a year, waking refreshed and wanting to run? Maybe he'll remember how it all happened by the time he reaches the park.

#

A couple of hours later, he steps from the shower and checks himself in the mirror as he towels off. His hair has grown back, and his arm is free of its cast. Yes, he's the same man who looked in here yesterday, but today there's something different. The run was a struggle, covering maybe three of his five-kilometre circuit. He had to favour his injured ankle and reawaken long-forgotten muscles. Today he has work to do: attack the wildflower project afresh, honour his wife and re-invoke the passion she shared with him for flowers, their garden, The Blue Aster and the park.

131

Over the past few weeks, he's tried to remain buoyed by Irene's encouragement to keep going when all he wanted to do was stop. He picks up Melanie's notes and begins to rewrite them to accompany his pictures, noting location, time and day, as well as weather and her personal quips like "lovely to see again," "a rare one," "common," "fascinating," "important" and "need more information." He pauses to read and reread the extra notation she's included in her notes for blue-eyed grass.

> As for man, his days are like grass,
> As a flower of the field, so he flourishes,
> When the wind has passed over it, it is no more,
> And its place acknowledges it is no longer.
> —Psalm 103:15–16

Now, when did she put that there? He finds similar quotations throughout the notebook. She loved her Bible, and she loved the creation, the value of flowers in the plant kingdom, in the life of the planet. He quietly acknowledges all she has taught him about how thrilling life is.

He adds the quotation to the batch of notes and pictures he emails to Clotilde. "See you this afternoon at the library," he adds.

Clotilde suggested the meeting, and although he knows it's to talk about the flowers and their project, it's a good excuse for him to see her again. Communication is challenging, and he knows he has to always remember to look at her when he speaks. But he must move his lips differently because a lot of the time, she doesn't get it. Maybe he mumbles too much. He writes notes and tries to put aside his mild frustration at the miscommunication.

She's a beautiful woman, and this causes him to feel a little uncomfortable, always looking directly into her face when he speaks. He wants to know more about her but doesn't know how to ask, and he shouldn't ask either. This is just another business meeting. *Let's face it, Brewster: you're attracted to her. Today will be a quick meeting. A check on the*

transfer of documents and progress to date on the goal of 100 wildflowers they'd
nominated for the book.

#

"Hello, Mr. McWhirtle. Nice day out there," the ever-cheerful Jane greets him as he enters his office. He smiles and thinks this must be some sort of code as Joel greets him from his office doorway.

They spend a quiet hour shooting the breeze and going through the business issues since their last meeting. All is well. Brewster is thankful his business runs so well with Joel at the helm.

"I should have all the paperwork to hand over the shop to Jo and Danny next week," Joel says. "Man, they are one excited couple at what you have done for them. Jo is over the moon. I've been able to settle everything out for a dollar."

Joel raises the issue of selling the building and is surprised when Brewster simply asks for more information, adding that perhaps he could send the inquiry to his email. "I know I said no deal last time, but perhaps we should take a closer look at the offer," he says. "I'll chew it over. Have they given us a time limit?"

"Not in so many words," Joel says. "I do have the feeling that they might be looking around in this area. They've upped the offer. We should look seriously because it won't come round again."

"I've no reason to sell, and Lord knows you've done all the work here for the past year," Brewster says. "I guess with Melanie gone, I've lost interest and just want to move on—to what, I don't know. Perhaps Harris needs some support in Australia. I'm not sure what Hannah will settle on after university. I doubt whether she will be back here. I have the wildflower project to keep me going at present, but in a few weeks that will finish. I'm a bit lost, I suppose. Send me the info, and I'll get back to you within a day or two. Oh, no—the project. I'm supposed to be at the library soon to meet with the deaf artist. Gotta run."

#

She's sitting at a table as he walks into the atrium. She looks up, smiles and stands. "Cappuccino?" Brewster nods and smiles back. *Good grief, she's beautiful. Dark hair and her soft olive complexion.* He finds himself looking at her shapely legs. He turns away, feeling guilty, as though he's seen something he shouldn't have. *Why does this woman have to be deaf?*

She sits across from him. She is radiant, and a slight whiff of perfume reaches him. He looks away, trying to focus. He hasn't felt like this in the presence of a woman for a long time. He's embarrassed as he reflects on all that he enjoyed with Melanie.

"I love your pictures and the notes," Clotilde says, a slight French lilt in her voice. She looks directly at him, and Brewster is mesmerized.

"Thank you," he mumbles, and realizes she could not hear or see his lips. He smiles and repeats, "Thank you."

Clotilde smooths out her file. "This is terrific. I have finished these 20 you sent, and they can now go to Louise for the park input and documentation. That leaves us with about 80 completed."

"Will we get there this summer?" he says, forgetting to look at her. He lifts his head, repeats and knows immediately that she did not get what he said. He writes a note and passes it across.

She smiles and nods. "I have sketch work done for the balance, I think. I've been down there most days, and I've been able to do the fieldwork I like."

Why is she deaf? he thinks again. *Why am I so rattled around this beguiling woman?* He mumbles and fumbles and scribbles a note to say that he will have the final 20 pictures and notes to her within a few days. Then his part will be done, and he can go back to his business. *Maybe.*

Clotilde looks at him. "Why did you put that Bible verse in?"

"It was in Melanie's notes," he says, this time speaking slowly. She nods. "Melanie used to write Bible verses in lots of odd places, like on photos of flowers or notes on the fridge. Just to encourage me and the kids, I think."

"What about you?" she says. "Do you go to church? Are you a Christ believer?"

"I used to go to church, until Mel got killed. I've been pretty upset since then, and I've just walked away. Nothing seems to make sense."

Clotilde nods with a look of understanding.

"I'm a bit shaky as a believer right now," he writes.

She reads and looks up. "Why shaky? I believe, and I want to go to church again like I did before I went deaf. Jesus is my life, really, but I haven't come across a church where I can be comfortable as a deaf person. What about your church?"

"Well, I, er, I don't know. But I'll find out for you."

"It is so difficult for me. I can feel the worship music and the singing, but I can't see the person who is doing the speaking. I have to rely on the closed captioning on the television. That doesn't always work for me, and I'm a bit wary." She laughs. "My husband used to say they were a bunch of bozos wanting money from shut-ins and blue-rinse widows. Not very kind. I went to one church, and they tried to tell me it was because of something I did, or that it was some sin of my parents. That's a lot of rot. I'm deaf because I got meningitis. It happens. Really, I'm comfortable with who I am. I'm not a victim, and I don't see myself as having a disability. I'm deaf—that's all. My only thing is that I'm alone since my parents died.

"I still have contact with Pierre—he was my husband—and my son Ben, but that's not the same. They live in Vancouver, and it's hard for them to communicate with me. We've tried things like FaceTime and Skype."

Brewster takes it all in. He feels a lot like a gawky schoolboy having to look into her face as he speaks, her dark shiny eyes smiling at him. He watches her tiny hands control the pencils as she gives a quick demo of how she draws. He notes her focus and delight as the colour shapes a petal. She has precision so exact that he can't really tell what she is adding.

What was it Irene said? Learn to sign.

Brewster wants to keep Clotilde engaged, keep her in front of him for a while longer even though their meeting is all but over. He talks about being alone. She nods. "I'm not so much lonely now that Melanie has gone, but I do feel totally alone." *Maybe,* he thinks, *I shouldn't let my life with Melanie overshadow or sour my liking for this adorable woman I have the good fortune to work with.*

Clotilde bundles up her files and stuffs them into her briefcase. "This is a good project," she says. "I'm enjoying the challenge and the deadline."

Brewster enjoys the openness and candour of his collaborator—refreshing and in no way telling him what to do. No demands. He enjoys walking beside her to the car park. There's that voice in his head: *Learn to sign.* He realizes this is a must if he wants to enjoy Clotilde's company after the project.

#

The day has been remarkable, and he finds himself very reluctant to go home to his empty house. He thinks about picking up a supermarket meal to go, or perhaps he should try the hotel trick again. Aloneness strikes, especially after what had turned out to be a warm and productive day.

Supermarket to go meal wins and he stops in to pick up a beef dish and salad. He adds a loaf of bread, vanilla ice cream and a can of apricots. The last thing he wants to do is eat on his own, but what else can he do? He sits at the coffee table in his big chair and slowly works his way through his package meal. He loads a dish with ice cream and apricots and clicks to CBC National on television. Not satisfied with that, he picks up Melanie's notebook, finds Claire's number and calls.

"Claire? Hello, this is Brewster. I just called to thank you for coming over the other day and saying what you did. I do hope I wasn't too rude to you. You spoke the truth, and I will try to get it all together. So, again, thanks."

"How about coming over for supper tomorrow night," she asks. "We'd love to have you over."

"Well, um, yes, I could," he says. " I've just demolished a meal to go from the supermarket, and my cooking is not great. You were obviously a good friend to Melanie, and I do appreciate your words of encouragement. I want to make that change." He begins to choke up.

"Okay, then, till tomorrow, say about 6:30 p.m.," she says.

He hangs up, visualizes a cake plate and wonders if the antique store would know what he was talking about.

Chapter Twenty-Three

"Hello, Irene. Brewster here. Please call me. I've got a man question." Brewster laughs at his own message. *"Man question." That'll appeal to her.* And sure enough, it does. That evening she calls him and responds to his simple question of what he should do when he visits Claire and Heath for supper.

"It's like this," he says. "A few days after Melanie's accident, this lady turns up at my door with yet another cake. I was angry and bitter, and the last thing I needed was to have to be nice and visit with one of Mel's friends. I waved my hands around and knocked the cake plate from her hands, and it lay in pieces on the concrete path. She left in tears.

"She bravely visited me the other day. I didn't recognize her at first until she smiled and said, 'No cake this time.' I apologized for my terrible behaviour and my rejection of her kindness. I thought maybe I should replace the plate. It's an old plate, and I'm sure I can find a replacement at the antique store. What do you think?"

"Off the top of my head, I'd say do it." Irene hesitates. "On one hand, it's not necessary; you've apologized. Then again, it might be nice to show you value their friendship."

"I found a piece of the plate still in the front garden," he says. "I'll go check it out and decide then."

#

Peering into the grass and undergrowth as he walks along a favourite path is a peaceful park pursuit for Brewster. He chats quietly

137

with the woman who'd made his life a joy each and every day, and he tells her about Irene's comments on grief and how it never leaves. "The big how, Mel, is handling it. What is emotional memory, and can it ever be erased? There's no reformat button that I'm aware of. Nothing to give me a reboot to peace and wholeness."

Park users distract him every now and then, and he wonders how many of them know about the flowers that thrive underfoot. A zooming cyclist startles him and all but pushes him into the blooming wild rose bushes. Crushed and furious, he's about to let fly but thinks better of it. The pathway really belongs to everyone, although he concedes that cyclists could slow down, ring their bells and exercise care. He takes a second look at the rose bush and tries to remember the difference between Alberta's wild rose and a prairie rose. Could be either; both are roses and both are a pink colour. Peering at the petals, he knows he should be able to tell the two flowers apart. "What, Melanie? What?" He speaks aloud and surprises a couple walking hand-in-hand along the path.

"You okay, sir?" the young woman asks.

"Oh, sorry. Yes, quite okay. Just talking to myself, trying to identify which rose this is."

She looks at it. "That's the wild rose, our floral emblem," she says. "It's also called a prickly rose."

"Yes, that's it," he says. "I get prickly and prairie mixed up."

She lets go of her friend's hand and reaches for a bloom. "Best way to tell is this is just one flower on the stem. Prairie has two or more. That's how I know."

"Well, thanks. My wife was the one who knew all the names," he says rather wistfully.

"I'm—well, we," she looks at her boyfriend and takes his hand, "are doing a biology degree over at St. Mary's Uni, and we do a lot here in the park. I want to go into environmental work somewhere."

Brewster wishes them well, and as they head off, she turns and says, "In case you're interested, there's a whole bunch of bracted orchids down in that ditch to the right. Lovely little things, but beware—heaps of mosquitoes."

Bracted orchid, he thinks. *Is that the one Melanie called a frog orchid?* He goes into the ditch to check and recognizes the surroundings where he photographed the summer before. He's happy the cyclist pushed him into the rose bush.

#

Melanie's bench is not occupied, and he sits down, glad it is there and thankful to the park people for acknowledging his request in such a timely way. The warm sunshine soaks in, and he closes his eyes, pondering the days he's spent bitter at God and angry and nasty to all the people who have reached out to him. These times in the past year are beginning to bother him now.

"How do I recover from this, Mel?" he asks. "Sure, I'm irritable and frustrated that now I have to live alone, but why pick on people who just wanted to express their love for you. Is this what depression is, just destructive pain?"

Enough. No pity party in the park. He crashes into a youngster on a bike when he gets up and turns onto the path

"Whoa, sorry there, young fella," he says, grabbing the bike's handlebars and keeping the bike upright. "Sorry about that."

"S'okay, Pops," the boy yells. He dances on the pedals and disappears.

Pops? Is that what I am now? Pops! Hannah and Harris will laugh at that one. At least that will give me something to talk about with the Rhodes tonight.

"Those kids in the park, hand-in-hand, were just like Mel and I used to be," he tells Claire, relating his adventures of the afternoon. "I hope they have what we had."

He looks at the table, all laid out for supper. The dishes, just like the one he broke. The same pattern. "Just gotta go out to the car." He dashes out the door into the rain. It doesn't take a minute to retrieve his plastic bag and the plate he'd picked up that afternoon at the antique shop.

After they're all seated, Brewster offers Claire the package. "For you," he says with a smile.

She places it on the table and invites Brewster to join hands with them. Heath says grace. "Thank you, Lord, for bringing Brewster to us tonight. May he find peace in your presence."

As Heath hands him the exquisitely prepared filet mignon, Claire opens the plastic bag. She puts her hand to her chest and exclaims, "Brewster!"

She runs round the table and gives him a hug. "You darling. Where'd you find it? I thought I'd never be able to replace the one that, er, accidentally ended up in the garden. Look, honey," she says, turning to Heath. "My missing cake plate."

It's a wonderful meal with tiny whole potatoes, crunchy carrots and a mixed green salad accompanying the filet. It's been a long time since Brewster enjoyed such a complete, home-cooked meal. They talk about politics, world events, city planning and Hannah and Harris until Claire rises, clears the plates and suggests they enjoy dessert. "You like lemon meringue pie?" she asks. Then she laughs and disappears into the kitchen.

"Quite the woman," Heath says. "I'm so glad we were able to work through things. Your Melanie was responsible for that."

Brewster smiles and gently changes the topic to the whereabouts of their daughters.

"Netball practice," Heath says. "Their coach picked them up tonight, so it worked out well we could have you over."

After the discussion he'd had with Claire just a few days ago, Brewster fully expects the coffee gabfest in the lounge after the magnificent pie dessert to be about his attitude toward God. But no. They enjoy light but energizing conversation about their children, the opportunities for them in today's world and their pending vacation before school returns.

As he is about to leave, Heath leans over and suggests that if Brewster is not comfortable about going to church just yet, maybe he wants to be part of their house group every other week. "There's only eight of us. We talk about the previous week's message, or whatever is on someone's mind. We don't have an agenda. It's about friendship and a few nibbles that everyone contributes, and we always wind up by 10:00. Call me if you need an evening in good company."

Brewster walks to his car. The rain has stopped, leaving everything smelling clean and glistening in the street lights. He drives to the reservoir, keen for a walk in the damp night air along the open pathways. He wants to stay in his warm, happy place, thankful that he knows people care about him.

No man is an island, he thinks, and he considers where that expression might have come from. He'll Google it later, just in case it's connected to something that might take him a step further in reining in his grief.

Twinkling lights across the lake add to his peace of mind. "Grief will always be with you," Irene had said. "It's part of your emotional memory, and in saying that, it must not be allowed to control you."

"Perhaps I have to let you go, Mel," he says. "I have to release you into your new life in that place you always said you wanted to be one day. This is so hard. I'm selfish. I want you to be with me."

Tiny spots of rain dab his cheeks, and he scurries back to the car, mindful that if he is to live at all, he must release his wife, smile for all the good times and be the man she knows him to be.

Chapter Twenty-Four

Hello Clotilde,

I was down at the park yesterday and revisited an old location to check on the bracted orchids. I do have some photos taken last summer, but think I might go back to see if I can get a better shot. I don't think I've passed this one to you as yet. Have you worked on this beauty? Melanie used to call it a frog orchid. Let me know, or I can give you directions to this little plot of wonder.

Brewster

Brewster clicks send and heads to the kitchen for his solitary breakfast. He pulls the yogurt and milk from the fridge. The espresso machine hisses, and the toaster crackles. It's pretty much the same routine he had when Melanie sat opposite him. He smiles at her empty chair. This was always a good time of the day. For the first time since the accident, he pauses for a short prayer of thanks, just as he used to do.

The day is filled at the computer, selecting and editing his flower pictures to give the best possible view to the passer-by keen to put a name to what they see. Melanie's notebooks provide general information. She's detailed simple things like what the stem looks like, how the leaves are arranged and the ground and surrounding growth. He laughs that his lack of specific knowledge means he has to guess which description belongs to which flower. Thankfully, the enchanting Clotilde has a much better grasp of the plant kingdom. It's a bit odd that he's the least knowledgeable, and yet it was through him that the project started. He's thankful for what Melanie taught him: to appreciate the ground he walks across.

The email pings—a message from Clotilde.

> Hi Brewster,
>
> I'm good with the bracted orchid. Lovely little plant, and quite shy unless you know what you're looking for. Thanks for the tip, but we have it. I look forward to seeing your new picture.
>
> C

Rats. That means I'll be on my own for the rest of the day. Oh, well. Lots to do here.

The email pings again.

> Brewster,
>
> Please call me when you have a chance.
>
> Irene

Odd, he thinks. Irene's not made this sort of contact before. He goes to the lounge, reaches for his phone and dials.

"Brewster, thanks for calling. Fast response. What are you doing?"

"Just editing another batch of photographs for Clotilde. What's up? Sounds like you have something on your mind."

"Yes, yes," she says, her voice quavering. "Can I come over?"

"Why, for sure. Now?"

"Yes. I'll be right there."

"Okay, see you soon. Oh, if you'd like to stay for supper, can you pick up a loaf of bread on the way? I'm all out."

Brewster's perplexed. Something is bothering his friend, and he's not sure he's the right person to provide any sort of help. Maybe he's just a pair of good ears. Well, with company coming there's time to do the dishes, tidy up and get some coffee brewing. He's not used to having people in the house. He looks around and sees he's living like a lazy slob. At least he can clean up the lounge and the kitchen and shut a few doors. He opens some windows to get a draft and freshen the air. He hasn't paid any attention to the house since Hannah left, since the big tidying-up of Melanie's belongings. Claire hadn't said a word either—another reminder to get his act together.

He's at the door as Irene pulls into the driveway. She has a loaf of bread in one hand and her purse in the other. He greets her, and as she says hello, she bursts into tears.

"Irene. What is it? Come on in." He hugs her trembling body. Without any words, he takes the bread from her, leads her to the lounge and sits her on the sofa. She's clutching an envelope. *Tissues, tissues. Where? Oh, right there on the coffee table.* Irene plucks one from the box.

"Black, no sugar, right?" he says, handing her a coffee.

"Thank you, Brewster." She gently dabs her eyes and dries the tears from her cheeks. "If I had a brother, he'd be you," she smiles, close to tears again as she sips her coffee.

Brewster sits in his chair and looks at her. How can he provide any comfort? Moreover, what has put this organized, easy-going person in such a state?

"Sorry, Brewster," she says. "I never thought this day would come. Somehow it seemed far away. I've been up all night and wanted to call you, but you have stuff of your own to deal with."

He has no idea what he can say or do to bring comfort. He gets up, sits beside her on the sofa and puts his arm across her shoulder. She leans in, sobbing.

Boy, this must be serious, he thinks. A few minutes later, he takes the half-empty cup from her as she gets up to use the bathroom. He quietly hopes it's clean enough for her, and he's glad that he'd put a fresh towel on the rack.

Irene returns after splashing her face with water. Her eyes are red, and her face is puffy. "I'll be okay now. Thanks," she says, attempting a smile.

Brewster is back in his chair, and Irene sits and curls her legs up on the sofa, tucking a cushion under her arm. She sighs deeply. "Bit of shock, really," she says. "All those years of waiting. All those years of hoping and yet always knowing it would probably come to this."

"What is it, Irene? It's like you've been hit by a tornado."

"When I got home yesterday, there was a message on my phone to call a company in Toronto. I thought it might be something to do with the Nicaragua thing, so I called the number. It was a lawyer." Her voice fades, and she's close to tears again.

"Is it about Mark?" Brewster asks. "Has something happened?"

"Yes." There's a long pause. "A lawyer. I hear it from a lawyer, of all people. I'm extremely upset, and now I'm so mad."

Almost without taking a breath, Irene relates what she'd been told: Mark wants a divorce as soon as possible. "I think he's somewhere in South America. The lawyer said that now I've confirmed my address, he'll courier a package to me this week."

"Good grief, that's a strange one," he says. "And you've never had any inkling of what Mark has been doing?"

"Nothing. Absolutely nothing for 20 years, and then I get this— from a Toronto lawyer, no less. He reckoned he'd been trying to find me for a couple of years. Didn't try very hard. Good grief, I'm even on Facebook and LinkedIn! Didn't try very hard."

"Well, now we know he's alive somewhere. Divorce? Wonder what's brought that on?" He just wants her to talk it all out.

"I was so blown away by what he was telling me that I didn't catch it all. Anyway, even the lawyer doesn't know it all. Just says that he's been favoured with instructions. Ha. Favoured with instructions from Mr. Steele. Ha."

"What are you going to do?"

"We'll see what's in the package the lawyer is sending me," she says. "I'm really sad—no, horrified and hurt—that my life has come to this, even though the writing has been on the wall for a hundred years."

She adds that she'd love to know what Mark has been up to all these years, but then again, she wouldn't. Irene continues to vent until there are no more words to say. She stretches and curls up on the sofa. Brewster watches as she falls asleep.

He gets a blanket, covers her and heads to the bedroom to make his bed and clean up other parts of the house. An hour goes by, and she's still sleeping. It's dark now, and he wonders if he should make a meal or leave her.

She'd said she'd not slept through the night. *She must be totally bagged. The shock and no sleep.* He gently lifts her from the sofa, carries her to the bedroom, lays her on the clean sheets and draws the covers over her. She barely stirs. He leaves her and quietly closes the door.

A boiled egg and toast from the bread she'd brought over provide him with a welcome supper. *If she wakes, I'll do the same for her.* He turns on the television and watches the news. That done, he tiptoes to his bedroom and peeps in. No movement. She is lost to the world.

The closet in Melanie's office yields a duvet, and he settles on the sofa. He's glad that his friend has a place to talk herself out. A rough night has smoothed into comfortable rest. He'll take the morning as it comes. "Been a good few years since I did this, Melanie," he murmurs. "Maybe when you had that gallbladder operation."

He wakes around 2:00 a.m. It takes a while to figure out why he's on the sofa. Then he remembers and peeks into his bedroom to see an empty bed. He looks out the lounge window.

Her car is gone from the driveway.

Chapter Twenty-Five

Three days later, Brewster closes the front door behind him and breathes deeply. *Home.* It's been a hectic but satisfying day at the office, catching up on business and sharing with Joel all the things involved in a possible sale of the building.

He puts his supermarket supper-to-go into the toaster oven to keep warm while he changes into his sweats. Tonight it's a rib dinner with mashed potatoes, gravy and peas. He takes the time to make up a salad of lettuce, carrots, slices of red and yellow peppers and raspberry vinaigrette. He even takes the time to set a place at the dining room table, lays out the newspaper he didn't get a chance to read that morning and settles in for his solitary meal. As he gives thanks, he asks God for wisdom while Irene works through her unexpected circumstances.

He thinks about a dessert and wishes now that he'd picked something up at the supermarket. The fridge yields a container half full of soft ice cream. He opens it; lots of crystals. He sniffs it, pokes his finger in and tastes. *Should be okay.* He scrapes away the crystals, puts a couple of dollops into a bowl, figures it looks lonely and adds a couple of teaspoons of raspberry jam on top.

"Colour is good," he says before stirring it up. "Well, at least it's tasty, but not sure I'll do this again."

He thinks he can hear Melanie laughing and saying, "Typical man. If you'd looked a bit further into the fridge, you'd have found a bottle of caramel topping."

Did he just hear her? He goes to the fridge anyway. Sure enough, there at the back on the second shelf is a bottle of caramel fudge topping, probably left (like the ice cream) by Hannah.

#

With his dishes washed and dried, he heads to his computer, where he finds two messages of immediate interest amongst the newsletters.

> Hello Brewster,
>
> I've got the package from the lawyer. I'd like to go through it with you tomorrow, if I can. He's asked for all the signatures to be done ASAP, but I want to bounce this off you before I do. Let me know a good time. I'm flexible all day.
>
> Irene

He rocks back on his chair. How to respond?

> Irene,
>
> How about we meet at my office? I have to be there all day tomorrow, so why not drop by about 10-ish? Happy to help you through this.
>
> Brewster

A brief, cheerful note from Clotilde. One more step in completing the wildflower project. He smiles as he reads.

> Hi Brewster,
>
> I'm down to my final drawings based on your previous attachment. I think we should get together and review where we are at. I think we need one or two more studies to complete the 100 wildflower theme. Can you do Monday at 11:00 a.m. at the library?
>
> Clotilde

Clotilde,

Fine by me. I look forward to the review of everything we have. Nice to know we're just about there.

Brewster

Clotilde's resourcefulness and the way she entered into the project makes him smile. He's certainly intrigued by this woman and how she has coped with the changes in her life. She can't hear the jets going over, the buses going by or the chirping and twittering of birds in the garden. He wishes he knew more about her. *Maybe one day.* He loves her drawings and knows that Melanie would be over the moon at what's transpired even though he was a total grouch and very uncooperative at the beginning. Working with Clotilde and wondering what it must be like living in her silent world has calmed him.

#

"G'morning, Jane," he says as he walks into the office, feeling very upbeat. "I've always liked Thursdays because that means tomorrow is Friday, and that's the end of the week." She laughs and tells him Joel will not be in until about 10:30, at which point he mentions that Irene will be in around 10:00.

"I've put the final papers on your desk for the transfer of the flower shop, and there are a couple of messages here for you to call tenants. Otherwise, things are quiet," she says. "But it's early yet."

He watches as she pirouettes her wheelchair around to put away some files. *Here's another woman who has overcome her difficulties. This is what a car accident did to her. Could Melanie have ended up like her?* He settles into his office and reaches for his in-tray. *Which is better, a wheelchair or a coffin? Handicapped or heaven?*

These dark thoughts are pushed aside as he tackles the paperwork Jane has laid out for him. He checks through The Blue Aster transfer to Jo and Danny and signs off. He's busy talking with one of his tenants when Jane wheels in and signals him that Irene is here and waiting.

"That's okay, Tom," he says. "Good to talk with you. I'll get Brian to drop in and follow through. Thanks for your comments." He hangs up the phone.

"C'mon in, Irene," he says, coming round from behind his desk. "Welcome to my world up here, the headquarters of BAM Inc."

"BAM?" she says.

"Well, our roots are the sheet metal and plumbing business, so we thought BAM was pretty good. Brewster and Melanie. Simple and catchy."

"Coffee or tea?" Jane asks from the doorway. "That's fresh water you have there in the pitcher."

"Very traditional admin you have here," Irene says. "I pictured you as one of those manager types who gets his own."

"Ninety-nine percent of the time, it's get-it-yourself around here," Brewster says. "But Jane said this morning that things are pretty quiet, and she likes to stay busy. Besides, you look important today in a suit. You must have a client meeting."

Irene acknowledges his accurate assessment and tells about her possible new client, in town from Seattle. "They tend to be a bit more formal than us Canadians." She takes the manila, letter-size envelope from her briefcase. "I have to sign these divorce papers—sign off on a lump sum settlement, and that's it."

He sees she is devastated by what has to be done. "Any word from Mark at all?" he asks.

"Very brief," she says, showing him a one-page letter. "He says he wants to marry the mother of his three—yes three—children, and he's been advised to settle his affairs in Canada." She pauses, bites her lip and looks away. "That means I am nothing but an affair. How can he say that? We were in love. We are married, we had a mortgage. I've waited 20 years for him. Good grief. An affair."

He asks about Mark's whereabouts, hoping to calm his hurting friend. She shakes her head. "Not known," she says. "Obviously not here in Canada, from the tone of the letter. That's not to say he wasn't in Toronto to meet with his lawyer."

Brewster walks to the door and asks Jane to have Joel look through the divorce papers as soon as he gets in. He looks at Irene. "I hope you don't mind me showing them to Joel. He has great eyes for detail and is more in tune with this than me."

Irene nods. "What should I do? He wants to pay me $100,000 to just sign and settle."

He thinks back to his days of rehab and what people had talked about: of bitter divorces, of relapse, of forgiveness, of depression, of not letting go. Then he reminds her of their conversations at Revelstoke. "You said you loved being on your own, being independent and fulfilled. You enjoyed the life of a bachelorette with a great circle of friends. Does this still hold?"

"Well, yes, I suppose it does. But this is like the clock has been wound back 20 years."

"My gut tells me that you should sign all this stuff and bring the whole matter to a close. Find peace in knowing what you have always held inside, anyway. This way you move on and develop your life wherever and with whomever."

He hopes his words have not hurt her any further. Before either of them can say anything, a cheerful Joel appeals in the doorway.

"Come in, Joel. Meet Irene Steele. Irene, meet Joel Cohen, my best friend, business partner and accountant."

Joel's timing couldn't have been better. The whole room seems to relax with his presence. He has that way, with his wide grin. "Two days running," he says to Brewster. "Glad to see you here in the office. And Anna wants to know if you're still on for supper tomorrow." He reads the legal documents. "These papers look fine to me, Irene. I've seen them before—kinda standard stuff, procedural and formal. No flaws or catches in here. Basically, Mark wants to end the marriage with the least amount of disruption in your life so that you can both embrace whatever life holds for you. He's offering you a lump-sum settlement."

Irene looks at the two men—probably two of the very few people familiar with her background. She asks for a pen and, with Joel as a witness, signs off on all the documents.

"If you like, I'll have Jane copy all these and get them into the courier this afternoon," Joel says. "Outta your hair, and you're on your way with your life."

"Hug?" she says, and Joel and Brewster suddenly find themselves swept into a group embrace. With teary eyes, she grabs her briefcase, smiles at each of them and dashes from the room, half-crashing into Jane.

Joel and Jane exchange glances and look at Brewster as Irene pauses, turns and lifts her hand to her ear, mimicking a telephone.

"You two an item?" Joel asks.

Chapter Twenty-Six

After a day dealing with finances and tenants, Brewster looks forward to a pleasant dinner at the home of his friend. It's Shabbat, the Jewish Sabbath, and in summertime Calgary that means arriving before the nominal sundown. Joel and Anna greet him at the door and welcome him in.

"Oh, Brewster. You okay?" Anna asks. She sees through his happy face veneer. "Come, take your troubles, put them in the pocket of your coat and hang it right there."

She lights the two candles on a table in the entryway. The unruffled atmosphere wipes away his tension as he's embraced in a very family affair. Anna gently moves her arms above the candles, drawing the light to her. She covers her eyes and quietly prays: "Blessed are You, Lord, our God ..."

She uncovers her eyes and hugs Joel. Their two children hug each other then leap and hug Brewster. "Shabbat shalom," they shout as they move through to the dining room. Brewster knows the ritual from the many times he and Melanie had been here together at this time of the week. The Shutdown at Sundown, he'd called it. With the candles lit, the Sabbath has begun in this warm-hearted home.

While standing at the dining room table, he notices the chairs and the place settings. There's one too many—six places instead of five. "That's the setting for our absent guest," Anna says, recognizing the look on his face. She doesn't say it, but Brewster knows she has included Melanie.

Joel says the blessing of the children. "May God bless you and keep you. May God show you favour and be gracious to you. May God show you kindness and grant you peace."

Anna and Joel kiss David and Naomi, and Joel softly sings the final verses of the Book of Proverbs, commonly titled "Eishet Chayil, a Woman of Valour," as a tribute to his wife. *Melanie you were a woman of noble character,* Brewster says to himself.

David and his sister fidget. Joel blesses the wine and offers a prayer of thanks for their day of rest. He passes a glass of grape juice to Brewster and the children, and a glass of wine to his wife. They say amen to finish and take a drink before scampering to the kitchen to wash hands. As learned from earlier visits, Brewster takes off his wedding ring and leaves it at his plate, just so there is no part of his hand untouched by the ritual water. Joel reminds him of the words of the blessing. He dries his hands and moves back to the table.

No words are spoken as the family follows the age-old custom of not speaking until everyone has been given a piece of bread. David and Naomi recite a prayer of thanks, the bread is cut and pieces are handed round.

A satisfying aroma drifts around the table when Anna lifts the lid from a casserole prepared well before sundown. Brewster senses the rest and spiritual enrichment of Shabbat.

He slips easily into the family warmth, and after their meal, he relaxes in their living room. "Joel, you asked me about Irene, and I gotta tell you there's nothing going on between us. She is a good friend, and we've enjoyed each other's company. She's been a great help to me as we talk about our different pathways. Don't get me wrong, though," he adds, noticing Anna's curious look. "I think she's a terrific person, and I wish her well in her life. I think we'll always be friends. Anyway, she might be off to a new job in Nicaragua soon."

"I certainly didn't mean to intrude," Joel says. "It's just at the office today, the two of you looked pretty cosy, familiar."

Anna reaches for her husband's arm. "Joel."

"Sorry, my friend," Brewster says. "We're just two people who connected when we shared our stories. Besides, I'm certainly in no shape to have feelings for another woman."

David and Naomi challenge him to the wordgame Upwords while Joel relaxes in his chair and Anna reads a book in her corner chair. He finds it a bit tough to fully concentrate and is soundly beaten by the two bright kids.

Later at home, Brewster sits quietly in the dark, reflecting on his business day and the significance of ritual to Anna and Joel. His house doesn't seem so silent tonight.

Sleep triumphs in the comfort of his chair as he prays, "Lord God, help me."

Chapter Twenty-Seven

Automatic doors swish closed behind him, and Brewster looks beyond the community centre offices and the many people in the concourse to see a small white dog in a red coat drinking from a blue plastic bowl in front of the large, floor-to-ceiling windows. Clotilde stands at the grey steel table, extracts some papers from her green briefcase and arranges a large black presentation portfolio on a chair. The associated snack bar shares its delightful smell of espresso coffee as he nears. Two foam-topped white china mugs are at a centre table. It's a busy little place with people coming and going from the library. Brewster feels like the silly schoolboy again as he grins widely and slips opposite her at the table. He puts his folio case and laptop on the table, and with a great deal of effort, he clumsily moves his hands to sign a greeting. "How are you?"

Clotilde beams and signs. "Great. We are close to the end." She follows this with another question, and when she sees he doesn't get it, she laughs and voices, "Nice work, Brewster. Where did you learn?"

"I looked it up online," he says, staring directly at her and hoping that his direct look didn't look like he's ogling. *She is beautiful.* At the close of each of their update meetings over the past few weeks, he's been increasingly eager to meet again and enjoy her remarkable quiet nature, her talent and her ability to overcome challenges—especially him. "I think that by the end of this week, I will have completed all my pictures for you," he says. "The 100 wildflowers on our list."

"You will be done? End of the week?" she asks. "I think I'm close too. I want to do a glossary—you know, plant shapes and forms. This will add to Melanie's notes and the botanical contribution from the park."

Brewster's mind is far away, thinking more about how he can get to know her better. He's found it difficult up till now to distinguish between her deafness and her seemingly intractable opinion on what their combined efforts should include. Their unwieldy system of communication, a combination of her voice and lip-reading skills with his note-passing, bugs him. He's curious about life beyond the project.

"There's one flower we do need in the project," he says. "I haven't given you the picture yet because I need to find it again for a classic shot of its beauty."

"You want one more picture?"

"Yep. We need a striped coralroot. The flower was important to Melanie, so I think we should have it." Tapping his chest, he adds, "My photo." Pointing directly at her, he says, "Your illustration."

Clotilde raises an eyebrow. He's not entirely sure she's understood. He scribbles a note. As she reads it, he scrolls through his computer photo library to find an image of the coralroot.

"I have to find this in the park," he says. "Those tiny striped flowers have an amazing translucent sparkle. The trick is to picture that."

She nods and repeats, "In the park?"

"Yes."

"Why don't we use that picture?" she asks.

"No, no. We must locate one in the park. The project, our guide, must only include the flowers we have found in the park." *I must be speaking too quickly,* he thinks. *I don't think she gets it.* He writes an abbreviated note, "Just flowers in the park. This picture is taken in Kananaskis."

"But don't they look the same?" Clotilde asks. "I haven't seen this. We could use this picture and not have artwork, perhaps."

Their strange mix of voice and note rolls back and forth as Brewster declares his point of view that this one flower is the most important. To Clotilde, a flower is a flower.

Frustrated, his emotions colliding through loyalty to Melanie and his inability to convince Clotilde, he slowly stands and through gritted teeth blurts that nothing, absolutely nothing, will be presented or published without a photo of the striped coralroot taken in the park.

Sensing that Clotilde has not absorbed the significance of his words or his notes, he explodes. "I can't work like this! This whole flaming exercise is just crazy!" Waving his arms, he stalks off down the wide-tiled atrium separating the library from gymnasiums, a swimming pool, the coffee shop and offices. He shouts and calls the world a stupid place.

Clotilde stares after him. She hasn't heard a word, but his actions speak louder. It's déjà vu, a repeat of the same frustration with Pierre in those first months of her deafness. In disbelief and shock at Brewster's theatrics, she sweeps her samples, the finished pieces and her pencils and sketchbooks into her folio case. Holding back tears, she tells herself she's finished. It's not the first time she's experienced this, but somehow she'd hoped Brewster might be an exception. She loves her work too much to allow some miserable, self-absorbed malcontent ruin the delight she finds in her botanical drawings.

She looks at Bebo, her very attentive friend. His eyes give that doggie, "Yes, I know how you feel" look. He stands, shakes and wags his tail.

"Yes," Clotilde tells him, "it's time to say goodbye to that handsome misfit."

The open laptop, a couple of books, a coffee mug and a folio case are all that remain.

Three women at the next table watch and resume their gabfest about what has just taken place. A man, a woman, a blow-up. They wonder what it is all about.

"They looked so happy just a minute ago," one woman says.

"Yes. I'd say they were working on a project of some sort," another says.

"I thought they were lovers," says the third. "She is so beautiful."

A librarian approaches Clotilde as she returns her mug to the barista. The women watch the silent conversation of moving hands and gestures, rarely seen and so different to their noisy world.

"They go fast, don't they?" says one.

"It's amazing how they do that," says another.

"I wonder what it's like—you know, not being able to hear anything," says the third.

Clotilde tells the librarian not to be concerned about the remaining articles at the table. "That man can stew in his own juice. I'll have nothing more to do with him," she signs. "No, we're not married or anything like that. We were working together on a field guide project."

The librarian signs that her son is deaf, and as a result she's learned to sign. They understand each other. Clotilde heads to the car park, finding comfort that she's made a new friend.

#

Brewster is at the far end of the atrium. He watches through the landscape windows as a couple of magpies strut about the grass. He's distressed that after several meetings, Clotilde would even suggest they use a photograph he'd taken of the striped coralroot at the Mount Lorette Ponds in Kananaskis. He is sure he told her right at the beginning that each flower must be actually photographed and drawn in the park, along with Melanie's notations. No ifs and buts, or sleight of hand. That was the way Melanie had seen their project, so that was the way it would be. Besides, it was what he'd said during his presentation: only Fish Creek Park specimens. The magpies hop, hit out at each other, and then continue together, presumably happy (or at least tolerant) of each other's company.

Feeling a bit sheepish about his behaviour, he turns back to the table, surprised to see Clotilde has left. His gear is still on the table next to the three women. A man holding a coffee mug and plate of food is looking round for somewhere to sit because all the tables are taken. He quickens his pace and waves to the man, indicating his table will be free. He stuffs his books and laptop into the folio case.

"She left a few minutes ago," one woman says.

"She talked with the librarian," says another.

"I think she was very upset," adds the third.

Brewster glowers at them, mutters a thank-you, shoulders his folio case and heads out.

"You'd think he'd return his coffee mug."

"Typical, man. Just leaves it for someone else."

"It wouldn't have hurt him to put it on the dirty dishes trolley," agrees the third.

#

Rain keeps Brewster indoors the next couple of days. He broods a good deal as he selects and edits his pictures, comparing his files with Melanie's notebook.

#

"You've hurt me, and I no longer want to be involved with the project—or you."

Clotilde shuts the door, leaving Brewster standing on the doorstep in the rain. He stares at the door, half expecting it to open again. He shuffles the package in his hands, opens the mailbox and drops it in. Sheltered under his red-and-white golf umbrella, he stands beside his car, looking back. The door remains firmly closed.

Perhaps she'll come round once she gets the peace offering, he thinks. It was a spur-of-the-moment thought he'd had while buying a fresh supply of birdseed for his backyard feeder. The dinner-plate-sized stained glass window hanging of a chickadee had instant appeal, and he recalled the many times he'd stood in the park, watching and hoping to capture the perfect picture of the ubiquitous chirping chickadee. He included a "Gee, I'm sorry" card he'd created.

What to do? he thinks. *Maybe the folks at the park will be able to keep Clotilde in the project. Maybe, just maybe.* Most of all he wants to know where he can find a striped coralroot. It's already July, and the chances of finding the plant are growing slimmer by the day.

#

"Well, look what the rain brought in," Louise says as Brewster once again crashes into the wrong door at the park offices. "We had a meeting this morning and were talking about you, Clotilde and the project. We wondered how everything is coming along."

"Well it was going okay," Brewster says. "But I've gone and messed up the whole thing. The other day, I quarrelled with her when she suggested we use a non-park picture of the striped coralroot. She's walked out and now refuses to have anything to do with me. Says she is no longer associated with the project because I have hurt her. She shut the door in my face."

Louise looks at him.

"Yes, I know," he says. "I was a bit blunt when I got up and walked away from her. We were at the library when things got the better of me. I probably embarrassed her as well."

"She's a lovely and talented artist," Louise said. "Have you apologized?"

"Yes. Well, I just went over to her place. As I said, she shut the door in my face. I left a small gift and written apology in her mailbox."

"Brewster, first off, I'm glad you came and told us so we can work out how to recover the situation," Louise says. "We cannot get involved in your differences; only you two can sort them out. My concern is bringing the book to fruition. As we have discussed earlier, we need to be assured that we can have everything finalized by the end of August—that's the drawings, the pictures and the text. We have people working on our side on that too."

"I understand," says Brewster. "I'm sorry this has happened. It's my whole attitude that caused the problem. I acted like a pouty schoolboy and should have known better."

"Put it this way," she says. "Where are you at as far as the photographs are concerned? It's not all that essential that you and

Clotilde actually work alongside each other. It's simply a matter of each knowing what the other is doing and how that interface works with our environmental group handling the script. Any chance that we might just have 99 pictures?"

"No. The blow-up came about because I insisted that we must have a park picture of the striped coralroot. I'd say I'm about 90 percent complete. At last count, I had about 90-plus individual flowers finalized. I have all the flowers except the striped coralroot. It is the only one outstanding, and it was the one flower in which Melanie was most interested. I'm determined to find it and photograph it right here in the park. To me, it's the key.

"Sounds good, Brewster. We're keen to make this happen. I'll personally connect with Clotilde to gauge her progress," Louise says. "She can work with us. Technically, this is a park project and will be a park guide. We have to keep our eyes on the big picture. I'll ask around to see if anyone has seen the coralroot. I've not heard it mentioned by the flora volunteers." She looks at him.

"Tell me, Louise," he says. "What's on your mind?"

"I just hope this is a temporary wrinkle," she says. "You're a successful businessman, Brewster. I'm sure you know what to do and can appreciate that we will not get involved in a squabble. Let me have the pictures as arranged. From the material you two have submitted to date, I can tell you it is an awesome project, and the book will be a major asset in our ecological work here. I'll work on how to bring it all together."

Chapter Twenty-Eight

From enthusiasm and excitement to utter sadness. Clotilde is perturbed by Brewster's behaviour. "How could he say that?" she says to Bebo. "Those things about me being deaf? Just like a lot of people think: deaf and stupid go together."

She tears as she realizes that what she thought might trigger a lasting botanical art career has been crushed. The question of how to get published looms large. She vows to withdraw completely from the wildflower project; her drawings will not form part of any book. "There will be no 'Created by Brewster and Melanie McWhirtle, with drawings by Clotilde Chiasson.' Never, *jamais, jamais*."

Bebo looks up at her from his comfortable spot in her lap. She wriggles the little dog's ears and resolves to recover and move on with the same strength and purpose she's applied to her many life changes. Brewster's peace offering and apology doesn't cut it. The double hurt is she genuinely fell for him—felt more than a warm connection as they worked together. Now his true colours show. The stained-glass chickadee is lovely and thoughtful, she concedes, but he can have it back. Each time she sees it against the window, she'll be reminded of his very public outburst. She wraps it up and puts it aside in her studio.

The book and the benefits that might result from her exposure is now a bust.

"Oh, Maman, what shall I do? There's nothing to keep me in Calgary now. Maybe I should take Cousin Ruth up on her advice and move to Cape Breton."

The trees wave their green branches at her as she gazes out, thinking of her many enjoyable holidays and the extended vacations there. But her parents were always with her and they bridged communication gaps in the extended family. To her knowledge, no one in the town signs. Maybe when she gets there, Ruth will pick it up. But which family? Her mother's Acadian heritage around Cheticamp on the west coast of Cape Breton, or her father's Mi'kmaq heritage at the Membertou First Nation at Sydney?

"You and Papa were always my inspiration," she says, looking at a photo of her parents on the nearby bookcase. "I loved the way you looked at each other in your everyday romance. That's what I thought would happen to me and Pierre. We had a fairy-tale meeting just like you did, when you found each other at the Nova Scotia Eastern Institute of Technology in Sydney. Just two ordinary people, Papa learning heavy equipment operation, and Maman learning secretarial."

Clotilde pauses and thinks about the possible raised eyebrows of the Mi'kmaq and Acadian romance. Perhaps it was different out there. Once they graduated, they married with the full support of their families. For a time, her dad worked in the fishery at Cheticamp because employment in the coal mines was sketchy at best. It was a period of great change, and she thought about her parents packing up and heading to the unknown west, where they'd heard good things about high-paying work in the Fort McMurray oil sands. In spite of the hardships, the burgeoning community at the confluence of the Clearwater and Athabasca rivers became their delight and life, especially when Clotilde entered their lives.

Camping in the surrounding wilderness, canoeing on the rivers, fishing and hunting were parts of her parents' adventure. Her dad worked in the oil sands, and her mom eventually found work as a typesetter at the new daily newspaper in Fort McMurray.

Clotilde enjoyed her out-of-school hours as a candystriper at the local regional hospital, graduated from high school and entered the nursing program at the University of Alberta. Filled with the same sense of adventure as her parents, Clotilde recalls the excitement she had finding employment at a Calgary hospital. That was where she met Pierre, an up-and-coming young lawyer who'd moved west from his native Montreal. He'd turned up in Emergency one evening with a broken leg from a climbing mishap.

"I wish you were around now, Pierre," she says. "It was good with *Maman et Papa* here. Now it's an empty house, a daily struggle. She always knew she'd be alone one day, but did it have to come so fast? Cancer took her dad after a four-year battle, and she was there to care for him in spite of her deafness. Mama went suddenly, just a year ago and a year after her beloved Papa. "A broken heart, *un coeur brise*." Now her high expectations for her art have evaporated. She trusted Brewster, liked him, liked being around him, wanted to be near him. She felt as though she was falling in love with him, like when she first met Pierre.

"Why am I deaf?" she asks Bebo. "You are my ears now. We're a great pair." She reaches for the pet bristle brush on the coffee table and sits on the floor. "Let's groom these knots out of the way."

"Toujours avoir confiance en Dieu," "Always trust in God," was a favourite expression of her parents whenever they saw her spirits drop, especially with the heartache of saying goodbye to her husband and then her son. She appreciated her parents' willingness to pack up, sell up and quit their well-paying jobs in Fort McMurray just to be with her and help her through the new challenges of life in a silent world.

"There's no need to argue with God or to question Him, *ma petite*," her mother had said. "You are who you are, a wonderful creation and our awesome capable, confident and creative daughter who's always given 110 percent. *Ne perds jamais ca,* do not lose that."

Bebo dances around and playfully tries to nip the brush as she drags it through the fur on his back. "Come on, now. See how nice you look." She lets the dog go and watches him dash around the room, shake and playfully run some more. "Are you smiling?" she says as she gets up from the floor, pleased that the distraction has helped to distance her from the closed art folio.

"Enough, Bebo," she says to the little dog at her feet. "Time for action. Let's go for a walk—*on va se promener.*" Bebo acts pleased and sits quietly as Clotilde dresses him for work in his red service coat. She will avoid the park and their usual walk, and she suggests to Bebo that they head for the Inglewood Bird Sanctuary for a pleasant walk along the pathways. She doesn't want to go anywhere near the subject of the artwork, which has been her focus for a couple of years.

Brewster has ruined that activity.

She's eager for a walk in the quiet sanctuary bordering the Bow River. But why is the car park so empty on this warm, cloudless day? One look through barrier fencing tells her why. The recent floods have had a major impact on the area, and the oasis has become a catchall for all the floodwater junk, including a kitchen sink. Viewing platforms and bridges have become muddied barriers and captured driftwood and debris for overworked city crews to clean up.

"Looks like we're out of luck on that walk today, Bebo," she says. "It's going to take a couple of years for that to be cleaned up."

Bebo has not been out and around people lately; she's been too engrossed in her work. A quick diversion to the Chinook Mall will benefit her four-legged friend. Clotilde's taken aback at the number of young people walking around. *These folks should be outside somewhere, soaking up the all-too-brief season of sunlight and warmth, with fresh air.* She remembers her own days at the same age: pickup ball games in the school grounds and sports fields, hiking or biking along pathways and through new neighbourhoods, camping at the lake or even tanning in the backyard with a good book. There were never enough hours in the day to volunteer, be with friends and take part in church group youth activities.

Ah, well. Each generation has its own culture, she rationalizes, hoping that the activities of today lead to productive and enjoyable lives in adulthood. She had the benefit of growing up in a small city in spite of the rapid growth brought on by the mushrooming oil sand industries. In those days, the city grew at a faster rate than the amenities, housing and infrastructure could cope with. Clotilde reflects on the painful decision to let her son grow up with his father. Overall it was a good decision because Ben loved the outdoors, the mountains and his sport, reflecting his dad's interests.

In the crowded bookstore, Bebo constantly attracts dog lovers young and old, wanting to know why he's wearing a little red coat with pockets. She asks people not to pet him because he's working, and she explains that the pockets contain his licence and registration as a service dog. Most people don't know about dogs assisting the deaf. The little fellow is well-trained, and as she searches the bookshelves, he sits quietly at her feet, alert to surrounding activity.

Her online reading group suggested she might enjoy the novel *Finding Dermot* because it deals with changes a family was forced to make to overcome adversity. It's not on the shelf, but a happy staffer greets her, finds the book in the computer catalogue and agrees to order a copy for her.

She browses the photography and art books to look at flowers. She's smiles as she compares the quality of her work against internationally known artists. She regrets her rash decision to pull out of the project with Brewster and the park. Maybe she can reconsider this one opportunity to have her work published and recognized. She can work directly with the park, maybe, and not be associated with Brewster.

When will he get over his wife's death? She has an inkling of his pain from the loss of both her parents, but *c'est très triste*—15 months, and he still doesn't know which side is up. She empathizes with his sad and tragic position, sure that somewhere down deep, he is a good man.

"Perhaps he'll find himself one day, Bebo, and learn how to put his grief in perspective. As mama said, *Toujours avoir confiance en Dieu*— always trust in God,"

#

Patients and visitors watch as she and Bebo enter the hospital. She smiles at them as she passes through the sliding glass doors into the main lobby and heads toward her friends at the admitting office.

"Clotilde and Bebo!" Edie, the charge nurse, hurries to them with a cheerful welcome. Even after all these years, Clotilde has a fondness for the familiarity of the hospital where she'd worked. She misses her nursing. "If you have time, Clotilde we have a man up in the heart ward who's deaf, and I'm sure he'd like to meet you and have a chat. He's a wee bit lonely by himself," Edie says.

Clotilde acquaints herself with the patient and then heads to the ward with Bebo, now quite comfortable with the hospital from their many visits. "Hello, Mr. Shaver," she signs. "My name is Clotilde, and I used to be a nurse here."

Joe Shaver's face lights up like a Christmas tree, and he answers in sign. A couple of ward staff stand in the doorway and watch the silent, animated conversation.

"I think we should learn to do that," one nurse says as they return to the nursing station. "There's a definite need here. I wonder if they teach that somewhere?"

Joe reveals that he's close to 70 and gets Clotilde to talk about herself. He's a bit of a rascal, and with a twinkle in his eye, he asks why she doesn't have a fella. "You're a looker—a real looker," he signs. "If I was young, I'd be after you in a flash."

"Oh, boy, you are a charmer. I did meet a man, and he's hearing, but we got off to a bad start. I do like him—well I did once. He was getting used to me until just the other day, when he blew up at me because I had an idea he didn't agree with. Something to do with his wife, who was killed in an accident."

She enjoys their chat in sign and tells him she'll be back in a couple of days to see how he's doing.

"Oh, don't worry," he signs. "I'll be outta here in a day or two. My wife will pick me up. She's deaf too, but we get along famously. Been 25 years now. Before that, we both hid in our deafness. So you get your fella—go get him. Don't hide like we did all those years."

Joe tells how he met his wife at the Spruce Meadows equestrian facility. "We met by chance one championship weekend. I couldn't make myself understood at a food booth and was getting frustrated, so she stepped up and was able to get my order across to the server."

"Hey, I came in here to cheer you up," she signs with a laugh. "Here you are, giving me a lecture on romance!"

Clotilde turns to leave, and Bebo steers her around the doctor as he enters. He looks at her, and Joe signs for her to stay. She begins to tell the doctor she's deaf and a nurse, but he smiles, looks straight at her and says the folk at the nursing station told him she was there. She signs for Joe as the doctor talks about what happens next with his heart condition. Joe is cleared to go home the next day.

#

Clotilde curls up in bed with her book, but the lines run together, and she finds it difficult to concentrate on what she is reading. Her thoughts are very much around what Joe said to her: "Go get him. I'm sure he feels bad. You need a fella. Don't be like us and hide away. Look at what we missed."

Perhaps Brewster will find himself one day, she thinks. *Perhaps he will be able to put his grief in perspective. But could he ever love again after experiencing the close intimacy and connection he obviously had with his wife?*

The depth of her own feelings for Brewster surprise her. He's done nothing to lead her on, but there is something about him she cannot place. He's grown on her since that first meeting at the park. *A bit of a charmer,* she thinks, *clever and a smart man to be with.* She found herself making excuses for them to meet. She admired the way Brewster always tried to communicate better with her, looking at her when he spoke, willing to try a few signs and repeating his comments when she did not detect his phrasing. He was quick with his notes for clarity, and he was usually very courteous. He even understood some of her French expressions. But why the blow-up?

If she did decide to get back into the project, she'd have to be a bit more guarded to avoid being hurt again. Hearts cannot rule in business, and the book is all about business. She finds it difficult to recall when she'd spent so much time with a man since Pierre left. True, she's flirted with doctors and male staff at the hospital from time to time, but nothing more. That is her workplace, and she means to keep it that way.

Who wants a deaf woman?

Chapter Twenty-Nine

Brewster freezes. Directly in front of him, a mule deer lifts his head and stares, transfixed. No movement. He holds the young buck's gaze and can see the fuzz on the sprouting antlers. This is beauty in the forest, and it's a treasured moment a camera cannot capture. The deer drops his head and continues to browse on the grassy meadow. *Wow,* Brewster thinks, not wanting to move. The deer lifts his head, unfazed, and quietly high steps into the shelter of the aspens.

Glorious morning. The sunshiny blue sky casts good light into the undergrowth. Maybe today the striped coralroot will show itself to the world. Brewster is energized.

"How I wish you were here, Melanie," he says, hoping the deer might still be within earshot. "You'd be able to see this plant. There has to be a specimen here somewhere. Please, please."

As far as he knows, Brewster has searched all of their frequented locations. He has not been able to pinpoint the spot where he'd photographed it before in the park. That one time Melanie had found it, the mid-afternoon light was so poor he'd not been able to get a macro photograph. There's no reference as to its whereabouts in her notes. If only he could remember where it was. He's searched for the past 10 days—in the rain, in the sun, regardless of the weather. He's determined to find the plant, photograph it, and then hopefully get Clotilde fully engaged again, drawing the plant in its natural Fish Creek habitat.

He is happy that Louise has been able to convince Clotilde to keep going. Her work is almost complete, save for the elusive striped coralroot. Like him, her interest over the past couple of years means that the hurdle of portraying 100 flowers of the forest is within reach.

One thing the blow-up has revealed is his liking for Clotilde. He wants to see her and be with her, though he knows he's carrying a lot of baggage, which at times doesn't make him a very good companion. Maybe when the tension of the project is over, they will find a new and better connection. Until then, he realizes he has a lot of thinking to do and steps to take to corral his grief. He's glad though that Clotilde levelled with him, calling him a self-absorbed nutcase and shut the door in his face. It was a good wake-up call about how his moods affect other people.

Brewster pauses on the gravel path. In front of him on the sunny side is a nice, healthy grouping of his blue asters—the showy aster, probably. He never could tell them apart. He looks around, and there's no one near. "Melanie? Are you signing me now?"

The only sound is the crunching of the tiny stones under his feet as he pulls his gear behind in the roller-wheeled camera case. *Another search day done. Perhaps tomorrow. But it's already mid-July. Too late?* Then again, the plant doesn't always show itself each year, and the spring floods may have ripped the plant away or buried it in the fine, choking silt. Like all orchids, the coralroot fascinates in that it needs fungi in the decaying forest floor matter to grow. If the fungus is not there, then there's no coralroot. And who knows what changes can occur from year to year? He is sure he's scoured every possible site. He begins to doubt his stance on finding the plant in the park. Should he acquiesce and use the Kananaskis picture?

Tomorrow. Maybe it'll show tomorrow.

#

There are only a couple of other vehicles in the car park when he arrives. Still early for much of the mid-week crowd. He feels as though he has this wonderful place to himself today. He sits on the tailgate, drinking his coffee and reviewing his plan of the pathways. The routes he's already searched have been marked. *Where else is there?*

Today, he's out to check a couple of places where they'd wandered deeper along the bike trails. His biggest discomfort may be mosquitoes. The trails of his new search cut through old and new forest, spruce and poplar. The undergrowth is largely dogwood, saskatoon, wildrose and wolf willow. Perhaps this is where he might find the elusive coralroot poking up through the decaying leaf and needle detritus.

He closes up his vehicle, pulls up the handle of his camera case and heads east, first along a paved trail and then on to the gravel path to a bridge over Fish Creek itself. He looks afresh at his reject pictures as he walks. The plant does not have leaves; it's a funny, pinkish-yellowy stalk sticking up maybe 30 centimetres or so. He smiles. He's really looking for a stick, and there are plenty of those around, so a flowering stalk would help. It's a beautiful morning, clear and warm. He's feeling good about things, but has no idea why.

He crosses the bridge and reaches his key point of interest. He heads off trail and carefully uses his hiking pole to push aside the undergrowth around and near the bases of the spruce. His search absorbs him, and he's thankful that there are fewer visitors around. He's left his black bag with the handle sticking up at the side of the path.

"What are you doing?" a small voice calls. "Have you lost something?"

Brewster looks across the undergrowth back to the path. "I'm looking for a plant," he says, thinking this is a pretty lame thing to say. He gently retraces his steps to see a girl about seven years old looking up at him from under a huge-brimmed pink straw hat.

"I thought you were Tigger," she says. "I'm looking for Tigger, but I think his house is back there in the big trees. Have you seen Tigger?"

Brewster thinks for a minute and reconnects with the adventures he had in the park with Harris and Hannah.

"I haven't seen him today," he says. "Perhaps he's gone to visit Kanga and Roo for lunch?"

"Yes," she says. "He does that a lot."

"Have you seen Pooh or Piglet around?" Brewster asks.

"Well," the little girl says, "not today. We just got here, so I haven't been to their place yet. What plant? You said you were looking for a plant."

"It's called a striped coralroot. It's an orchid, and it looks like this," he says, handing her his photographs. "Are you lost? Where's your mom and dad?"

"Oh they're over on the bridge. They said I could go for a walk 'cause there aren't many people around. But I have to stay on the path."

"Let's go see them," Brewster says, wondering how to end this encounter. "Um, what's your name?"

"I'm Lily," she says without looking up from the pictures. "I've seen this pretty flower over by Owl's house—it's all stripey. I'm not allowed to pick it, my Mom says. Not allowed to do that in the park 'cause it will die."

Brewster smiles at the girl's imagination, reminding him of Hannah at the same age, full of wonder as she played in the park with Harris. The same games.

"Well, there you are, young girl. You had us worried."

Brewster looks up to see a woman coming along the path with a man in a wheelchair.

"This is my new friend," Lily calls. "He says Tigger has gone to Kanga's house for lunch."

"I'm sure he's right," the man says. "We're going over to a picnic spot by the river for lunch. Sorry if our Lily has been a bother to you," he says to Brewster as he spins the wheelchair around.

"No worries," Brewster says. "I'm searching for a particular flower to photograph for a book I'm working on, for the park administration. It's about the wildflowers that grow here. I'm determined to find this one, last plant because it was important to my wife."

"It's just like my fairy flowers by Owl's house," Lily says again, this time tugging his sleeve. "I can take you there."

There's an awkward silence. Brewster grabs the handle of his case and makes a move.

"Please, Daddy. We can all go to Owl's place, and then we can go have lunch," Lily says. "This is really special. Please?"

"We're the Palmers," the woman says. She smiles and offers her hand. "I'm Holly, and this is my husband, Wendell."

"Brewster," he says, shaking her hand. "Brewster McWhirtle."

"Come on, Lily. Take us to Owl's place," Wendell says, and they follow her back across the bridge, past the barns and along the path that borders the river. Lily skips ahead and darts into the undergrowth towards the riverbank.

"Here," she shouts. "Here it is! Just like your picture."

Brewster is overwhelmed as he bends over the tiny plant, nothing more than a cluster of easily missed, pinkish sticks in the ground with a cascade of striped flowers. He looks at Lily's parents. "I'm dumbfounded. How did she know? I would never expect anyone, least of all a little girl, to spot and remember this plant," he says. "I've spent the past 10 days wandering around and looking for it. I think I was here in this same spot just a few days ago. There was light rain though."

"I lost my ring here," Lily says. "But we had to go home before I found it. Yesterday, Owl showed me to come here by these fairy flowers." She sits beside them, smoothing out her colourful cotton sundress. She holds her hand out in an almost reverent touch to the coralroot.

The lighting is perfect to create an eye-catching vignette. Brewster lifts his camera and asks Holly and Wendell if he can take the photograph. They nod and watch him as he quietly shoots several frames. "I'll print you a copy," he says, standing back to take some general location shots.

Holly and Wendell smile. "She has quite the imagination," Holly says. "We were here a couple of days ago, and Lily was skipping through here hoping to see a garter snake when she lost her chunky star ring the hospital gave her for being brave. It's very special to her."

Brewster nods and smiles, not sure what to say or do. "Thanks, Lily," he says. "I'm coming back tomorrow to take some more pictures of that plant, and I have to tell the parks people to invite their artist to come and make some really great drawings for a flower book."

Lily beams and points at nothing more than her imagination up on the nearby poplar tree. "Thanks, Owl," she calls. "See you tomorrow."

They walk back to the parking lot, and on the way Holly and Wendell open up about their daughter, the illness that keeps her in hospital and the car accident that put Wendell into the wheelchair.

"It's been a rough couple of years," Holly says. "But we are so thankful for every day we have together. Wendell may never walk again, and we trust God that Lily will get better. She loves these short visits to this park. She's free, and if tomorrow is sunny and warm, we might get to have her here again. She never wants to go anywhere else."

Chapter Thirty

My Dearest Melanie,

This has surely been an interesting spring and summer, and one in which your presence has been sorely missed. I have not known which way to turn. It doesn't matter where I look; I see you with every bunch of blue asters I come across. I wake in the night, and my hand feels across the bed for you, but it is empty. I'd give anything to feel your arm around me, to wake in the morning to hear your sleepy "Good morning, sweetheart." When people mention you, I tend to tear up. It is so hard to find myself alone and without the one person in this world who knew me perhaps more than I know myself.

I felt like escaping the city a couple of weeks ago, and I headed down to Waterton. I'm so glad I did. You and I loved it there. It was quiet, even though it did get a bit windy. It was a lovely afternoon on the first day, so I took a trip on the boat down the lake reliving the time when we did it together. Saw a moose and a couple of bears. Lot of people on the boat. Comforting, really, that I was amongst people who did not know me or you. Glad I took a couple of chocolate bars with me and a bottle of water. Next day, it was really windy and the water choppy. I know it would not have been a day for you on the boat. I was tempted to go out again just for the thrill, but I opted more for a drive up to Cameron Lake. Not as windy up there. Found a beautiful crop of glacier lilies that we called the dogtooth violet. I took a few pictures with the small camera. Wind was troubling, but I did get a couple of good pics after sheltering them with the golf umbrella we keep in the car. I had a feeling something or someone was watching me lying there on the ground, and I looked up to see a Steller's jay sitting on a spruce branch. He looked gorgeous, and I managed to get a couple of shots away before he took off. I'm glad it wasn't a bear taking an interest in my activity.

I got back home and found the shock of my life. Our place was transformed. I plead guilty, my love, to the fact that I've not lifted a finger to look after the gardens and the lawns, because you are not here. The place was looking really ragged compared with the way it bloomed under your tender care. There's been no one to go out and water in the mornings, no one to talk to the flowers. Weeds have had a bit of a field day. The grass was long and unkempt. I hadn't even trimmed the back hedge. I'm so sorry I let it all go. But here I was, turning into the driveway to find five large paper bags stuffed with the work of an unknown group of people.

I confess to be being a bit ticked at first that these fairies had interfered in my life. After walking around the place, though, I calmed down and muttered a quiet word of thanks to God for whoever was caring enough to give up their time to make a difference.

I must confess to being a bit selfish, only thinking of myself and what I was feeling. A lot of people miss you. Hannah and Harris miss you. I'm slowly learning that life goes on and that people are dying every hour of every day; "passing" seems to be the favourite word these days in the obit columns. I often wonder if they had such a violent departure from this world. I think I'm learning to accept that Jesus was there with you in that blink of an eye between this world and where you now find yourself. If only I could be sure.

The gardens look really nice today. We've had a bit of rain, but today the sun shines. The chickadees and the nuthatches are back at the feeder now that I've taken the time to buy more seed and fill it up for them. I remember how you used to say that every time you went out to the garden, the chickadees arrived with their music. Now when I go out there, I'm joined by their cheerful chirping. I'm happy that I've found you in the garden, poking around, pulling weeds or dead-heading some of the blooms. You are part of the garden.

I told you in a couple of my earlier letters that Jo is overjoyed at taking over ownership of your beloved Blue Aster. She stopped by with young Mikey the other evening after closing up. She brought a couple of arrangements because she figured the house probably needed some new colour. She really is our extra daughter. She chattered along and reminded me of you as she outlined her new promotion plans and how the shop is doing better this year. You certainly laid a good foundation there, Mel. Your touch is everywhere.

I found out this week that the garden fairies were Claire and Heath and some of their friends. Heath wouldn't say who, but I guess they were all part of that prayer group you used to be with. When I asked, he said something about how the left hand doesn't need to know what the right hand is doing. He smiled at me and told me to accept what I'd been given. I'm not too sure how to take that, and I wonder if there's a deeper meaning.

I think I told you about selling the business. That will go ahead, I believe. Joel is taking care of the nitty-gritty. I'm still going over to the Rhodes for their small group night. I'm not much of a contributor; still very cynical and questioning the presence of God. Might get back to the church sometime soon. I think I've come to realize that perhaps my faith is still intact, even though I've been off the map all this time you've been gone. I've questioned and fought, wallowed in a mixture of bitterness and anger that is not doing anyone any good. I've allowed my emotions to rule, and now I've slowly come to terms with the fact that it was not God who left me—I left Him. I'm so sorry, dear, sweet Melanie. Your love for Jesus was so real.

I really made a mess of things with Clotilde too. She won't have anything to do with me now, and the only way our book is going ahead is because she works directly with the park people and not with me. Her illustrations are awesome, and I wish you could see them. I know she could hold her own in any botanical art circle. And she's self-taught too. Picked the style up from her fascination with the detail in medical drawings. Really odd transition, isn't it?

I'll send her a note and hopefully encourage her to reconsider. A sick little girl showed me the location of a striped coralroot she'd found in her Tigger's forest. It's a good example, and I'm hoping Clotilde will come down and do her work. It's all because of this flower, a favourite of yours, that I blew up at her. To me, the striped coralroot is the most significant flower in the book. It's a lonely and a strikingly beautiful plant. I want my new pictures to show up the red striping and the pink-yellow translucent sparkle of the tiny flower.

I know Clotilde will be excited about the plant if I can just get her to come and look.

I'm thinking of selling up everything now and moving away once the book is settled. I might take a look at somewhere on Vancouver Island. I'll take a trip and see what the business opportunities are like. Some sort of a fresh start to keep busy and interested in life. Not really sure what I'll do. Our wildflower book has been my focus this year. Hannah is off to Europe this winter, and Harris is enjoying himself and doing well in the warm waters of northern Australia. I think he's given up on the big boat racing idea since the capsize and his close encounter in renegade seas. Not sure we will see our boy back here again; he does enjoy his sailing and the sun. I'll suggest to Hannah that she and I head down there when she's finished at Acadia. We've talked about it, and I've now come to realize that you will be with us too. You will always be wherever we are.

This has been a long letter today, Mel. I know you will read it as the expression of my lonely heart. I don't think I'll write any more, so this is my final letter to you, my love. I want to release you to your new place. You kept your vow of till death do us part, so now I must let you go, happy to know that one day we'll hug again.

Love goes on and on, forever.

Brewster

Chapter Thirty-One

It's still dark when Brewster wakes. He thought his restless nights were a thing of the past, but here he is, wide awake. His first thoughts are of Clotilde. He gets up, showers and goes to his computer. He stares at it, working up the courage to write her an email about yesterday's miraculous find. He wants to reach out to her and hopes to see her again, to be involved together and bring the project to completion. *Please, please, Lord. Help me.*

> Hello Clotilde,
>
> Great news. I've found a striped coralroot in Fish Creek Park. Well, I didn't find it, but a seven-year-old girl found it and took me to it. It was by Owl's house, she said. She's imagined Winnie the Pooh and Tigger down there in her own fairy-tale place. Ever since I blew up (and I apologize over and over for that), I've been down at the park looking for the orchid. I had to find it, and Lily, the little girl, led me to it. I'm sure it will be around for a few days yet; flowers are still forming, and it's in a relatively safe place.
>
> Please come and have a look. I know you will be delighted. The plant cluster is not far from the barns, toward the river and along the pathway to the snakes. I think you might find it a good location to get your

drawings. I promised Lily and her parents I would be there tomorrow for detailed photographs. Probably around noon, when the sun is high and the light is best at ground level. I'm hoping Lily can be there, but she only gets out on day passes from the hospital, so it really depends on her condition.

Do let me know. I think you'd like drawing this striking little plant.

Brewster

It's 7:00 a.m. when he finally sends the email. He's dithered a bit, contemplating whether he should email or call on Clotilde, and wondering if she is still mad at him to the point of total withdrawal from the project. He thinks about Holly's comment that they trust God for each day with Lily's illness and their hope for a miracle. *Such a bright child,* he thinks. How sad for them—leukaemia. As Brewster prepares his breakfast, he recalls Harris's very serious and meaningful comments before he returned to his life in Australia.

"Dad, when I was out there floating around in a stormy ocean, there was only one thing I could think of, that if this was the way God wanted me to die . . . .well, I didn't have a choice, did I? You and Mom taught us to believe in Jesus Christ, so that's where my mind was as the huge waves lifted and broke over me. I could hear the emergency whistles of my mates, but I could not see them. When a wave carrying me crested, I could see the hull of our broken yacht and tried to head toward it. Nothing was happening. I just prayed and sang any old hymn I could think of. I must have lost it somehow, because the next thing I know, I'm being hoisted into a rubber ducky—you know, a Zodiac. So I say, Daddy dear, that I'm here today as a result of God's hand. All of us were picked up, and I always see God in our rescue. So get with the program, Pops!"

Brewster smiles. Harris's rant has touched a spot deep down, and even though he has yet to truly accept Melanie's accident, he sees now that she has broken through this life and into the new; she is with her

Jesus in the very place He promised her. His lips move in a whisper as his eyes close, seeking help to embrace the day.

#

He breakfasts out on the patio with the chickadees. There's been no response from Clotilde. Perhaps she's not home, but he knows she always takes her phone with her and that Bebo will have heard the email come in. It's after 11:00 a.m. when he heads to the park. He does not want to miss this fresh opportunity to spend time getting all the striped coralroot pictures he will need. He imagines the picture on the wall of the park administration building.

Lily was delightful in the way she told him about Owl. *The faith of a child.* Melanie often spoke of them being children of the living God. *Not many people in the park again today. That's good. Fewer interruptions to my challenge.*

The coralroot looks gorgeous, and the natural light is as he likes it. The dime-sized flowers sparkle in their translucent beauty. He pushes some of the undergrowth away to allow the filtered sun onto the tiny plant, poking maybe a foot or so above the dark, moist, ground clutter. He has plenty of room to move around, setting up his tripod and camera. He positions his homemade reflector to improve the lighting under the flowers and unrolls his vinyl picnic cloth so he can lie down to minimize ant attacks and avoid prickles. The mosquitoes haven't found him yet, but they'll come soon. He pulls on his mesh mitts. He's lying down and composing his photograph on the digital screen before seeing it through the viewfinder. He's lost in the closeup beauty of the orchid. He wipes away stray twigs and grass crowding the frame.

"Hello, Mister Brewster." It's Lily, cheerful and smiling from under her big hat. "Owl told me in the car park you are here, and Mom and Dad let me run down to see. They'll be here soon. We've got lunch."

Brewster looks into her shining face. He invites her to kneel down and look through the lens at the flower. He shows her how to click the shutter and take her own picture.

Clotilde reaches the barns and recalls the message that the plant is somewhere along the path near the garter snake hibernaculum. She knows every inch of the park and heads straight for the place where she thinks Owl might live in the imaginary Hundred Acre Wood. Brewster jumps up when he sees her, embarrassed, and he offers yet another apology as Lily bends to touch Bebo. Clotilde asks her not to pet the dog because he's at work; she explains quietly that Bebo helps her by listening. Lily stands back, silent and watching, while Brewster shows off the coralroot. Clotilde greets him with a smile. He inwardly melts as she shows her excitement at seeing this very striking flower.

"Let's go find your parents," Brewster says to Lily. He expects Clotilde will need about an hour to do her work with the plant. Further photographs can wait for different lighting. He's quietly thrilled Clotilde has come and is obviously back in touch with the project.

Lily races around the grassy picnic area, chasing the ground squirrels into their burrows. Then she lies quietly on her tummy, watching them pop out again and call to one another as they dart from hole to hole. Her squealing laughter drives them all underground again. She rolls on to her back. "Mister Brewster, can we go and see that lady now?"

"She's getting a bit tired," Wendell says. "I'll ride her down." Lily doesn't need any prompting. As fast as a ground squirrel dives down it's hole, Lily is up on her dad's lap, snuggled against him as he wheels round and heads down the path.

Brewster and Holly pack away the picnic gear, and he helps her stow it in their vehicle. She tells him more about Lily, and about Wendell's past few months in a wheelchair.

"How do you handle it all?" Brewster asks.

"We were faced with the utter bleakness of everything that was happening to us. My neighbour came over one day and said matter-of-factly, 'Why don't you give it all to Jesus?' What about you, Mr. Brewster?"

"Yeah, well, I don't like to talk about it."

As they walk toward Clotilde, Brewster realizes that he's been extremely rude to a person who has opened her family to him. He's just about to speak when Holly tells him he'll drive himself to an early grave if he keeps everything inside. Surprised at her bluntness, he apologizes and tells how he and his wife were well established in their church, and he really thought he was a true believer until the accident. "I could not understand why Jesus took her away from me. Where was God?"

"So you've spent the past year being totally miserable to yourself and everybody around you," she says. "How does that make you feel? Any better?"

"With what's happened in the past few weeks, I've come to the conclusion it's me," he says. "I slammed the door and wallowed in my own misery. I'm the one who has to open up."

Their footsteps on the loose gravel remind him he has to buy cornflakes on the way home.

"I'll be honest, Brewster. Our lives were shaken to the core when Lily first got sick. Then there was Wendell's accident. Our world was crumbling. Wendell took my hand one night when I was visiting him in the hospital. 'Don't worry,' he said, brushing the tears from my cheeks. 'Let's pray.'"

They turn onto the soft, needle- and cone-strewn path to Owl's place. Brewster tiptoes into their quietness. "You are an astonishing family, Holly. The coralroot has introduced us, perhaps for a purpose we've yet to experience. Look." He pauses and lifts his camera to his eye. Lily is standing with her arm draped across Clotilde's shoulder. Sunlight bounces off her big pink hat, contrasting sharply with the green of the trees and the dark brown of the pathway angling across and behind them. Clotilde sits on her portable camp stool, her sketch pad across her knees. Her floral dress drapes to one side, providing a snug spot for Bebo. "This is a Rockwell moment if ever I saw one," he says. He positions and repositions, shooting from all angles to capture the backlit moment.

"Mommy, I want to draw like this lady," Lily says. "I can put the pictures on my wall."

Clotilde senses Lily's interest. She rummages in her bag, brings out a small sketchbook and offers it. She gently pushes Bebo to one side to make room for Lily, who squats on her knees, takes a green pencil from Clotilde's case and begins drawing the coralroot.

Brewster and Holly leave them and join Wendell nearby at the river. He hushes them as they approach and points to a garter snake wriggling its way upstream on the opposite bank. They spot another in the shadows.

"Sure is a magical day," Wendell says. "Twenty minutes here in the sun beside a lazy, wandering river has given me new energy." He turns to Brewster. "Lily has really taken to your artist friend."

"Speaking of Lily," says Holly, "we'd better get back and get her home."

Lily sees them coming, jumps up and starts yelling. "Look, look! The lady says it's really good. I made my stalks green—much better green."

"She reminds me of my Hannah at that age," Brewster says, realizing that this is the first time he's spoken of his children. "She's doing an earth and environmental sciences degree at university in Nova Scotia. We used to come here and do the same things. She loves the wild plants, just like her mother did."

"Mr. Brewster, this lady—I've seen her at the hospital. When she reads a book, she waves her hands like this, and Anil the deaf boy knowed what she was saying."

"Her name is Clotilde," Brewster says. "Look at her when you talk and she will know what you are saying. Clotilde is deaf too, and when you talk she can read words on your lips. Cool, eh?"

Bebo frisks around as Clotilde packs her things, and the Palmer family heads toward the car park. It's been an interesting and happy time, and Brewster wonders where it's all heading. Clotilde is very matter-of-fact, all business. *She obviously doesn't want anything to do with me.* He mutters something about his turn now, and he looks at the flower and considers his best angle. With a perfunctory "I'll be in touch," Clotilde and Bebo are gone. The silence of the woods surround him as he settles down with his cameras, and for half an hour he loses himself in his favourite pursuit, reminiscent of his times scrabbling in the underbrush as Melanie poked around looking for other hidden gems.

He elbows his way up to sit on his knees and unclamps his shoulders. He has the feeling he's being watched, but there's not a person in sight. A deer? No, there's not a sound.

"Why don't you give it all to Jesus?" Holly's question dangles in front of him. Harris' outburst sits on his mind. He tries to brush them aside. "Give what?" he asks, directing his question to the coralroot. "Me? I tried that, remember? But I wake up every morning." Pins and needles tingle and prickle his legs. He gets one leg up and leans forward on his left arm to stand. He looks around, certain now that he's not alone. He pulls his camera case over and leans on it to pull himself up. His legs throb as nerves rearrange their pattern. It's time to get back to the car park.

Give it all to Jesus, give it all to Jesus, give it all to Jesus. The words clang in his head. "What?" he screams. "What?"

"Hey, Brewster. You okay?"

José is about 30 feet down the path. "Oh, hi, José. Boy, you startled me there. It's just pins and needles and a bit of cramp." Brewster's words rush out in an embarrassed ramble. "Look, we have the striped coralroot."

"Man, that's cool," José replies as he comes alongside. "How'd you find that? Looks as though it would have been very well hidden until you started trampling all over the ground." He grins.

"Clotilde was here, and we had a family with us. It's been a good day," he says, fluffing up and rearranging the disturbed ground cover.

As they stroll back to the parking lot, Brewster talks about how he'd been led to the plant by a small girl's imagination.

"Pretty remarkable, I'd say. Sounds like one of those God moments," José says. "Well, I'm due over at the centre. Good to see you, Brewster. Glad the project's going well."

Brewster slowly packs his gear into the Jeep, methodically closes the tailgate, locks the vehicle and wanders over to the picnic table he'd shared a couple of hours before with the Palmers. "God moment," he murmurs. "What the dickens did he mean by that?"

Chapter Thirty-Two

Brewster wakes with a wild idea to paint the lounge and dining room. He looks around the room, and halfway through his breakfast, he gets up and rummages through a drawer where Melanie had carefully stowed the paint chips they'd decided on. The work will keep him busy while he waits on word from the park.

Hello Harris and Hannah,

I think I've gnawed my fingernails to the quick while waiting for word on the project. Today I finished painting the lounge, like your mother always wanted. It's the colour she chose, a warm sandstone. Looks good and fresh, but I think it needs a contrast wall somewhere. I can remember your mom talking about it, but I don't think it was ever decided. You guys might know more next time you are here.

Well, I just got a call from Louise at the park. We have a book meeting set for Friday afternoon. Sounds good to me, and then I'll be able to report on the next step in getting this work done. To say I'm a little bit excited is an understatement. I'm sure your mom will be pleased that her work and interest will see daylight in a glossy, full-picture book to be enjoyed by many users of the park and beyond.

The business is good, and when I last checked, Joel has successfully filled all vacant space. We have an insurance company as a new ground-floor tenant. A large company is pressuring us to sell them the building. We're into some heavy negotiations, but Joel is confident the sale will go through.

Must give Jo a call at the Blue Aster. Haven't seen her for a couple of weeks now.

Harris, you asked me about Irene. To bring you up to date, she finally heard from her long-lost husband because he wants a divorce. Joel and I helped her with her papers to get things settled. She was a bit distraught, as you can imagine, with her husband leaving on an overseas assignment and not coming back. She may pull out of Calgary and take a contract job with the Nicaragua canal project. Massive undertaking, and she may be working with a British company on some environmental aspects. Good opportunity for her.

As for me, I'm doing good and getting things together. Been going to the Rhodes for their small-group meeting. I've met too many people recently who by chance happen to tell me to "give it all to Jesus." So there you go. I'm following your advice too. One day I'll talk to you about all the blue asters showing up wherever I am. Not sure I've ever seen so many in one season. Makes me think there's something going on. But that's crazy talk.

Would love to hear from you soon. Thanks so much for your emails.

Dad

Brewster is sad that Clotilde is not at the meeting. As he understands it, she's closed up her house and moved her world to Cheticamp in Cape Breton, for an extended stay close to her parents' families. He hasn't seen much of her since the coralroot finding, and he recalls the day they bumped into each other at Louise's office when she mentioned very briefly she was leaving the city. His chin had dropped to his knees, or maybe the floor, saddened to lose all contact with her. He'd love to be with her, talk with her and hear her voice. The possibility of seeing her again has kept him attending his sign language training program.

"... But we're extremely disappointed to tell you, Brewster, that we will not be printing the book this year."

Brewster sits bolt upright. He'd fogged out for a minute as the discussion revolved around how wonderful the work is and the amount of work done to present the final draft. The technical information has been added, and the book is ready for final editing and design.

"Excuse me?" he says. "Did you just say that the book is not going ahead?"

"Yes, you heard that. We're so sorry to have to tell you that the budget monies we'd set aside have to be diverted into further flood recovery work. Our department considers that catering to the physical safety of our visitors has a higher priority."

"I don't believe it," he says. "I just can't believe it. All that work, our whole summer wasted. What happens now? Who owns the book now?"

"Well, technically we do," the department manager says.

"Technically? What do you mean?" Brewster feels the deep body blow and fights to keep control of himself. He sits and looks around the boardroom table. Louise, who has been their point person throughout the summer, looks down and fiddles with her papers. She must have known about this.

She looks up, her face serious. "I'm sorry, Brewster. I know what you're thinking: why didn't I speak up sooner? But you see, I think we all figured that somehow the funds would be found somewhere. Sure, we knew the project was in jeopardy, yet we kept on working at it."

The manager cuts in and explains that as the park requested the drawings and photographs for the publication, and that department staff had provided the scientific and botanical information, ownership of the work resides with the department.

"You mean to say you now own all of Clotilde's artwork?" *Keep calm, keep calm,* he tells himself as he feels the heat rising. "I know I gave you my pictures in Melanie's memory and love for the park; it was a voluntary donation. But Clotilde's work …"

"We did have an arrangement with her," the manager says. "She participated mainly for the exposure and a quantity of the books. Now, we'll have to check. It may be that she retains copyright, in which case we'll have to return them."

"There's one thing, Brewster," Louise says. "At this stage, we have not lost hope that the book will yet be published. Possibly next year, and we'll draft the new budget year accordingly. We may be able to find a grant for it. We want to see it done. As we have always said, this popular urban park needs it."

"Thank you," Brewster says. He has to leave. He picks up his briefcase. "I'll make contact with Clotilde."

He sits in his Jeep, fuming and feeling abandoned. *Clever of them to call the meeting for the end of the day.* He drives straight to his office.

"Joel, just had a bit of bad news. The park isn't in a position to publish the book. They blame it on budget. What if we publish it, or at least provide the funds? I just can't let it disappear into some bureaucratic filing system."

"Off the top, it shouldn't be problem," Joel says. "Be just like the Blue Aster. We'll form a division of BAM Inc. The only issue I see is the government and whether they will release it for private publication. But I think that will be a technicality that can be worked out."

It's Friday, and that means Shabbat begins at sunset for his Jewish friend.

"Okay, Joel. Get going home. That's all I needed to know at this stage. I'm going to speak with Clotilde tonight. Love to Anna."

Brewster sits at his office desk and sends a quick email.

> Hi Louise,
>   You certainly gave me a jolt today. I need to meet with you at 9:00 a.m. on Monday at your office. I think I may have a solution.
>
>   Brewster

He sits back and contemplates putting the call to Clotilde through from his office or from home. *I'm on a roll now—might as well try from here. Let's see, Three hours' time difference means it's about 8:00 p.m. there. Should be good.*

He reaches for his phone as his email dings.

> Brewster,
>
> Sounds good. Can we make it 9:30? I'm really sorry about things. I hope you're not too mad at me.
>
> L

> Louise,
>
> It's a deal: 9:30 it is. I'm not mad—bit hurt, maybe. But I was totally blown away. More surprised, really. All good. Enjoy the weekend.
>
> Brewster

He's only made a TTY call once before, and he's glad he kept a phone number for Clotilde. He feels new energy at the challenge as he speaks with the relay operator and explains his call. Technology that allows him to speak, the operator to type to the TTY, Clotilde to read and perhaps voice back to him. He hopes she will speak. He does want to hear her voice.

It takes a while for the connection and the explanation of the service from the operator. Brewster tells her about the sudden turn of events, in short and structured sentences. He listens to the operator's keyboard, and to Clotilde's quietly measured responses. The call is magic. His nervousness washes away when Clotilde finally says she's glad he called.

With that encouragement, he fires ahead and outlines his growing idea to have a new division of his company publish the book in cooperation with the park department. "I'll aim to have you and I hold the full copyright for the book. You retain your originals and all copyright for your artwork," he says. "I think the park should undertake a major role in promotion."

"It sounds like you have it under control, Brewster. I'm happy with that approach. Any chance we can have it by Christmas? I was hoping for Christmas presents, you know."

"We've got a lot of work to get through." He listens to the operator keying his words for Clotilde. "I'll have my lawyer draft it up once I finalize these ideas with Louise on Monday. We'll make it happen. How's life in Cape Breton?"

"Interesting," she says. "Different from what I imagined it would be. I've spent a lot of my time getting to know the various branches of the family and learning to lip-read their accents. Some of them have trouble realizing I can speak, so why can't I hear? No signing. I'm not sure this was a good move, but I'll get used to it. Nice people here, and my relatives are great."

"I know you've only met the once, but Hannah, my daughter at Acadia University, might come visit you. I mean, if that's okay with you."

"Would she? That would be terrific. I'd really love that."

#

He grabs a notebook, locks up the offices and heads to the elevator. No use going home to eat; a noisy restaurant might be the ticket. He doesn't want to lose this fresh surge of energy that's been slowly building since Lily first showed him the striped coralroot.

The Vietnamese place is good—not too busy and offering light food. Curry chicken and steamed rice are all Brewster needs as he makes notes for his talk with Louise on Monday. Gaillardia Press, a division of BAM Inc, has a nice ring to it. He's pleased with this name suggestion from Clotilde. In a follow-up text after the phone call, she said the flower was dramatic, a survivor in the prairie dry seasons. *Truly vibrant—like you, Clotilde*, he thinks.

A plate of food and two pots of green tea later, he sits back, arching his back against the floral cushions backing his booth. He reads the outline he's made to give to his lawyer.

"Is this worth an evening call?" he says to his server. She looks totally bewildered, smiles, collects the dishes, leaves the bill and walks away.

Brewster is eager to move on the book. With the time now nearing 9:00, he ponders briefly if it's too late to call Horton. The phone barely has time to ring before it's picked up.

"Hello, Brewster." The ever-cheerful voice of Margaret. "I bet you want my husband. Hang on; I'll get him. Horton, it's Brewster."

"Quite the PA system you have there, Horton."

"Sure is," the deep bass voice of his lawyer says. "Margaret is downstairs watching a movie, and I'm upstairs making a pot of tea. Not really my kind of movie, but it's entertaining."

Brewster outlines his plans for Gaillardia Press and the reasons behind the proposal. "I have a meeting with the park on Monday morning. Is there any chance I can send you my thoughts to see if there are any red flags?"

"No problem. This is a good weekend to do that because I have to be in the office tomorrow anyway, to get a couple of tough things out of the way. I'll have Abby in, and she can take a look; I'll review it."

"Thank you, Horton. You're a pal."

"Yeah, yeah. How're you making out? You sound a bit like the old Brewster tonight."

"I seem to have a bit of energy around this venture," he says. "I want to see it work, for Melanie and for the artist, Clotilde. I'll leave you with your tea and a movie, and I will email you my notes tonight. Thanks."

It takes Brewster another two hours to transcribe and expand on his notes, hammering out a basic proposal as he sees it. He reads it through, makes a couple of word changes and attaches it to his email with copies to Clotilde and Joel.

Satisfied he's done all he can tonight, he closes the computer, sighs, turns out the lights and heads to the bedroom—always the worst part of his day. He hates going to bed alone and is reminded of the advice of a close friend. Tomorrow he'll follow up on that idea and buy some new bedding to make the room comfortably his.

Will he ever get over feeling like just half a person?

Chapter Thirty-Three

Brewster picks up a box of Timbits on his way to the park office. "Morning break," he says as he offers the box to Louise.

"Well, this is surprise," she says. "You're looking very upbeat on this dull morning. I was a little afraid you'd come in all agitated and ready to give us a going over. Come help me get the coffee. I alerted Tanya, and she would like to join us, if that's okay with you."

The three of them sit down in the boardroom and enjoy the donuts and coffee as Brewster runs through his proposal. He's pleased with the work Horton did on his notes, tightening up and cutting out some of his wiffly-waffly expressions.

"We see that as there is nothing on paper between the three of us, Gaillardia Press would like to take the book on and publish it, in conjunction with the park by giving you full acknowledgement of your botanical contribution. We suggest the title as *Underfoot: 100 Wildflowers*. You've expressed a need for the book, and we really want to see it published. This is perhaps the best way to achieve both our objectives," he says, getting up and walking over to Louise. He picks up the box in front of her, lifts the lid and takes out a couple of pages, a Clotilde drawing and one of his photos. "This is a brilliant work and just has to be done."

Tanya, the senior education officer, wipes icing from her lips, smiles and nods. "This is an encouraging offer. I'm sure the department will go for it. We have much to gain from it, and the partnership you have outlined is very detailed. You've shown us all through the summer how we can work together. I'll talk to Edmonton this afternoon, and hopefully they will agree with your approach. Gaillardia Press, eh? I like it."

"How did you pull all this together over a weekend?" Louise asks. "It's a very detailed proposal."

Brewster is thrilled. "My undertaking to donate the photographs still stands," he says. "You will be able to use them at will, and even decorate your walls. The one thing I do ask is that we work together to get the book edited, designed and printed in time for the Christmas market. I can take care of all of that, and of course you will get to review the final proofs."

His feet barely touch the ground as he walks to his Jeep. He sends a brief text to Clotilde: "Success."

He calls Horton. "The meeting went very well," he says. "They understand the approach you helped me describe. I'm so glad you reviewed my proposal and made changes before I talked with them. Thank you. If all goes well, I expect to hear today. It's a win-win for us all. Once I explained our financial position, they relaxed, knowing that we wouldn't be coming along with cap in hand in a few weeks' time."

"You certainly have an interesting career, Brewster," Horton says. "In all the years I've known you, you've gone from being a tradesman, entrepreneur, business owner, property developer and now a book publisher. Me, I'm still a lawyer."

"And a brilliant one, my friend. You've been through everything with me; it's just that you're on one side of the paper, and I'm on the other. Thanks again for disrupting your weekend and making mine a turning point. When you draw up the legal papers, put Clotilde in as president, and Holly and Hannah as directors. I guess you, Joel, and I are in there ex officio through BAM Inc. Now I've gotta go tell Joel about all the excitement."

Joel is talking with Jane in the front office as Brewster walks in, beaming.

"Well, look at you," Joel says. "The most cheerful I've seen you looking for a long time. You even ironed your shirt."

"Good meeting. Looks like Gaillardia Press lives. I'm hoping we'll get approval in principle this afternoon. We are moving into the book publishing business." The three of them high-five, and Jane pirouettes in her wheelchair.

Brewster spends a couple of hours working in his office, emailing back and forth with Clotilde. She's elated that the book will get a wider exposure under Gaillardia with new retail opportunities. He sits back and thinks of Melanie and how much she would have liked to be part of this new venture, the realization of her concept and drive. The only way forward now is to get it done and share the beauty of the wildflowers with others. He relives the thrill she got each spring when they went out to find the wintergreens and check up on the variety of orchids. The flowers in the meadows, beside the streams, in the bogs and along pathways seemed to call out to her.

Not wanting to lose the momentum of the day, he drives to the mall for new bedding—something that's him and not the past, something different from the constant reminder every evening and every morning. "Make your bedroom cosy and you," is the advice he's been given. But he'd always been so wrapped in his own misery that he'd denied himself that switch.

"Something masculine, maybe natural tones and cosy," he tells the bewildered shop assistant. "You know, maybe bamboo colour? Yeah, maybe bamboo. A pattern is good."

"My husband would like these ones," she says. "He often says our sheets are too girlie." She laughs. "How would your wife like these?"

"Um," he hesitates. "Well, she died a year ago, and I've been told I should make my room different to make it easier to survive without her."

"Yeah, I've heard that before," she says. "I had a lady in here last week, I think, saying the same thing. I'm sad for you. Now, what about these? I think they go with you. These sateen sheets are really good quality, nice and soft. Queen or king?"

The afternoon draws on, and he hasn't heard from Tanya or Louise. He goes home with his new bedding and before he can doubt himself. He puts the sheets, pillow slips and matching duvet cover into the washing machine. While that's happening, he raids his freezer to see what it might yield. *Mmm, not much.* He picks out a small package of ground beef. *Looks like a pasta night.*

With one of Melanie's ABBA CDs on her aging boom box, he makes up his new bed with warm, freshly laundered and dried sheets. He likes the look of it—now it's his bed. He stuffs the old bedding into the washer to be cleaned for the OpShop.

Bing, bing, bing. His cellphone. Where? Oh, yes, still at the kitchen counter.

"Hello, Brewster here. Tanya? Yes, great afternoon."

"I've made the pitch to Edmonton, and they like the idea—a definite win-win," she says. "They have a couple of concerns on the legal side of things, such as liability. I suggest your lawyer and our legal dudes put their heads together and come up with an acceptable agreement."

Brewster doesn't know what to say. This is what he was waiting for, and he's speechless. "Great," he finally says. "I'll speak with Horton tonight, and he can contact your people. Can you email me the contact there?"

"Will do, Brewster," she says. She pauses and adds, "I'm very glad about this. Will you drop down tomorrow and pick up the full manuscript? We've added and placed our contribution in both the hard copy and the digital file. I'm sure you'll want to jump on this as soon as possible."

"Thank you, Lord, thank you," Brewster says as he slips the phone into his pocket.

He texts this golden moment to Clotilde. How he wishes she was here in person. He calls Horton and tells him the good news, adding that he is now Gaillardia's front man with the department legal beagles.

"It's a pretty simple solution, really," Horton says. "You mapped out your proposal very well, and with your financial ability, it makes it a no-brainer. We'll make the park folks shine."

Horton adds that he does not anticipate any issues in the agreement, which is aimed at safeguarding their participation in the book and resolving any question of liability.

Brewster chalks the successful day up to his changing view of grief. The gap will always be there, but he knows that he must plough on for Hannah and Harris—and perhaps one day, grandchildren. He knows now that Melanie will always be with him in the memories of their adventures and everything they accomplished together. He has to make the shift from then to now, otherwise he'll be no good to anyone. The book will keep him busy.

The pasta works out okay. His meatballs fall to bits, but it's not an issue tonight. Gourmet chef he is not, and that makes him think about the laugh he'd recently had trying to remember a password for one of his apps. He had to correctly answer security questions, the third and final of which was what was the first thing he'd learned to cook?

"An egg."

Chapter Thirty-Four

The dust hanger is still there. What did he expect? Of course the ceiling looks the same. Brewster moves his arm out of pure habit to the left side of the bed. No one there. It's been a good night, and he slept right through for a change. New bedding? Surely not.

With the stimulation of a new business venture, he's ready for action and determined to move into the day with a fresh attitude—a realization that he's been whining for far too long. "Stay busy," Joel and Anna have told him. He has plenty to occupy himself.

Horton anticipates the immediate needs of Gaillardia Press and *100 Wildflowers,* and he refers the names of a couple of editors, probably clients, and an introduction to a local book printer.

Louise greets him and hands over the manuscript. "I'm going to sit on Melanie's bench and have a good read," he says. As he avoids crashing through the main doors, Louise grins and says that in her very private opinion, everything is turning out for the best.

He sits in the morning sunshine and slowly reads through each page, utterly fascinated by what he holds in his hands: the culmination of their collective efforts. The flowers are broken out into families and then listed alphabetically. A glossary has been added as part of the botanical information, complete with Clotilde's pen drawings of flower structure, leaf type and leaf arrangement.

"Melanie, I so wish you were here to see how your vision has turned to reality," he says. "I'm just kinda blown away."

"Hello, Mr. Brewster." He turns to see Lily, her big blue eyes looking out at him from under her yellow straw hat. "I've been looking for you," she says. "Mom just said you were too busy, but I just knowed you'd be here one day and sitting here." She gives a thin, pale smile.

Her sparkle, he thinks. *Where's her sparkle?*

"Whatcha got, Mr. Brewster? Mom and Dad will be here soon. Mom's getting a picnic done, and Dad—well, he's not doing too good. His legs hurt a bit. Mom said we couldn't come today, but Dad said we should try 'cause I wanted to see you."

Brewster smiles at the courage of this sick little girl, ashamed of his own moods over the past few months. "I'm so happy to see you, Lily," he says. "Come up here on Melanie's bench and look at what I've got." He helps her up onto the bench. "This is a draft copy of the book on flowers I was telling you about last time. See? Look at this picture drawn by the deaf lady, Clotilde. Remember her?"

"Yes. But she doesn't come to the hospital now. I guess she waits for a deaf kid, but we haven't got any." She traces her tiny fingers around the drawing. "It's so nice, Mr. Brewster. Is she coming today?"

"Lily must have an extra sense, Brewster," Holly says as she wheels Wendell closer to the bench. "She was so insistent that I had to give in. It's … well, it's while we can."

"You mean before the snow," he adds, knowing full well what she meant.

Wendell nods and agrees. "An opportunity not to be missed, although it's pretty hard on Holly, and I'm not in the best of shape these days."

Lily has been carefully turning pages, absorbed in the pictures and the drawings. "This is the deaf lady's book," she announces. "And look—there's my flower!"

Brewster gets up and invites Holly to sit down so she can look through the box with Lily. He grabs the wheelchair and he pushes the wheelchair along the path. The two men talk, and Wendell opens up that Lily's prognosis is not good. "We're waiting on the results of more tests to see if full recovery is really possible. She's a brave little soul. We take it one day at a time. We have to. Things are a bit complicated too. I've been told they might have to amputate my left leg because of some infection."

Brewster gently probes deeper into the family's circumstances and learns that they are just scraping by. Holly had to quit her job as a proposal writer just to look after Wendell and take advantage of the time they could be with Lily.

"Yeah," Wendell says. "It's day-to-day, and I have to get this leg stuff sorted out so I can look for a job. Holly is stretched to the max, and it's starting to show. She's always been a very sunny person, but there are more cloudy days now."

Back at the bench, he finds both Holly and Lily engrossed in the book. Lily wants to learn to draw like Clotilde. Holly wants to advance her skills as a graphic designer.

Brewster carries Lily back to the picnic area. Her hat falls off as she tucks her head into his neck. Wendell carries the book and Holly pushes the wheelchair. "It's not much, but you are very welcome to share our lunch," Holly says. "We'd love it if you could. Just sandwiches and stuff."

Holly deftly turns the conversations away from health issues and talks of the hope they have that all will be well. Lily falls asleep in his lap. He carries her to the car, wraps her in a Tigger blanket on the back seat, looping the seat belt over her tiny body. Holly slips into an old, grey cardigan as he steadies and helps Wendell into the passenger side and then stows the wheelchair. They give Brewster their address and suggest he call ahead before visits to their home. "We spend so much time at the hospital that we are hardly ever home."

He waves and watches the family leave the parking lot. *Some people have it really hard. Oh, Lord, how can this be?*

At his office, he sends a quick email to Clotilde, telling her about the book and his encounter at the park with Lily and her family. He sends a copy of the note to Hannah, adding a personal bit at the end about his new bedding and the fact that he's eaten at home three days in a row.

Jane dumps a pile of folders on his desk. "Joel says they are self-explanatory," she states with a smile as she wheels toward the door.

"Just a sec, Jane," he says. "Could I get your help with something?"

He spends a few minutes talking about Holly, Wendell and Lily and their meeting at the park. "I don't know much about them and their circumstances, but I think it must be pretty grim," he says. "Here's their address and phone number. That's all the information I have. Do you have any way of learning a bit more about their situation without making any contact with them? I'd like us to do something for them if we can." He also asks after Joel.

"He's not in today," she says. "I think it's some event or registration at the school."

Brewster remembers that now and puts his mind to work on the work of business laid out so efficiently in front of him. An hour later, he packs up, grabs the flower book and gives the folders to Jane.

"All done," he says. "I'm off to the lawyer's, then to a book printer place here in town. Not sure I'll be back, but you know how to find me. Otherwise, I'll see you tomorrow."

He has a light bulb moment in the car park that causes him to abandon his afternoon plans and arrange to see Holly and Wendell instead. He calls Holly and finds out they are at home after taking Lily back to the hospital.

Chapter Thirty-Five

From the address, the Palmers do not live that far away, though they're in an older, more historic area of the city. He's at the underpass at the Bow River, sees a couple of kayakers suiting up and slows when his hands-free phone announces an incoming call. He has the road to himself, and he makes a fast switch into the picnic area.

"Hi, Jane. Just a sec. I'm pulling off the road."

"Just a couple of observations so far," Jane says. "I tried Facebook, and sure enough, Holly has a site, but as far as I can see, nothing has been posted there for at least six months—probably soon after Lily was first diagnosed with leukaemia. The last post was simply that Lily was sick and that the family would like prayers. I read the comments and from that found their church. I called there, and the reception lady said they were a lovely family, but she had not seen much of them for some time. She did say that one of their pastors visited them regularly, and I should talk with him. She understandably did not want to break any confidences, but after we chatted for a bit about the nature of my inquiry, she let on that things were pretty grim."

Brewster gets out of his car and walks to the river, where the now wetsuit-clad kayakers are pushing off for a cruise downstream. After talking with Jane, he begins to wonder if he's really doing the right thing, or if he's interfering. He decides to go with his gut. As he pulls into their driveway, he gets an inkling of why Holly had sounded a little reluctant to have him stop by late in the afternoon. Jane's findings and his knowledge about Lily add up to some devastating news.

Wendell opens the front door before Brewster walks up the crude plywood ramp covering the front steps. They greet each other warmly, and Holly invites him in. Their little house is sparse and not equipped for any sort of wheelchair traffic. Wendell laughs and shows off the collision points where he's negotiated the tight spots. "We had to sell our house because it was a two-storey, and we couldn't get up the stairs," he says. Brewster figures that means they could not keep up the mortgage payments. "So we're renting this one until I get on my feet."

Holly looks at him. There's a deeper sadness in her face than what he'd seen at the park just a few hours ago. She's been crying. He asks, "How's Lily?"

"We've just been told that her tests show little progress," Wendell says. Holly moves to the wheelchair and puts her hand on her husband's shoulder. "So we're not too chipper right now."

Brewster changes the subject, not wanting to add to their sadness. "You know, Holly, you said the other day that you were a proposal writer for a large environmental company but had to quit to keep things going here at home. You also told me you'd like to do more graphic design. Tell me if I'm out of line here, but I asked Jane at my office to check your LinkedIn profile, outlining your career background and experience."

"No, Brewster, you're not intruding," Holly says. "That's all public stuff. We've grown quite fond of you, especially Lily, and we've really appreciated the fact that we've been able to pray for you and see God at work in your life these past few weeks."

"Have you considered working from home until things settle down?" Brewster says. "I have an idea that might just suit you. When you and Lily looked through the book, what did you think?"

Wendell jumps right in. "She said it was awesome and couldn't stop talking about it. She wishes she could do something like that, instead of proposals. Design and communication really are her thing. It's how we met. She came into the dealership where I worked, wanting material and pictures for a new company website. She came over and talked to me about what I was doing to the car engine. I must have had a clean shirt on that day." Wendell laughs at the memory.

Holly's cheeks flame, embarrassed by her husband's outpouring of support.

"Yes, I've thought of working from here, but it's not what I can do as a proposal writer. I have to be in constant contact with people, resources and meetings. Besides, I no longer have a computer at home. That had to go, and we don't have Internet or cable."

Brewster asks if they have time to talk about his idea before they leave for their evening visit with Lily. "We maybe have an hour or so," she says. "We can perhaps have supper there."

"Let's order in—pizza or Chinese, or whatever. Your call, my treat."

Holly leaves the room to make the call. Wendell looks up. "She is very down, Brewster. I'm not sure how much more she can take. She does it all on her own—my appointments, the worry with my leg, very little income—and now Lily seems to be worsening. Our church helps. And there are some days folks come round to help with basic housekeeping and groceries. Not sure where it's all going. There's some silly holdup with the insurance for my leg, and if they have to amputate, it will take longer."

Holly is gone for a long time and finally enters the room. She's changed, but he can see she has been crying again—something the fresh makeup has not been able to mask. "Chinese," she says. "Be here in about 10 minutes because they are just round the corner. Irregular hospital visits have turned us into regulars."

Brewster goes to his car and gets the book box and his thumb drive. He looks at the house, a low-cost rental if ever he saw one. Peeling paint, roof tiles lifting, rusting eavestrough and a lawn in need of a mower. And yet in direct contrast, on either side of the ramp are flower boxes of flourishing blue, yellow, orange and red annuals, marigolds, petunias, violas, nasturtiums and geraniums. *A reflection of the hope inside,* he thinks.

"I like your flowers," he says as the doorbell rings. "I'll get that."

Holly puts out plates and cutlery as he opens up the Chinese takeout on the table.

"Looks good. What have we got?" In turn, they dip into the boxes and load their plates. It's a good-looking feast, particularly with their smiles and light laughter. Ginger beef, steamed rice, noodles and sweet-and-sour chicken go down just fine.

"That was great," Brewster says, "but time is running short before you have to take off for the hospital. What would you like to see, Holly?" he asks as he lifts the lid off the *Underfoot* manuscript box.

"Is this a test?" she says. "The book is terrific." Brewster sees the sad longing in her eyes as she pauses and looks up. "Not sure what you want me to say."

"How would you like to take it to final design? Design it, lay it all out, add what needs to be added like keys and colour—you know, turn it into something, turn it into a real book?"

Holly screws up her nose, puzzled and looks to Wendell. Then she looks back at the book where she flips another couple of pages.

"I can't," she says. "Been several years since I did book design, and that was in an earlier life, before I got into proposal writing to earn real money. Now, I don't even own a computer." She rushes from the room in tears.

Brewster feels a bit of a chump. "Wendell, I didn't mean to upset her like that. I figured she can do the job, so I asked. Someone has to do it, and when I saw her and Lily the other day, I saw she has the desire and the interest."

Holly returns when she is composed, and she clears away the dishes and takeout packets. She sniffles and avoids eye contact with her husband and Brewster. The two men watch her. Wendell reaches out, touches Brewster and puts a finger to his lips. They wait, twiddling fingers and looking at the table. Dishes clank and clatter into the sink. Leftover portions are boxed and placed in the fridge. *Another day, another meal*, Brewster thinks. *There's no such thing as waste in this house.*

"We'd better go, Wendell," she says finally. "Brewster, I'm sorry. Of course I want to, but I can't see how. C'mon, Wendell. I'll take you to the bathroom, and then we should be off."

As Holly manoeuvres the wheelchair into the passageway, Brewster recovers the thumb drive and asks Holly to chew it over and give him a call sometime. "Please say hi to Lily for me."

#

Brewster stands at Claire and Heath's front door. He needs to talk this through. "Please, Lord. Holly and Wendell need help, and their ship seems to be sinking very fast. First Lily, then Wendell. God help them."

He's about to hit the doorbell when Claire opens the door. "Look who's here," she says. "Saw you pull up in the driveway. You eaten yet? We're having supper, but there's plenty for all. Come in, come in."

"Thanks," Brewster says, "but I just ate with Holly and Wendell. But I'm up for dessert."

Brewster enjoys their company and the friendly banter until Heath interrupts. "You don't look as though you dropped in out of the blue just for berries and ice cream. What's on your mind?"

Brewster opens up about Holly and Wendell and their situation. "You know, I thought I had problems, but these folks are such an amazing couple with a beautiful daughter—and look at their situation. I think they're flat broke. They're struggling. Where is God in their lives?"

"I'll come to that, maybe," Heath says. "But I'd say you've been put in a very special position in the lives of this family. Think about how you met, and how a small sick little girl solved your problem. So what do we do with disappointment, when accidents happen and we feel so lonely we can't go another day? When faith conflicts with emotion? What are you doing about it, about the loss of Melanie?"

Brewster looks at him. Maybe he should have just gone home. "Thought you'd know, is all."

"Listen, the only thing we know is what we learn from the Bible. I don't think there's a lot God can do if we wallow in self-pity or get just get mad at Him," Claire says. "Faith allows us to reach beyond ourselves. Stretch out a hand for God to hold. Remember, He says He will never leave us. Have you left Him?"

Their conversation ranges back and forth, and each time Brewster questions his faith, Claire or Heath respond with an encouragement that they say comes from a life with Christ. "Think about it, Brewster. You attended all those meetings with Melanie. Think about what you heard and what you learned, what Melanie learned."

"But what about Holly and Wendell? Look at them. They might lose their daughter. And what about this infection Wendell has? How far will that go?"

"Brewster, we don't know the answers. Our confidence comes from bringing the matter before God. Our faith, difficult though it might be from a human perspective, is to leave it with Him and to trust that He is listening," Claire says.

"The final word from me in this, Brewster, is that we must listen. What is God telling you? You want my take on the blue asters you keep seeing? Let's see it as a reminder of God's promises that He's always around."

Heath and Claire walk Brewster to his vehicle. It is a lovely clear night, and they comment on the sliver of a moon. He contrasts the Palmers' house with the Rhodes' tidy, neat bungalow on a tidy, neat street.

With no answers, he mutters as he steers his way through the darkened neighbourhoods. *Never any answers.* He waits for the garage door to open, drives in, and switches off the car as the overhead door slowly closes. He thumps his steering wheel with both hands and screams, "Why, God? Why?"

He bursts into tears.

#

A couple of days later, Brewster dashes into his silent house to grab the ringing house phone. "Greetings," he says, slightly out of breath.

"Hello, Brewster," says Holly, barely audible. "I'd love to be part of your project, really, but I just ..."

The blaring toot-toot of a car horn takes him to the street window. It's not for him; a skateboarder crossing in front of a pickup makes a fist at the driver and rolls on to the sidewalk. *Crazy people.* "Holly? Holly? You still there?" he says.

"Hi, Brewster. Wendell here. Sorry about Holly's call—she's kinda beside herself right now. Not so good a report today about Lily, and yesterday ... Well, it looks like I'll be saying goodbye to my leg after all. They're scheduling surgery time."

"Wendell, thanks for calling. I just don't know what to say. Want me to come over?"

"It's okay, Brewster. We'll get through this, I know."

Brewster asks if it is okay to talk. "I want to bounce an idea off you. I'd like to send our techie over and put a new computer into your house for Holly to use. It's a new iMac with all Holly's preferred software that she talked about the other night. He can bring it in when Holly is not home. Maybe a surprise for her."

"Sounds like a bold plan, but you don't have to do this, you know."

"I understand. But listen, it's a way for a bit more independence. I'll pay Holly her going rate, and when the book is done, I'm sure it will lead to more work. That way she can be home for you and Lily. We need a designer for the book, so it might as well be Holly." He pauses. "And what if we get someone in to help with the daily chores? You know, ease the load a bit?"

Brewster encourages Wendell to think about it. "There's no need for an immediate answer. Just work it through and call me back. The more I think about it, Wendell, the more I'm satisfied that this is an answer to our prayers, that God brought us together. I was at a prayer get-together with some friends the other night, and everyone agreed this is not some random thing."

They're about to hang up when Brewster adds, "I've spent the past 15 months or so governed by my own out-of-control emotions. It's not the way I want to live."

Chapter Thirty-Six

Hello Clotilde,

You'll be amazed at what is happening with our book. Holly is making solid and exciting progress on the layout and design. We met yesterday with the park team as well, and Holly reviewed her progress. The attached is a review for you, so let me know any concerns or suggestions you might have. I'd like us to add a dedication page and want you to send me your ideas.

As for the family, Lily has stabilized, which is really good news. Wendell likes—if that's the right word here—having lost his leg. He's looking forward to the time that his stump heals and he gets a prosthetic so he can walk. He's already tried standing on the other leg and moving round with crutches.

With Lily's steady improvement I wonder if you'd like to send her a note or something from you. She hasn't had any day outings for a while now, and she keeps asking when you're coming back because she wants to draw flowers like you. Perhaps a sketchbook and pencils, and a wee note on how you started drawing, or even how you begin working on flowers. She has lots of fresh flowers in her hospital room. It's just a thought.

She was so thrilled the other night when I went up for a visit to give her the photograph I took of the day you two met. It's a lovely shot (I've attached it) of you sitting and drawing the striped coralroot on the plaid blanket, with Bebo beside you. Lily is standing beside you, watching, with her arm resting on your shoulder. I took it as Holly and I walked along the path toward you, and I noticed how the sun was lighting this little scene amongst the spruce trees. The picture I took of her kneeling in the grass sniffing a gaillardia is a beauty too.

Hannah told me all about her visit to Cheticamp and how much she enjoyed the tour up the Cabot Trail. She says she's heading your way again for Labour Day weekend and your family get-together. She says being with you all helps her French before her Europe trip.

Let me know your thoughts on the draft layout and design. I think you should plan on being out here when we review the printer's proof and do our final liaison with the park. At that time, the park wants to talk about the book launch. Gaillardia Press will arrange your bookings nearer the time.

I look forward to your email. I miss your laughter and your smile.

Brewster

Attach two pictures. Click. Send. He sits back in his chair, rolls his neck, and chews over the conflict of his faithfulness to Melanie and his deepening fondness for Clotilde.

Jane wheels in at the right moment to interrupt with some tenant files. She says Joel would like to drop in.

"Now's good, whenever," he says. This is crunch point with the future of his building. Joel wants an answer for the prospective buyers. "Where are we at, Joel?" he says as his friend slumps on to the leather couch by the window. "Is this the time?"

"I think so," Joel says. "They've upped their price three times now, so we either do or don't. I say we do. They've agreed to keep me here running the place for up to five years. Their plans to move into the building will not happen right away. They've accepted our submission on behalf of the tenants too."

Brewster looks out the window and gives a silent prayer. "What'll we do next?" he says.

"Ha! I don't think that's a worry. We have plenty on the go, and I'm sure you will have something new come along sooner or later."

"You're right. Has that landscaper fellow cleaned up his lot and paid his lease?"

"All fixed up. Devi went over, helped him through and got him on the right track. The city won't bother him again, and we've helped put his accounts and invoicing in order. They're an excellent couple in a new, flourishing enterprise. They just got lost in their work and forgot the business side of things. We did that at no charge or penalty, so I think they'll keep their accounting with me."

"I like your style, Mr. Joel," Brewster says with a smile.

An hour later, Brewster is out for some quiet, mid-afternoon exercise. He figured on a slow jog, but a few muscles screamed at him about that. He hasn't been near this pathway for some weeks. *Start slow and warm up.* There are small sailboats out on the water, the aspens are golden and leaves crunch underfoot—a beautiful, fresh afternoon. Wild blue flax wave their blooms, partially protected by the higher grasses. *Late*, he figures. *A double crop this season. And the pale blue flower only lasts a day.*

He dismisses the sudden urge to pick up a meal-to-go at the supermarket on his way home and opts for a home-cooked meal of whatever he can find. Melanie's mystery freezer still yields surprises, and tonight it's a lamb chop, which he grills and lines up with boiled potatoes and a salad he's still reaping from last week's head lettuce.

The day has been profitable, and as he eats, his iPad dings.

Brewster,

C'est merveilleux. Holly is doing a wonderful job with our book. I love how she's combined all the elements just as we first envisaged. Can we have a dedication to both Melanie and Helene—you know, for their inspiration and initiative? Maybe Holly can word that for us.

I'd love to come out with Hannah to see the printer's proofs.

C

P.S., I miss you and your energy.

The message is more satisfying than the meal, and he finds himself eager to have the proofs done so he gets to see her again. He'll practice his sign language in front of the mirror tonight. He's six weeks into the 10-week course, and he wants to build his vocabulary. *She'll be surprised.*

Five-letter word for twig junctures. He enjoys the newspaper crossword: simple and quick. *Nodes,* he prints into the squares. *Hunt and peck? Mmm, only four letters. Of course—my style at the keyboard: type. Canal and lake? Erie.*

He gets a phone call. "Hello, Joel. Not usual for you to call at night. What's up?"

"Well, it's Anna's insistence, because you said you're heading over to see Holly in the morning. One of the townhouses BAM owns in the southwest is up for rent. The tenants have done a run. Devi and Brian were over there this afternoon. We've got a bit of a cleanup to do, but we thought Holly and Wendell might like to move in."

Brewster thinks for a bit. "Not a bad idea, but my mind goes to the extreme. I'd love them to have it. I've even thought of buying them a place, but I'm a bit cautious about overpowering them. They're a very humble and private couple."

"That occurred to us too," Joel says. "I thought we'd rent it to them for what they're paying now. Sure, that's less than market value, but they need a break. Paying the rent helps them to maintain their benefits while Wendell heals. I hear he figures on going back to his work as a service tech at his old firm."

"That's his plan, all right. Not sure how long it takes to be fully mobile with a prosthetic, but he's a fighter. I'll raise it in a general sense and see what the reaction is."

The following day he pulls into the driveway of the sad looking house. Holly opens the door just as he's about to knock. "You're late," she says. "It's two minutes past 10:00 and you said you'd be here at 10:00."

They laugh. This is the happiest he's seen her in a few weeks. Before he has time to get through the door and make a comment, she blurts out, "Lily's new tests are good. Her oncologist reviewed them with us last night. He cautioned us not to get our hopes up too high, but he conceded that things are looking good—really good."

Brewster closes the door and gives her a hug as loud language erupts from the lounge area.

"Don't mind him," Holly says. "Wendell figures he's training for a triathlon, so his ego gets a bit bruised when he falls over. I've told him he's going too fast and too soon, but he insists. I must say, he's doing really well."

Brewster tells them about his visit with Lily at the weekend and the picture poster he'd made for her of the striped coralroot she'd found. He'd added an owl into the tree and had a Tigger looking out from the undergrowth.

"Oh, she loves that picture," Wendell says, demonstrating how good he is at standing on one leg. "We put it in a picture frame last night. Her nurses love it and wanted to know all about it. Our little girl can tell an amazing story."

Holly closes off their book discussion with the comment that she figures about one to two more weeks at her current rate of progress. Then it will be in shape to go to the printer.

"One other thing I have for you," Brewster says. He outlines Joel and Anna's suggestion they move to the single-level, ground-floor townhouse his company owns in the southwest. "Same rental payments as you have here," he says. "It's a really nice place, but the tenants we had didn't look after it, and it needs a bit of a cleanup. Our building guys are looking after that now. What do you say?"

Holly and Wendell look at each other. "This can't be true," they say. "A new house?" Holly squeezes Wendell's hand. "Yes," she says. "I can't stay here much longer. Anything would be better than this place. We actually had a break-in the other night, when we were at the hospital. We surprised them when we came home. Fortunately, they didn't get the computer because I always put it in the closet when we go out. The police came but couldn't do much."

"Sad to hear about that," Brewster says. "I think you'll like the new place. Quiet street, and not that far from the park. We'll draw up a contract, but don't worry, there's no money required. It will be for your protection as well as ours. Our building folks will look after your moving."

Holly recaps the book progress, and they agreed it could be three, maybe four weeks to get a printer's proof. She asks if Clotilde should come out to review the proofs.

Wendell chips in and gets a dig in the ribs from his wife when he says, "We're not sure if it's just the proofs you'd like to see her out here for."

They have a good laugh at Wendell's wry humour as they walk to the front door. Brewster turns, gives each of them a hug and steps out.

"My car," he says. "My car—it's gone! In broad daylight, too."

Chapter Thirty-Seven

The cyclist sits astride his mountain bike, one foot on the armrest of the park bench. He drinks from a tube to the water bag on his back. His wheels are thick with mud, his shoes and legs are splattered, and there are flecks on his face and arms. Brewster grins at the sight. "Looks like you've been having a bit of fun off trail."

"Yeah," the cyclist laughs. "Big bog in there." He screws around on his seat to point down the trail. "I came around this sharp corner, heading downhill a bit, and there it was. *Wham*, I hit it hard. Thought I was going to come off face first, but I managed to find a bit of traction and pedalled out. Powerful, man."

He pedals off down another semi-concealed trail, and Brewster wipes the mud from Melanie's bench. He sits at the opposite end to enjoy the late afternoon sun. A young jogger paces past, her ponytail flipping side to side through the gap in the back of her ball cap. She skirts to one side to allow room for three women and their strollers to move past on the paved path.

This park is always busy, he thinks. The shadows slink ever closer to his feet, stretched out into the grassy patch. He grins at the blue aster at the edge facing into the sun—the park's late bloomer. *This has been quite the summer, and this seat started a startling sequence of events. My life continues to change.*

He looks at his phone. "Hello, Holly. I'm down in the park, at Melanie's bench. It's a great spot at this time of the day."

"We're all moved into the new place," she says. "We can't believe how nice it is. It's such a marvellous change from where we were." There's a short pause. "Lily is over the moon. She got a surprise package of art materials and a nice letter from Clotilde today. It made her day. We haven't seen her so happy for some time." Another pause. "Clotilde also had a note in there as to how she started her drawing."

Emotion moves through the air, and Brewster jumps in. "It's a nice place, and I always liked how it is situated to the sun throughout the day. Glad you like it. It'll be great for your budding artist when she comes home." He immediately regrets making this comment, in case …

Holly says, "I have a meeting with the printer in the morning so I'll update you with the progress then. I just had to tell you how grateful we are for this house. It takes away a huge worry and gives Wendell time to get healthy. Almost forgot—my final thought for today. Clotilde told Lily that she misses us all."

He sighs and pockets his phone. "Well, Melanie, what do you think? It's all happening, and your dream of a book of the park's wildflowers is entering the home stretch."

The late afternoon solitude is broken with the dings of his cellphone. "Brewster?" It's Claire. Heath's got the barbecue bug. You'd better come over and taste some of his outdoor cuisine."

An hour later, he's sitting on the Rhodes' patio, knowing that one of the best things about the barbecue will be dessert. Claire's contribution to the evening feast tonight is key lime pie.

"Superb," he says. "You two certainly know how to make that barbecue hum! Melanie wouldn't let me near ours after the time I burned my nose and singed my eyebrows."

Their conversation is wide-ranging, from Brewster's day in the park to progress on *100 Wildflowers* and the likelihood that Clotilde and Hannah will be out to review the proofs.

"How is Clotilde liking it in Cape Breton?" Claire asks. "She's in Cheticamp, I remember you saying. We had lunch there when we toured the Cabot Trail—10 years ago, was it, Heath?"

Brewster tells them about the email he received a few days prior from Clotilde. "I get the feeling she's rethinking her decision to move there. She wrote about how she spends hours sitting in an historic and very beautiful church, thinking. Says her extended family is very supportive, but she finds the place too far away. She's not found a way to be involved with anything."

"It'll be interesting to hear what she has to say when she gets back here," Claire says. "And Hannah's coming too?"

"There's a growing friendship between them, and they reminisce a lot about Calgary. Hannah's been up to Cheticamp, and Clotilde toured her round that Acadian region."

Heath looks at Brewster. "You really like her, don't you?"

"Mr. Rhodes, that is none of your business," Claire says. "Leave the man alone."

"Well, you said it the other day," Heath says, looking at her. "Besides, what's wrong with saying it? Brewster?"

"Not sure what's going on here, but it seems everybody wants to know the answer to the same question. First, Joel's giving me Anna's opinion, then Irene and now you two. Clotilde and I have merely worked on a project together. We've had our ups and downs, and we're pleased to see our efforts coming together. End of story."

"Yeah, yeah, buddy," Heath says. "But still—you have a tender spot for her. She's a looker too."

Claire scolds, "Heath Rhodes, you stop that at once, or I'll be thinking it's *you* who has a thing for her." She turns to Brewster. "Anyway, if you like her, tell her and don't let her get away. You can't spend your life alone. You're just not built that way."

Brewster is puzzled as he drives home. Both Irene and Claire used almost the same words to him: "Can't spend your life alone. You're not built that way." *Is this women's intuition?*

That night he decides to write another letter.

My Dearest Melanie,

I said my last letter would be the last, but it just cannot be. Not yet, my sweet Melanie. This ache and longing lies deep inside. I've been living in this confused state of my faithfulness to you and a desire to not be alone anymore. I've got to stop hanging on to the bitterness of you being yanked out of my life. I feel guilty every time I'm with Clotilde, yet I look at her and have the same experience with the same feelings I had when you and I first met. I remember too how you blew up one day and said we would not get married if I kept drinking. Yet we did get married, and I continued drinking until the blackouts started, when I couldn't remember where I'd been or how I'd made it home. Then I realized God had a call on my life, and I quit cold turkey. Your love and the love of Christ prevailed and brought me to my senses. I owe you my life and what we built together, and yet you are no longer in it.

Perhaps it's because I'm avoiding the issue, but suddenly people have wanted to know about my relationship with Clotilde. There is none. We are good friends and enjoy each other's company. Something must show of my regard for her. Claire tells me to stop mooning about, yet I didn't know I was. I'm so sorry to tell you this, but you're the only person I know who'll listen. Clotilde and I have never been anything but collaborators on the wildflower book. She and Hannah are getting along really well, but I think that's because Clotilde feels a misfit in Cheticamp, too isolated and regretting her move there.

The book is all but done now. We have a proofing round with the park in maybe two weeks, and then you'll see your concept rolled out. It will certainly get a good launch and publicity because I'm sure the park will put it on their mailing list.

I wish you were here to see it.

I wish ...

Chapter Thirty-Eight

They stand gazing up at the sandstone cliffs. Fish Creek murmurs by in a lazy, end-of-summer, low-flow way. *No worry, no hurry. What a story these cliffs have.* Possibly as a level of subtle preservation, the main park pathways don't lead this way. Yet just a bit further down the pebbly beach are the charred remnants of a campfire.

"These banks are part of the Porcupine Hills formation," Irene says. "Millions of years old. Also, I understand the banks were used as a buffalo jump."

Underneath the pathways, beyond the trees and the flowers and buried in the cliffs, are stories to be told and secrets to be kept.

"It is truly a fascinating area and a city gem," Brewster says. "And it is so well used year-round."

They find a rock to sit on and Irene pulls a couple of cans of pop from her backpack along with a chocolate bar each. "Thought we might need a snack," she says. "It's so gorgeous here today, 'Far from the madding crowd ...' Soon I'll be in a different environment altogether. You haven't asked me about my trip to London."

"I gather that's why we're down here in the park," Brewster says. "I figure you have something to say, but I'm not sure whether it's to do with the lawyer and Mark, or with the canal project."

"You're just far too cautious. C'mon, we're friends. I have news on both fronts. Which do you want first?"

"The good."

"Both good. All the stuff with Mark is signed, sealed and over with. The lawyer did everything, and the divorce will be complete in the near future. I'll be single again, and I have money in the bank. The new twist is that there was a letter from Mark, held by the lawyer until I'd signed. I read some parts but couldn't deal with it. I put it through the shredder. It was one of those apologetic things—no substance, all about his needs, and he even said we shouldn't have married in the first place. That made me feel real good, I can tell you." She snorts. "I loved him, Brewster. I really did."

The river picks up her words and carries them into the past, as it has done through the years with this ancient hunting ground, farmland and recovered wilderness.

"As for the interview and the possibility of leaving for the tropics, that's all go. I've accepted and will head out for orientation in a couple of weeks. Then it's back again to close up my things and hand over my clients to others in the office, and I'll be gone. Not sure for how long, but it will be a mixture of fieldwork and analysis."

"Congratulations on both fronts," Brewster says. "I'm really glad for you and this terrific opportunity. Just from the little I know about you, the work will stretch you into new areas."

"Oh, it'll stretch," she says, as she stows the empty cans and papers into her pack. "It'll stretch. Now, how's the book?"

Brewster fills her in on the twists and turns of progress while she has been out of town. "I'd like to think it's possible to get Clotilde and Hannah out from Nova Scotia in a few weeks to review the printer's colour proofs. If all goes well, we might have books in our hands inside a couple of months."

"You really like that artist, don't you? I can tell by the way you look when you say her name. Good for you." He blushes and looks away, suggesting they should probably be on their way. "If you like Clotilde, then tell her," Irene insists. "I'm sure Melanie, from her current view, would be very pleased for you. Don't get into the memory thing. You're not a man to spend the rest of your life alone."

He gives her a peck on the cheek when they reach her vehicle, and they agree to a dinner date some night before she leaves town. He says,

"If it works out that Clotilde and Hannah are here, we could make it a foursome—three exceptionally beautiful women, and a lonely slightly bewildered man."

She laughs, waves and drives away.

Chapter Thirty-Nine

A keen buzz fills the park meeting room. The printer's proofs are all laid out on the table. Clotilde, as president, introduces the Gaillardia Press group, Holly as designer, and Hannah and Brewster as directors. Brewster knows all but two of the park attendees and supposes they are down from head office; possibly they're connected with the material the park has supplied and any legal ramifications.

This is Holly's show. She's confident as she reviews her design elements, which were developed in consultation with the park's Calgary-based education group. She explains the process she'd like them to follow in checking the proofs for colour, placement, page numbers and the physical look of the finished book. Editing changes have been completed in earlier rounds and were rechecked. Hannah hands around different coloured stickies to each person to place where there is a question or comment.

As Holly starts to move the pages around the table, a head office person suggests that the final colour proof process is premature because the legal team has not yet seen the page proofs.

Brewster inwardly groans at this totally unexpected turn of events, but Louise jumps right in and, referring to her notes, says the page proofs were sent in on the 3rd of the previous month and returned with changes on the 12th. It is her understanding the proofs were fully reviewed and signed off by all head office personnel, as previously advised.

Tanya looks across at him as he sits up in his seat. Her brow furrows, and she mouths to sit tight. He does. The speaker says he has not seen the proofs and wants to know who in his office signed off on them. Louise refers to her notes and reads out the names of the department approvals. She passes the earlier proofs across the table.

Holly continues and suggests the proofs go round the table for any general comments. She volunteers to leave them at the park for further review and pick them up at the end of the day. "We will do what we can to make everyone comfortable," she says.

Brewster leaves the room for a break and walks along the corridor to the main entrance, looking at the selection of his pictures, now mounted and brightening the office walls. He stops to look closely at the Western Canada violet, a beautiful little flower. He smiles, recalling Melanie doubling over in laughter the time he'd called it a mariposa lily.

"Get it right, Brewster," she'd said. "About the only thing they have in common is they're white." His recollection of plant names had been a constant source of amusement for them both.

Footsteps break his musing, and he turns to see Clotilde heading outside on a bathroom break for Bebo. When she returns through the main doors, he slowly plucks up courage to sign, "How is progress in there?"

"Brewster, you sign!" She rushes forward and throws her arms around his neck. "When, how?"

With sign and voice, he hesitatingly explains how he's been attending sign classes for the past few weeks just so he could communicate better with her if and when they ever met again. "I wanted to sign when I met you and Hannah at the airport, but I decided that was too public. And at home, well, I just wanted to wait for the right moment."

Clotilde and Hannah had arrived two days earlier, and it was good to feel the house busy again. Clotilde enjoyed baking, and this morning they'd had a feast of fresh muffins with coffee. Evening meals were special now, and both Clotilde and Hannah eschewed any idea of his to eat out. "You eat out too much, Dad," Hannah had said. "And I miss home cooking."

"Clotilde," he starts.

But she puts her finger on his lips and then signs, "Not now—we should go back in."

Hannah looks up from her proof sheet. "Um, I'm not as good as Mom, but I think we might have a whoops here. From what Mom told me, I think the prickly rose—that's Alberta's wildrose—and the prairie rose have been switched. Clotilde, you might be able to tell from your drawings."

Tanya gets up from her chair and moves to Hannah. "Let's see here."

Everyone looks up as Tanya compares the pages and the drawings with the flowers.

"Good catch, Hannah," she says. "We need to have either the artwork pages switched or the photograph and information pages. What do you say, Holly?"

"I'll have them corrected. No problem," she says. "I'm just glad that they're sequential pages."

When Holly senses that the proofs have been given a thorough workover, she stands and says she will leave the proofs with the park, returning at 4:00 p.m.

Tanya thanks her, compliments Hannah's eagle eye, and agrees with the suggestion for extra time to have a final read through, cover-to-cover. "We'll go through them again because I'm sure we all agree this is too marvellous a resource to have even the slightest error."

#

"That went really well, though I was a bit worried when that head office guy raised a flag at the beginning," Holly said once they were all in the car park. "What's everyone going to do for the afternoon?"

"I'm going to pick up my new Jeep," Brewster says, "and then I'm not sure. I feel like going for a walk in the park, maybe from Voiter's Flats. Should be nice through there."

Clotilde says she wants to see Lily and agrees to go with Holly, who is also heading to the hospital. Hannah wants to be dropped off at the Blue Aster to spend the afternoon with Jo, amongst the flowers.

"Good, we all have plans," Brewster says. "Let us know how you get on when you pick up the proofs, Holly. I'm sure everything will be okay. I'm glad you gave them the opportunity for their own private viewing and discussion. All good."

They go their separate ways, fully believing that their combined efforts through the summer have paid off. Brewster has unvoiced reservations, knowing from bitter experience how life can turn on a dime. In the words of Yogi Berra, "It ain't over till it's over." He's worried about the head office representative, who he'd noticed did not really enter into the process. Perhaps he's being oversensitive.

He tries to pay attention as the sales manager goes over the features of his new, beautiful Jeep, replacing the one stolen from Holly and Wendell's place a few weeks earlier. Things are different from his now-mangled, 2-year-old, written-off and junked vehicle. It had a sad end. Like a lot of things in his life, the theft and wreckage was not only unexpected, but also something that had not happened to him before. Driving off the lot, he admits he didn't want a new vehicle. The now-wrecked one was fine, and it was something he and Melanie had bought together. It was as much hers as it was his; they were a one-car partnership. If only she'd taken the car that day, or even if he'd picked her up after her appointment she'd be here today.

"Uncharted," Irene had said when they were at Revelstoke. "Life is uncharted—no blueprints, topo maps or GPS."

Heath disagrees with this view. For him, the only charts needed are available in God's word. "Emotions might swing a bit," he says, "but the pathway is as true as Route 66."

Brewster pulls into his driveway, switches off the car and sits looking at the house he had shared with his wife. The gardens and lawns are once again maybe three points above unkempt. He'll have to get a service in, not his friends, to spruce up the place and get it back to where it was: a colourful oasis in the street. He feels bad that he's not maintained the place since Heath's workforce did so much earlier in the summer.

In less than 24 hours, he'll be on his own again as Clotilde, her Bebo and Hannah return to their lives in Nova Scotia. *It's been brilliant having them. Good meals, great company, lots of laughter. Tomorrow, night all will be quiet.*

"Whatcha doin', Dad?" says Hannah, as she climbs into the passenger seat. "Nice wheels. Same colour and everything as the last one. I thought I was seeing things."

"Hi, kiddo. Had a good afternoon with Jo at the flower shop?"

"You bet. I'm glad I went, and moreover, I was needed. That is some busy place."

They walk into the house. "Gonna be very quiet here tomorrow night, with you two gone," he says. "That's what I was thinking about while sitting in the car."

"Just one day at a time, Dad."

Holly's car pulls into the driveway. Clotilde is driving. Holly has her face in her hands, sobbing.

Chapter Forty

A very irritable Brewster pushes the visitor bell inside the park administration building and waits. He feels a nervous dampness under his arms.

"Hello, Brewster," comes a voice from behind him. Louise. "We're down in the meeting room. I think I know why you are here. Come on through; it's just Tanya and me. Let me get you a coffee."

He looks at Tanya, and when he sees how subdued the two women are, he takes a deep breath to calm down. "What on earth is going on?" he asks. "What did that fellow mean that Gaillardia Press, in so many words, is a bunch of amateurs, a wealthy businessman, a university student, an unemployed deaf nurse and an unseasoned graphic artist? I hope there's a good explanation, otherwise I'm here to pull *Underfoot: 100 Wildflowers* away from the park, remove all reference to your work, and go it alone. We are absolutely shattered after all we have done together. First the budget, and now the bureaucracy.

"I hear you, Brewster. We feel the same. Shattered," Tanya says.

"I showed him the agreement that the lawyers drew up. We explained our processes, that everything had been done in accordance with the agreement," Louise adds. "We're flabbergasted with his response. He took the proofs with him even though Holly specifically asked him not to."

"Everything was going so well, and now this," Tanya says. She shrugs and holds her hands out in apology. "It's beyond our control now. We showed him everything—all the head office contacts, proofs and sign-offs—but they've assumed control."

Brewster looks at them and slowly sips his coffee. Three deer walk past the picture windows, pause and look in. They continue their browse before stepping daintily into the trembling aspens. "Role reversal," Brewster says. "They're outside looking in at us, three miserable plant lovers trapped behind a glass wall. We are the wildflowers."

Tanya and Louise smile at his comment.

"Okay, then, here's what I'll do. I'll have Horton, my lawyer, get clarity. Let's see how that works out. I'm sure your bureaucrat will be a little bit wiser as to what has been created," he says. "I'll let you know as soon as I hear anything."

Horton is stunned at the news, remains calm and tells Brewster to leave it with him. He'll call his contacts in the department who were associated with drawing up the original agreement. "Don't worry. I'm sure it's just a misunderstanding."

Brewster knows he's supposed to let go. He's being told to let go of a lot of things lately. "What do you think of this pickle, Lord?" he says as he heads home to take Clotilde and Hannah to the airport. "I know, I know. You'll just tell me to trust you and be patient. So okay, Lord. I'll wait now until Horton calls me. Over to you."

There's not a lot to talk about in the 30-minute drive to the airport: the weather, the long flight, the great proofs and Holly's design skills. In their shared sadness, they agree it'll be a drop and drive at the airport; no waiting around. Hannah, Clotilde and Bebo will check in and head to the gate. The hard-working little dog needs to take it easy before getting on the plane. Clotilde's hug seems to have a little more depth and warmth, a closeness Brewster's not sensed before. Hannah holds him tight and whispers, "She's loves you, Dad. Please think about it." He watches them disappear into the terminal.

"Sir, no waiting—you'll have to move along."

He looks at the security person, smiles and says he's on his way. "They're two special women," he says.

"I'm sure they are," the security woman says.

#

Another day slips by, and another. He's anxious but remembers he'd said he would wait. "But how much longer?" He immediately realizes his impatience. "Oops. Sorry, Lord."

Uppermost in his mind these days is what the future holds now that he's sold his building and principal business interest. Essentially, he's free and in his early 50s. He sits on the rocks down by the Bow River—a lazy afternoon in the sunshine. He watches an angler fly fishing and contemplates whether that might be an interest he could develop. It looks so peaceful, a tranquil pursuit where a person could find that sweet spot in a day. He tries to recall if he'd ever discussed that with Melanie. His cellphone rings.

"Hello, Horton. You should be down by the river here with me in the sunshine instead of being up there in your tower watching the world go by."

"You sound chirpy for a change," Horton says. "Somebody has to look after your affairs. Anyway, I've got good news. All is well. The fellow you spoke about, Stan, was a bit taken aback. I guess he was on vacation and hadn't been briefed on the project by his associates. Bit of tension in his department, by the sound of things. His main concerns were whether the department publications group had been involved, and he wanted an assurance that the book will be up to department standards. He also wanted to know about the ability of the printer. To cut it short, his staff said the printer was well-known for high quality."

"He needn't have been so rude about our gang," Brewster said. "Still, it's all sorted out, and that's all we need to know. Thanks for lifting this load."

The fisherman has moved downstream a bit. Brewster watches the line flick in and out, rest on the water and repeat. *Must be quite an art to it,* he thinks. *Catch and release.* He's about to walk over to the angler for a closer look when his phone buzzes again.

"Hello, Wendell."

"Wonderful news here, Brewster. Holly's up at the hospital, and we think Lily might be home with us very soon—this week, even. She hasn't had one negative test for a couple of weeks, so it looks like the treatment is finally working. We're very hopeful."

"Excellent, Wendell! We might get another picnic in at the park before the snow flies," he says. "How's the leg?"

"Funny thing is I thought it would be easy, that the stump would heal up, they'd give me a new leg and I'd be walking. Not so. Now I find it's going to take a good, long while. Basically, I have to learn to walk again. But if athletes can run on their bionic legs, then I will too. Odd, though: I still think the leg is there. Everyone says one day at a time. I'm getting a bit tired of that expression."

"I hear you. I've been hearing that far too often these days too, but I'm learning to smile and be patient, thanks to people like you. The good news today is that all is okay with the book—let's say a good, old-fashioned bureaucratic wobble. Our proofs should be back at the park tomorrow. Please pass that along to Holly. She'll be happy."

He switches the cellphone to silent. He's not really in the mood for more calls. The angler swishes his line: flick, flick, rest. Brewster watches as the filament arcs into the sun and lands on the water. The artificial fly floats on the ripples and drifts with the current. *Must be a metaphor in there somewhere,* he thinks. Time to go. Horton has given him some good news to email to his partners.

Hannah and Clotilde had shopped for him, and he guesses something will fall out of his magic freezer tonight to provide a tasty measure of sustenance. A container of what looks likes stew. *Mmm, that's new.* Must be an extra from one of the meals he'd enjoyed earlier in the week with his recent guests. He runs the container under hot water and dumps the frozen lump into a pot on the stove. The only side tonight will be his usual raw carrots, mixed into a salad and topped with raspberry vinaigrette. He wonders if he'll ever get used to this lonely meal factor. No matter how hard he tries, he can't get excited about cooking. For all that, he enjoys his little supper while sitting in front of the television news in which he has little interest, but it does provide noise.

#

Hi Dad,

Thanks heaps for helping me buy into the company. This is a terrific investment for us. You will hear and see what it's about when you and Hannah come down in April or May next year, for the wedding.

That's right, Dad—I said wedding. Vicki and I (nice new pic attached) are going to get married. We'll set the date so that you guys can come. I've already checked with Hannah, and she thinks that's about the right time for her, before she has to start looking for a job. You'll like Vicki. We only met a couple of months ago at the church. She lives with her parents and works in their resort complex. This place is growing so fast and attracts people interested in eco or adventure sailing.

Now, Dad. Something I just have to tell you and get off my chest. Been worried about you for some time, especially since we moved some of Mom's things out. Anyway, Tom, the fellow who started this company, lost his wife Sophie, a couple of years ago. She was a very experienced sailor, so everyone was devastated when she was knocked off a vessel in bad weather during a race down south. Tom fell apart. They'd been sailing together and in business together since school. They too met at church, or it may have been Bible school somewhere. Well, he just wanted to sell up and disappear. The business all but crumbled while the guys he employed and sailed with held it together. To make a long story short, he met Polly. She was here for a holiday from New Zealand maybe four months ago, and she stayed. They became an item very quickly and married within weeks of meeting. They're a terrific couple. Personally, I think it was pretty brave of Polly to marry the moody widower.

Because I was worried, I confided in them about your situation. Their advice, passed on from their pastor, was to simply trust in Jesus and go with your heart. You'll always have memories, Dad, and you've got Hannah and me. We're in your corner.

I'm out sailing most days with really excellent passengers. One-day cruises, usually, but I do take the odd overnighters out as well. You've helped me into a remarkable life, which I often recollect beginning with my tearful, cold and windy days learning to sail out on the reservoir. I think I'll be forever awed at the power of the wind as the sails fill, and I feel the surge beneath the hull. That's what got me, even sailing the little Optimists and the Lasers. Now look where I am.

This is a long note for me, Dad, but I just had to tell you about Vicki, and about Tom's situation. He has this terrific helicopter photo of his Sophie standing at the helm of a 60-footer under full sail.

I can't wait for you to meet Vicki. She's one exceptional gal who loves sailing and being with people. Most Sundays she's helping with the toddlers at church. Think April. Hannah will be in touch soon with her schedule, so you can make the appropriate bookings. We'll build the actual date around you snowbirds. I hope you bring Clotilde (ha ha). Hannah has told me all about her.

Love you, Dad. Take good care of yourself.

Harris

My son, getting married. How life moves along. One generation to the next. Brewster muses about the youngster in the Optimist at the sailing club, and the races they had in the two-man boats and of those long ago holidays sailing down at the coast.

"Pick up the phone, Dad. I know you're there." He hadn't heard the house phone ring, and he jumped at the sound of Hannah's voice.

"Hello, daughter," he says. "How's it going out there?"

"Just great. I want to graduate with honours, so I'm doing all I can to keep up my studies. Looks like I'll be away over Christmas and New Year's for about two weeks in Europe. The study tour is coming together, and we're pretty excited about that. I just had an astonishing FaceTime with Harris. He's getting married!"

"Me too. I've just finished reading a long email from him," he says. "Harris sounds pretty excited, and it's nice they're planning the date for when we—well, really you—can get there."

"Vicki is really lovely. She was on too. They look suited to each other, and they want me in the wedding party," Hannah says. "That makes me feel special. Harris said something about me being best man. Do you think he was joking?"

Brewster thinks about this and says, "Well, you know your brother. Doesn't hold too close to tradition, so he's probably for real, otherwise he wouldn't have said that. I hope he doesn't expect you to be in a morning suit and top hat!" They laugh at the image. "It'll be good for Vicki to have clarity early, so there's no surprises about Harris. And you should know that I don't have a problem with you being best man, and I don't think your Mom would either."

With the book finalized and his business life changing with the sale of the building, he talks about going away on another road trip into British Columbia. *Maybe go for a couple of weeks this time See what's out there. Holly will take care of the book.*

"Be honest, Dad. Are you okay?"

"Sure am, most days. I'm still trying to adjust to the bachelor life. Evenings are the worst times, but I'm sure I'll get used to it. Good grief, it's been almost 18 months since ... you know, since."

"Well, you must be doing something right," she says. "You looked well enough when we were home last week. Gotta go, Dad. Beddy-byes and a long day of lectures tomorrow."

It's quiet in the house again, so he taps out a reply to Harris, congratulating him on his wedding plans, commenting on the photo and thanking him for his candour. He thinks how fortunate he is to have children who love him and are not afraid to express their concern.

He looks up from the keyboard at the picture he has of Melanie and their kids on top of the bookcase. "They're treasures, Mel," he says. "You must be proud of them and how you shaped them."

He looks around his desk for the letter he'd crafted to Melanie just a few days ago. He'd left it there, unfinished, with his pen sitting on top. The pen and empty letter sheets are all that remain.

Where is the letter?

Chapter Forty-One

Clotilde looks up at the brilliant frescos and stained-glass windows in the historic L'Eglise Saint-Pierre, built in Cheticamp some 100 years after the first settlers arrived, when they were tired of their wanderings and searching for peace. These first Acadians are part of her heritage, refugees from the tragic Great Expulsion of the mid-1700s. These days she finds it comforting to sit in the church for the quiet, with the southern sun streaming through stained-glass windows creating a warmth of rainbow colour in the sanctuary. The best days are when the parish priest stops by to talk about her Acadian-Mi'kmaq heritage. He's fluent in American sign language, and he communicates freely about life in the largely French-speaking community, but he's also encouraged her to consider her own faith more deeply.

"I'm not part of a Catholic community, Father," she signs. "My parents brought me up in a Baptist congregation in Fort McMurray."

He says, "But we look to Jesus Christ in much the same way."

She tells him about her deafness, and though she loves her family heritage, she feels lost and lonely. She feels a need to return to the West. "I only leased a place here for three months, to see if this is where I should be now that both my parents have died," she says. "My cousin Ruth encouraged me to come. But you are one of the first to sign with me."

"You have a son," the priest signs. "You should be nearer to him, though he has lived with his father. One day he will marry, and you will want to be near him. Keep looking to the Cross. There you will know the peace you seek and the path to overcome whatever you think you have lost." He looks straight at her as he speaks. "But I think you have gained, not lost. Realize the gift you have."

Ruth does not understand when Clotilde says she will not renew her lease on her little cottage. Why do you want to leave this place?"

"The West is where I was raised. *Mon fils est là-bas*. My son is out there. I should be closer to him."

Chapter Forty-Two

It's day 13 since he left Calgary. He stopped travelling when he reached British Columbia's Christina Lake. It's 10 days since he moved his travel bag into the large cedar plank house overlooking the lake. Most days he lounges out on the wraparound deck following the sun. There's a clear, idyllic view of the lake, framed by the pines towering up on either side of the house. Underneath the deck is a large carport; it's calm. For the first time in a long while, Brewster finds a peace within himself at this lakeside oasis in the pines. "Is this it?" he asks. "Is this my place?"

A week later, he's in Calgary. Without hesitating, he calls Brad, his realtor. He speaks with Horton and checks with Joel. His house will be on the market in about a week. Brad's expertise takes over. Gardeners arrive to tidy up the yard, an estate sales specialist takes control and a house-staging couple add their marketing savvy. All the furniture will be donated, along with the kitchenware, dishes, pots and pans. The contents of his well-equipped workshop, along with all his garden tools, will go to Habitat for Humanity. The special boxes of keepers will go to storage until he settles into a new home.

Brewster boxes the art and Melanie's knick-knacks. He assembles them in the garage, ready take back to his lake house. He's very thankful that Hannah had pushed him to put together their keepsakes. He aggressively cleans out his own closet and drawers.

"It's a clean sweep, Brad," he says. "A fresh start."

Holly and Wendell pull up in his driveway. "Wow, what are you doing?" they ask, taken aback at his efforts to expunge a period of his life.

He says, "I've come to realize that life is about today. It's all we have. Yesterday is gone, and tomorrow has not yet come. Today is the present. That came from a message we had in church some time back. It's funny how things pop back into mind at the oddest of times." He invites them to help themselves to anything they see. Wendell says he'll get his friend with a pickup to come move some of the stuff they could use.

"And Lily—I put these aside for her." He lifts two large, mounted flower photographs and a volume of Winnie the Pooh from a special box of gems "Think she'll like these?" he asks. "I used to read Winnie to the kids when they were small."

Holly beams. "I'd say so. Doctors are getting more confident each day that she's in remission, but it'll take a few years before we can declare that. Will you tell us where you are going so we can visit?"

"Well, duh," he says. "I expect you to come when I'm all settled. I'm leasing a place at present right on Christina lake. I may end up buying it, or something similar. Next summer, for sure."

After they leave, he's aware they did not discuss the book at all, and so he assumes all is well. Holly had said in her recent email that printing was underway. She'd rechecked colour proofs and the cover, and she expected the fully bound initial shipment of *Underfoot: 100 Wildflowers* by the end of the month.

The one thing that bothers him in his clean-up and clean-out excitement is the unfinished letter he'd written to Melanie. In all the activity in his office, stacking and packing books and files, the letter did not show. No one ever went into his office. How did it fade away?

Weird, he thinks. *Just too weird.* He's sitting in the sun, sipping a coffee to the background hum of cleaners and packers in the house, when Joel finds a space in the busy driveway.

"Shalom," Brewster says. "What brings Mr. Joel out on a sunny day?"

Joel says, "Just you. Couple of weeks ago, you were a moody son-of-a-gun. Then you burst back into town, put your house on the market, tell everyone you're leaving and poof!"

"Don't be worried—it's all good. I've just gotta move along, and I know in my heart that all this change is the way to go." He describes the house he's leasing and may possibly buy. There are three levels. A carport and utility rooms are on the bottom. The main floor has a three-sided deck looking out over the lake, and there's a bedroom floor with clerestory windows for maximum exposure to light and sun. The house is angled into a rock face and surrounded by trees.

"Sounds great," Joel says. "But what are you going to do to stay busy? You and Melanie were always doing something."

"I'll just email you 10 times a day," he jokes. "Not sure yet, but that'll come. If I like the area and decide to stay there and buy the place, I might look at investing in or developing an RV resort."

"It'll be different, that's for sure. Anyway, with that said, Anna wants you to come over for Shabbat on Friday."

"I'd love that. Six o'clock, right?"

By the end of the week, his home of 27 years is a shell of its former self. He's astounded at the change after a few days of frantic activity by a lot of people. To him, it has that unlived-in look. *Staged* might be the term realtors use, but to him it's more *unloved*. The laughter has gone from the walls, a family's presence extinguished. He's chosen to live in a nearby hotel for a few days and to leave the house in its pristine state for the realtor's open house at the weekend.

Brewster's about to lock up and leave when he has the urge for one more walk-through. He pauses in each room and sees their babies and their teenagers. He sees their junk and their untidy rooms. He sees their friends and the many noisy sleepovers. He sees their birthdays. He sits in the tidy lounge and lights a candle the stagers left on a table. Brewster watches the flame and whispers a prayer of thanks for what has been and what is to come. He prays for the buyers and hopes that this house will become their home as it was for his family.

He gently blows out the candle, walks out and locks up.

Chapter Forty-Three

The welcoming noise of people encompasses Brewster as he enters the church lobby. People greet each other, and children run and dodge the clusters of adults. Hands grab his shoulders from behind. "So good to see you." It's Heath and Claire. He turns and gives each a hug.

"Yeah, been awhile," he says. "But today is the day I decided to be brave and return to the fold. I think it's the result of being with Joel and Anna and their kids for Shabbat, and seeing the tranquillity in that home. Their ritual, their faith, their belief and their absolute assurance of the presence of God in their lives. They don't search—they know."

Brewster sits with his friends in the sanctuary. He enjoys the low lighting and the sense of closing out distractions. They stand and sing, and he's once again transported into a world of praise by the exceptional talent of the band and singers on stage. Today's message leaves him in a very introspective mood. He files out silently into the chattering crowd in the lobby. People must be thinking like him. *Where is God?* is the question. *God is there in our sorrows, reaching out,* is the answer.

Brewster talks with his friends about his new plans to move away and begin a new period in his life. He shares Harris's wedding plans and adds that he will head south with the newly graduated Hannah to join in the nuptials.

"You're a different person from just a few weeks ago," Claire says. "What's happened?"

"I went over a few things and realized that nothing's going to get any better. I became conscious of the fact that I'm far from unique in my pain. I decided I could not write God off as I had done, and there was not a lot He could do if I was going to wallow in some sort of self-pity. Like our pastor said this morning, faith allows us to reach beyond ourselves and really reach out to God."

Heath looks at him. "You're not going to turn into some hermit way out in the woods, are you?"

"Ha! Not on your life, my friend. But for now, I'm going to enjoy a change of scenery, enjoy the tree house and the lake and see where life takes me. I may look for a new investment or business I can get involved in, to stay busy. I'd say there's lots of opportunity around that part of the world."

"What about Clotilde and the book?" Claire asks.

"All taken care of. I'll be leaving things to Holly at the outset, and she will work with the park. For me, my part is done. Melanie's initiative is complete. Clotilde will no doubt help; as far as I know, she's settling into life in Cape Breton. I've not heard from her since she went back a few weeks ago."

"That's it?" Claire says. "You're just going to leave things there?"

Brewster reaches for her hand. "Dear Claire, I have to get myself sorted out before I think about putting anyone else into my life. Besides, I have Harris and Hannah to think about."

Signs are on the front lawn, and Brad's listing has already attracted some interest and at least one walk-through. Brewster is impatient to leave, to move past the intersection of death, to walk beyond the park and once again find and enjoy new discoveries.

Chapter Forty-Four

Dear Harris and Hannah,

I hope this does not come as too big a surprise to you, but I've put the house on the market. All our treasures will stay with me, and the boxes of keepers will go into storage. I'm moving to Christina Lake in BC. I'm leasing a nice little place that I may decide to buy once I've settled our affairs in Calgary. In a few weeks or so, I'll figure out my permanent base and be in touch. Internet may be patchy where the house is, but I will be in and out of nearby Grand Forks, so I'll make sure I stay in close contact.

Please do not worry. I'm feeling very refreshed and energized to begin a new chapter. Your Mom remains the most important part of my life, but I know I need to quit mooning around and realize that life has to be lived. Your Mom gave the three of us a huge example. You two live it, and now I have to as well.

I'm looking forward to our visit and your wedding, Harris, and to see your corner of the wide, wide world. It'll be nice to sail in one of your big boats.

You two will be the first to hear from me when I figure out the new Internet with my computer and phone. I hope it doesn't take too long. I expect to be travelling back to Calgary now and then, and I'll keep my current addresses just in case.

Attached is a picture I took from the deck overlooking the lake. The view is superb. It's like living in a tree house.

All this might sound a bit impulsive, but I assure you both I've really thought this through. Now each of us has plans: Harris a wedding, Hannah a trip to Europe and me living in a tree hut!

Love you guys,
Dad

Chapter Forty-Five

Three weeks later, Brewster lounges on his deck in the mid-afternoon sun, tilted back in his chair and his feet resting on the railing. The year is ending, and he will begin afresh. He lovingly traces his fingers over the striped coralroot picture in *Underfoot*. It's a picture of memories and the first page he turned to when he opened the carton of books Jane had shipped to him hot off the press.

"Holly," he says on his cellphone. "The book is beautiful and more than I ever imagined it could be. You have done an amazing job. A million thank-yous for seeing this project through to the end."

"Tanya and Louise love it," she says. "They bought a whole bunch; Joel has the numbers. They are only sending copies to their VIPs at present. They are holding off on any official launch until the spring. I think that's the right way to go, when the flowers will also be making their presence known in the park."

"I got a sweet call from Jo this morning," he says. "We put a carton of books into the Blue Aster and she tells me they are all sold. The grumpy supplier she had trouble with just before she took over the shop bought five of them. I emailed Jane a list of our special friends, and I've sent a few off to Harris in Australia. He'll be really proud that his mother's initiative has been fully realized with great success. Hannah has taken some to Europe with her. I'm so glad that Lily is doing well and is now at home full-time. Is Wendell up to marathons yet?"

"Not quite," she replies with a laugh. "He's very mobile now, though, and it won't be long before he will be able to go the full day. He's been in touch with his old firm, and things look positive there."

"Um, any word from Clotilde?" he asks.

There's a long pause. "Only that I think Jane was going to contact her to arrange shipping," Holly says. "I gather you've not heard from her?"

"Not since I've been out here," he says. "But I've found the Internet a random thing. I just hope she's doing okay and enjoying the miracle of seeing her work in print."

The afternoon drifts slowly by. Brewster sits with the book tipped forward to his chest. Jo's comment about naming the shop rolls across his mind. "I always remember why Melanie called the shop the Blue Aster," she'd said. "It's a common little flower and is always around, just like Jesus promised when he said, 'I will be with you always.'"

His eyes close, and in his sleepy state he listens to the birds in the surrounding trees and the occasional distant sound of a powerboat on the lake. It's very peaceful.

The sound of tires rolling across the new gravel in the driveway stir his happy state. He's not expecting any visitors, so he waits and listens. A car door slams, followed by footsteps. He slowly gets out of his chair, shakes himself awake and peers over the deck railing, high above the driveway parking pad.

A petite, dark-haired, olive-skinned woman with eyes like melted chocolate and a white curly-haired miniature poodle in a red coat look up at him. He pauses halfway down the 10 steps and looks at her for a second or two. In the silence of his forest home, he slowly moves his hands and signs:

"I am so glad, so very, very glad to see you."

Author's Note

"I want to always have an open mind so that new ideas may come in. In the mind of an expert, there are few possibilities, but in the mind of an amateur they become endless. This is a God given gift and I value it greatly. If I am able to bring emotion, understanding, comfort, or joy into another's life then I am using it wisely in His glory." —Olaf Schnieder, artist.

This book has been hugely rewarding to write because of the number of people who willingly helped me to imagine and bring words to the page. I am continually amazed that in this day and age, I can lift the phone or send an email to a person I've never had contact with and get the answers I need to lift my imagination. I thank them all, near and far.

My thanks go to: Julia Millen, Jessica Twidale, Vivian Jonathan, Sue Melin, Diane Chisholm, Ferne Watson, Jamie Hall, Sherri Turner, Tim McFarland, Angela Bentivegna, Alan Jones, Jack Heffron, Colleen Thorpe, Karyn Wog, Shula Bancik, Irwin Huberman, Fiona Connell, Rebecca Thorpe, Kevin McCartney, Sara DesRoches and Robert Sinclair.

I am deeply indebted to Terry McKinney, who as a profoundly deaf friend, inspired and helped me bring Clotilde to life, likewise Heather Forsyth and her delightful hearing dog Quill. My granddaughter Veronica Fukuda has been my on-call French tutor.

I have been utterly blessed to know Nancy Mackenzie, who has provided her editorial services above and beyond and has encouraged me to think about words and the worlds they can take us to.

Finally, where would I be today without my wife, Lois, and our ever-expanding family, from three daughters to eight grandchildren and now two great-grandsons. They are all my stars.

Printed in the United States
By Bookmasters